"What you call 'Earth' is an island . . .

. . . one of a few isolated lines in a vast blighted region. If you succeed in crippling this scout, you'll precipitate us into identity with an Earth which might be nothing more than a ring of cinders around the sun, or a great mass of fungus . . ."

A mass loomed across the lens. My imagination reeled at the idea that perhaps Winter was telling the truth. I stared horrified at the tiny cowlike head which lolled uselessly from the slope of the mountainous creature.

"Yes, it's a cow," Winter said. "A mutated cow which no longer has any limits on its growth. It's a vast tissue culture; the rudimentary head and limbs are quite useless . . ."

"I've seen enough," I said. "Let's get out of this!" I pushed the pistol back into my pocket. I thought of the bullet hole I had put in the instrument panel and I shuddered.

Look for all these TOR books by Keith Laumer

KEITH LAUMER

WORLDS OF THE IMPERIUM

Special Bonus Stories
"The War Against the Yukks"
and
"Worldmaster"

A TOM DOHERTY ASSOCIATES BOOK

WORLDS OF THE IMPERIUM

Acknowledgments:

"Worldmaster," copyright © 1965 by Galaxy Publishing Corporation.
"The War Against the Yukks," copyright © 1965 by Galaxy Publishing Corporation.

First Tor printing: September 1982
Second printing: June 1984
Third printing: January 1985

A TOR Book

Published by Tom Doherty Associates
49 West 24 Street
New York, N.Y. 10010

Cover art by Bob Petillo

ISBN: 0-812-54379-3
CAN. ED.: 0-812-54380-7

Printed in the United States of America

0 9 8 7 6 5 4 3

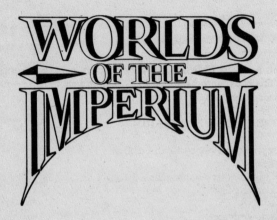

Chapter 1

I stopped in front of a shop with a small wooden sign which hung from a wrought-iron spear projecting from the weathered stone wall. On it the word Antikvariat was lettered in spidery gold against dull black. The sign creaked as it swung in the night wind. Below it a metal grating covered a dusty window with a display of yellowed etchings, woodcuts, and lithographs, and a faded mezzotint. Some of the buildings in the pictures looked familiar, but here they stood in open fields, or perched on hills overlooking a harbor crowded with sails. The ladies in the pictures wore great bell-like skirts and bonnets with ribbons, and carried tiny parasols, while dainty-footed horses pranced before carriages in the background.

It wasn't the prints that interested me though, or even the heavy gilt frame embracing a tarnished mirror at one side; it was the man whose

reflection I studied in the yellowed glass, a dark
man wearing a tightly-belted grey trench coat that
was six inches too long. He stood with his hands
thrust deep in his pockets and stared into a dark-
ened window fifty feet from me.

He had been following me all day.

At first I thought it was coincidence when I
noticed the man on the bus from Bromma, then
studying theatre announcements in the hotel
lobby while I registered, and half an hour later
sitting three tables away sipping coffee while I ate
a hearty dinner.

I had discarded the coincidence theory a long
time ago. Five hours had passed and he was still
with me as I walked through the Old Town,
medieval Stockholm still preserved on an island in
the middle of the city. I had walked past shabby
windows crammed with copper pots, ornate
silver, dueling pistols, and worn cavalry sabres;
they were all very quaint in the afternoon sun, but
grim reminders of a ruder day of violence after
midnight. Over the echo of my footsteps in the
silent narrow streets the other steps came quietly
behind, hurrying when I hurried, stopping when I
stopped. Now the man stared into the dark
window and waited. The next move was up to me.

I was lost. Twenty years is a long time to remember the tortuous turnings of the streets of the Old
Town. I took my guide book from my pocket and
turned to the map in the back. My fingers were
clumsy.

I craned my neck up at the stone tablet set in the
corner of the building; it was barely legible:
Master Samuelsgatan. I found the name on the
folding map and saw that it ran for three short
blocks, ending at Gamla Storgatan; a dead end. In

the dim light it was difficult to see the fine detail on the map. I twisted the book around and got a clearer view; there appeared to be another tiny street, marked with crosslines, and labeled Guldsmedstrappan.

I tried to remember my Swedish; *trappan* meant stair. The Goldsmith's Stairs, running from Master Samuelsgatan to Hundgatan, another tiny street. It seemed to lead to the lighted area near the palace; it looked like my only route out. I dropped the book back into my pocket and moved off casually toward the stairs of the Goldsmith. I hoped there was no gate across the entrance.

My shadow waited a moment, then followed. As I was ambling, I slowly gained a little on him. He seemed in no hurry at all. I passed more tiny shops, with ironbound doors and worn stone sills, and then saw that the next doorway was an open arch with littered granite steps ascending abruptly. I paused idly, then turned in. Once past the portal, I bounded up the steps at top speed. Six leaps, eight, and I was at the top, darting to the left toward a deep doorway. There was just a chance I'd cleared the top of the stair before the dark man had reached the bottom. I stood and listened. I heard the scrape of shoes, then heavy breathing from the direction of the stairs a few feet away. I waited, breathing with my mouth wide open, trying not to pant audibly. After a moment the steps moved away. The proper move for my silent companion would be to cast about quickly for my hiding place, on the assumption that I had concealed myself close by. He would be back this way soon.

I risked a glance. He was moving quickly along, looking sharply about, with his back to me. I

pulled off my shoes and without taking time to
think about it, stepped out. I made it to the stairs
in three paces, and faded out of sight as the man
stopped to turn back. I leaped down three steps at
a time; I was halfway down when my foot hit a
loose stone, and I flew the rest of the way.

I hit the cobblestones shoulder first, and followed up with my head. I rolled over and scrambled
to my feet, my head ringing. I clung to the wall by
the foot of the steps as the pain started. Now I was
getting mad. I heard the soft-shod feet coming
down the stairs, and gathered myself to jump him
as he came out. The footsteps hesitated just before
the arch, then the dark round head with the un-
cut hair peeped out. I swung a haymaker—and
missed.

He darted into the street and turned, fumbling
in his overcoat. I assumed he was trying to get a
gun, and aimed a kick at his mid-section. I had better luck this time; I connected solidly, and had the
satisfaction of hearing him gasp in agony. I hoped
he hurt as badly as I did. Whatever he was fumbling for came free then, and he backed away,
holding the thing in his mouth.

"One-oh-nine, where in bloody blazes are you?"
he said in a harsh voice, glaring at me. He had an
odd accent. I realized the thing was some sort of
microphone. "Come in, one-oh-nine, this job's
going to pieces . . ." He backed away, talking, eyes
on me. I leaned against the wall; I was hurt too
badly to be very aggressive. There was no one else
in sight. His soft shoes made whispering sounds
on the paving stones. Mine lay in the middle of the
street where I had dropped them when I fell.

Then there was a sound behind me. I whirled,

and saw the narrow street almost blocked by a huge van. I let my breath out with a sigh of relief. Here was help.

Two men jumped down from the van, and without hesitation stepped up to me, took my arms and escorted me toward the rear of the van. They wore tight white uniforms, and said nothing.

"I'm all right," I said. "Grab that man." About that time I realized he was following along, talking excitedly to the man in white, and that the grip on my arms was more of a restraint than a support. I dug in my heels and tried to pull away. I remembered suddenly that the Stockholm police don't wear white uniforms.

I might as well not have bothered. One of them unclipped a thing like a tiny aerosol bomb from his belt and sprayed it into my face. I felt myself go limp.

Chapter 2

There was a scratching sound which irritated me. I tried unsuccessfully to weave it into a couple of dreams before my subconscious gave up. I was lying on my back, eyes closed. I couldn't think where I was. I remembered a frightening dream about being followed, and then as I became aware of pain in my shoulder and head, my eyes snapped open. I was lying on a cot at the side of a small office; the scratching came from the desk where a dapper man in a white uniform sat writing. There was a humming sound and a feeling of motion.

I sat up. At once the man behind the desk looked up, rose, and walked over to me. He drew up a chair and sat down.

"Please don't be alarmed," he said in a clipped British accent. "I'm Chief Captain Winter. You need merely to assist in giving me some routine information, after which you will be assigned

comfortable quarters." He said all this in a
smooth lifeless way, as though he'd been through
it before. Then he looked directly at me for the
first time.

"I must apologize for the callousness with
which you were handled; it was not my intention.
However," his tone changed, "you must excuse the
operative; he was uninformed."

Chief Captain Winter opened a notebook and
lolled back in his chair with pencil poised. "Where
were you born, Mr. Bayard?"

They must have been through my pockets, I
thought; they know my name.

"Who the hell are you?" I said.

The chief captain raised an eyebrow. His uniform was immaculate, and brilliantly jewelled
decorations sparkled on his chest.

"Of course you are confused at this moment,
Mr. Bayard, but everything will be explained to
you carefully in due course. I am an Imperial
officer, duly authorized to interrogate subjects
under detention." He smiled soothingly. "Now
please state your birthplace."

I said nothing. I didn't feel like answering any
questions; I had too many of my own to ask first. I
couldn't place the fellow's accent. He was an En-
glishman all right, but I couldn't have said from
what part of England. I glanced at the medals.
Most of them were strange but I recognized the
scarlet ribbon of the Victoria Cross, with three
palms, ornamented with gems. There was something extremely phoney about Chief Captain
Winter.

"Come along now, old chap," Winter said sharply. "Kindly co-operate. It will save a great deal of
unpleasantness."

I looked at him grimly. "I find being chased, grabbed, gassed, stuffed in a cell, and quizzed about my personal life pretty damned unpleasant already, so don't bother trying to keep it all on a high plane. I'm not answering any questions." I reached in my pocket for my passport; it wasn't there.

"Since you've already stolen my passport, you know by now that I'm an American diplomat, and enjoy diplomatic immunity to any form of arrest, detention, interrogation and what have you. So I'm leaving as soon as you return my property, including my shoes."

Winter's face had stiffened up. I could see my act hadn't much impression on him. He signalled, and two fellows I hadn't seen before moved around into view. They were bigger than he was.

"Mr. Bayard, you must answer my questions, under duress, if necessary. Kindly begin by stating your birthplace."

"You'll find it in my passport," I said. I was looking at the two reinforcements; they were as easy to ignore as a couple of bulldozers in the living room. I decided on a change of tactics. I'd play along in the hope they'd relax a bit, and then make a break for it.

One of the men, at a signal, handed Winter my passport from his desk. He glanced through it, made a number of notes, and passed the booklet back to me.

"Thank you, Mr. Bayard," he said pleasantly. "Now let's get on to particulars. Where did you attend school?"

I tried hard now to give the impression of one eager to please. I regretted my earlier truculence; it made my present pose of co-operativeness a little less plausible. Winter must have been accustomed to the job though, and to subjects who were abject. After a few minutes he waved an arm at the two bouncers, who left the room silently.

Winter had gotten on to the subject of international relations and geopolitics now, and seemed to be fascinated by my commonplace replies. I attempted once or twice to ask why it was necessary to quiz me closely on matters of general information, but was firmly guided back to the answering of the questions.

He covered geography and recent history thoroughly with emphasis on the period 1879-1910, and then started in on a biographic list; all I knew about one name after another. Most of them I'd never heard of, a few were minor public figures. He quizzed me in detail on two Italians, Cocino and Maxoni. He could hardly believe I'd never heard of them. He seemed fascinated by many of my replies.

"Niven an actor?" he said incredulously. "Never heard of Crane Talbot?" and when I described Churchill's role in recent affairs, he laughed uproariously.

After forty minutes of this one-sided discussion, a buzzer sounded faintly, and another uniformed man entered, placed a good-sized box on the corner of the desk, and left. Winter ignored the interruption.

Another twenty minutes of questions went by. Who was the present monarch of Anglo-Germany? Winter asked. What was the composition of the royal family, the ages of the children? I exhausted my knowledge of the subject. What was the status of the Viceroyalty of India? Explain the working of the Dominion arrangements of Australia,

Northern America, Cabotsland . . . ? I was appalled at the questions; the author of them must have been insane. It was almost impossible to link the garbled reference to non-existent political subdivisions and institutions to reality. I answered as matter-of-factly as possible. At least Winter did not seem to be much disturbed by my revision of his distorted version of affairs.

At last Winter rose, moved over to his desk, and motioned me to a chair beside it. As I pulled the chair out, I glanced into the box on the desk. I saw magazines, folded cloth, coins—and the butt of a small automatic protruding from under a copy of the World Almanac. Winter had turned away, reaching into a small cabinet behind the desk. My hand darted out, scooped up the pistol, and dropped it into my pocket as I seated myself.

Winter turned back with a blue glass bottle. "Now let's have a drop and I'll attempt to clear up some of your justifiable confusion, Mr. Bayard," he said genially. "What would you like to know?" I ignored the bottle.

"Where am I?" I said.

"In the city of Stockholm, Sweden."

"We seem to be moving; what is this, a moving van with an office in it?"

"This is a vehicle, though not a moving van."

"Why did you pick me up?"

"I'm sorry that I can tell you no more than that you were brought in under specific orders from a very high-ranking officer of the Imperial Service." He looked at me speculatively. "This was most unusual," he added.

"I take it kidnapping inoffensive persons is not in itself unusual."

Winter frowned. "You are the subject of an offi-

cial operation of Imperial Intelligence. Please rest
assured you are not being persecuted."

"What is Imperial Intelligence?"

"Mr. Bayard," Winters said earnestly, leaning
forward, "it will be necessary for you to face a
number of realizations; the first is that the govern-
ments which you are accustomed to regard as supreme sovereign powers must in fact be considered tributary to the Imperium, the Paramount
Government in whose service I am an officer."

"You're a fake," I said.

Winter bristled. "I hold an Imperial Commission as Chief Captain of Intelligence."

"What do you call this vehicle we're in?"

"This is an armed TNL scout based at Stockholm Zero Zero."

"That tells me a lot; what is it, a boat, car, airplane . . . ?"

"None of those, Mr. Bayard."

"All right, I'll be specific; what does it travel on,
water, air . . . ?"

Winter hesitated. "Frankly, I don't know."

I saw it was time to try a new angle of attack.
"Where are we going?"

"We are presently operating along coordinates
zero-zero, zero, zero-six, zero-ninety-two."

"What is our destination? What place?"

"Stockholm Zero Zero, after which you'll probably be transferred to London Zero Zero for
further processing."

"What is the Zero Business? Do you mean London, England?"

"The London you refer to is London B-1 Three."

"What's the difference?"

"London Zero Zero is the capital of the Imperium, comprising the major portion of the civil-

ized world—North Europe, West Hemisphere, and
Australia."

I changed the subject. "Why did you kidnap
me?"

"A routine interrogational arrest, insofar as I
know."

"Do you intend to release me?"

"Yes."

"At home?"

"No."

"Where?"

"I can't say; at one of several concentration
points."

"One more question," I said, easing the automatic from my pocket and pointing it at the third
medal from the left. "Do you know what this is?

"Keep your hands in sight; better get up and
stand over there."

Winter rose and moved over to the spot indicated. I'd never aimed a pistol at a man point-
blank before, but I felt no hesitation now.

"Tell me all about it," I said.

"I've answered every question," Winter said
nervously.

"And told me nothing." Winter stood staring at
me.

I slipped the safety off with a click. "You'll have
five seconds to start," I said. "One . . . two . . ."

"Very well," Winter said. "No need for all this;
I'll try." He hesitated. "You were selected from
higher up. We went to a great deal of trouble to get
you in particular. As I've explained, that's rather
irregular. However," Winter seemed to be warm-
ing to his subject, "all sampling in this region has
been extremely restricted in the past; you see,
your continuum occupies an island, one of a very

few isolated lines in a vast blighted region. The entire configuration is abnormal, and an extremely dangerous area in which to maneuver. We lost many good men in early years before we learned how to handle the problems involved."

"I suppose you know this is all nonsense to me," I said. "What do you mean by sampling?"

"Do you mind if I smoke?" Winter said. I took a long brown cigarette from a box on the desk, lit it, and handed it to him. "Sampling refers to the collection of individuals or artifacts from representative B-I lines," he said, blowing out smoke. "We in Intelligence are engaged now in mapping operations. It's fascinating work, old boy, picking up the trend lines, coordinating findings with theoretical work, developing accurate calibrating devices, instruments, and so on. We're just beginning to discover the potentialities of working the Net. In order to gather maximum information in a short time, we've found it expedient to collect individuals for interrogation. In this way we quickly gain a general picture of the configuration of the Net in various directions. In your case, I was directed under sealed orders to enter the Blight, proceed to Blight-Insular Three, and take over custody of Mr. Brion Bayard, a diplomat representing, of all things, an American republic." Winter spoke enthusiastically now. As he relaxed, he seemed younger.

"It was quite a feather in my cap, old chap, to be selected to conduct an operation in the Blight, and I've found it fascinating. Always in the past, of course, I've operated at such a distance from the Imperium that little or no analogy existed. But B-I Three! Why it's practically the Imperium, with just enough variation to stir the imagination.

Close as the two lines are, there's a desert of
Blight around and between them that indicates
how frightfully close to the rim we've trodden in
times past."

"All right, Winter. I've heard enough," I said.
"You're just a harmless nut, maybe. But I'll be
going now."

"That's quite impossible," Winter said. "We're
in the midst of the Blight."

"What's the Blight?" I asked, making conversation as I looked around the room, trying to pick
out the best door to leave by. There were three. I
decided on the one no one had come through yet. I
moved towards it.

"The Blight is a region of utter desolation, radiation, and chaos," Winter was saying. "There are
whole ranges of A-lines where the very planet no
longer exists, where automatic cameras have re-
corded nothing but a vast ring of debris in orbit;
then there are the cinder-worlds, and here and
there dismal groups of cancerous jungles, alive
with radiation-poisoned mutations. It's frightful,
old chap. You can wave the pistol at me all night,
but it will get you nothing. In a few hours we'll
arrive at Zero Zero; you may as well relax until
then."

I tried the door, it was locked. "Where's the
key?" I said.

"There's no key. It will open automatically at
the base."

I went to one of the other doors, the one the man
with the box had entered through. I pulled it open
and glanced out. The humming sound was louder
and down a short and narrow corridor I saw what
appeared to be a pilot's compartment. A man's
back was visible.

"Come on, Winter," I said. "Go ahead of me."

"Don't be a complete ass, old boy," Winter said, looking irritated. He turned toward his desk. I raised the pistol. The shot boomed inside the walls of the room, and Winter leaped back from the desk holding a ripped hand. He whirled on me, for the first time looking really scared. "You're insane," he shouted. "I've told you we're in the midst of the Blight."

I was keeping one eye on the man up front, who was looking over his shoulder while frantically doing something with his other hand.

"You're leaking all over that nice rug," I said. "I'm going to kill you with the next one. Stop this machine."

Winter was pale; he swallowed convulsively. "I swear, Mr. Bayard, that's utterly impossible. I'd rather you shoot me. You have no conception of what you're suggesting."

I saw now that I was in the hands of a dangerous lunatic. I believed Winter when he said he'd rather die than stop this bus—or whatever it was. In spite of my threat, I couldn't shoot him in cold blood. I turned and took three steps up the passage and poked the automatic into the small of the back that showed there.

"Cut the switch," I said. The man, who was one of the two who had been standing by when I awoke in the office, continued to twist frantically at a knob on the panel before him. He glanced at me, but kept on twiddling. I raised the pistol and fired a shot into the instrument panel. The man jumped convulsively, and threw himself forward, protecting the panel with his body.

"Stop, you bloody fool," he shouted. "Let us explain!"

"I tried that," I said. "It didn't work. Get out of my way. I'm bringing this wagon to a halt one way or another."

I stood so that I could see both men. Winter half crouched in the doorway, face white. "Are we all right, Doyle?" he called in a strained voice. Doyle eased away from the panel, turned his back to me, and glanced over the instruments. He flipped a toggle, cursed, and turned over to face Winter.

"Communicator dead," he said. "But we're still in operation."

I hesitated now. These two were genuinely terrified of the idea of stopping; they had paid as little attention to me and my noisy gun as one would to a kid with a water pistol. Compared to stopping, a bullet was apparently a trifling irritation.

It was also obvious that this was no moving van. The pilot's compartment had more instruments than an airliner, and no windows. Elaborate ideas began to run through my mind. Space ship? Time machine? What the devil had I gotten into?

"All right, Winter," I said. "Let's call a truce. I'll give you five minutes to give me a satisfactory explanation, prove you're not an escapee from the violent ward, and tell me how you're going to go about setting me down right back where you found me. If you can't or won't cooperate, I'll fill that panel full of holes—including anybody who happens to be standing in front of it."

"Yes," Winter said. "I swear I'll do all I can. Just come away from the control compartment."

"I'll stay right here," I said. "I won't jump the gun unless you give me a reason, like holding your mouth wrong."

Winter was sweating. "This is a scouting machine, operating in the Net. By the Net, I mean the complex of Alternative lines which constitute the matrix of all simultaneous reality. Our drive is the Maxoni-Cocini field generator, which creates a force operating at what one might call a perpendicular to normal entropy. Actually, I know little about the physics of the mechanism; I am not a technician."

I looked at my watch. Winter got the idea. "The Imperium is the government of the Zero Zero A-line in which this discovery was made. The device is an extremely complex one, and there are a thousand ways in which it can cause disaster to its operators if a mistake is made. Judging from the fact that every A-line within thousands of parameters of Zero Zero is a scene of the most fearful carnage, we surmise that our line alone was successful in controlling the force. We conduct our operations in all of that column of A-space lying outside the Blight, as we term this area of destruction. The Blight itself we ordinarily avoid completely."

Winter wrapped a handkerchief around his bleeding hand as he talked.

"Your line, known as Blight-Insular Three, or B-I Three, is one of two exceptions we know to the general destruction. These two lines lie at some distance from Zero Zero, yours a bit closer than B-I Two, B-I Three was discovered only a month or so ago, and just recently confirmed as a safe line. All this exploratory work in the Blight was done by drone scouts unmanned.

"Why I was directed to pick you up, I don't know. But believe me when I say that if you succeed in crippling this scout, you'll precipitate us into identity with an A-line which might be nothing more than a ring of radioactive dust around the sun, or a great mass of mutated fungus. We cannot stop now for any reason until we reach a safe area."

I looked at my watch again. "Four minutes," I said. "Prove what you've been telling me."

Winter licked his lips. "Doyle, get to the recon photos of this sector, the ones we made on the way in."

Doyle reached across to a compartment under the panel and brought out a large red envelope. He handed it to me. I passed it to Winter.

"Open it," I said. "Let's see what you've got."

Winter fumbled a moment, then slipped a stack of glossy prints out. He handed me the first one. "All these photos were made from precisely the same spatial and temporal coordinates as those occupied by the scout. The only differences are the Web coordinates."

The print showed an array of ragged fragments of rock hanging against a backdrop of foggy grey, with a few bright points gleaming through. I don't know what it was intended to represent.

He handed me another; it was similar. So was the third, with the added detail that one rock fragment had a smooth side, with tiny lines across it. Winter spoke up. "The scale is not what it appears; that odd bit is a portion of the earth's crust, about twenty miles from the camera; the lines are roads." I stared, fascinated. Beyond the strangely scribed fragment, other jagged pieces ranged away to the limit of sight, and beyond. My imagination reeled at the idea that perhaps Winter was telling me the literal truth.

Winter passed over another shot. This one showed a lumpy black expanse, visible only by the murky gleam of light reflected by the irregularities in the surface in the direction of the moon, which showed as a brilliant disc in the black sky.

The next was half-obscured by a mass which loomed across the lens, too close for focus. Beyond, a huge sprawling bulk, shapeless, gross, immense, lay half-buried in tangled vines. I stared horrified at the tiny cowlike head which lolled uselessly on the slope of the mountainous creature. Some distance away a distended leglike appendage projected, the hoof dangling.

"Yes," Winter said. "It's a cow. A mutated cow which no longer has any limitation on its growth. It's a vast tissue culture, absorbing nourishment direct from the vines. They grow all through the mass of flesh. The rudimentary head and occasional limbs are quite useless." I pushed the pictures back at him. I was sick. "I've seen enough," I said. "You've sold me. Let's get out of this." I pushed the pistol into my pocket. I thought of the bullet hole in the panel and shuddered.

Back in the office, I sat down at the desk. Winter spoke up again. "It's a very unnerving thing, old chap, to have it shown to you all at once that way."

Winter went on talking while I tried to assemble his fragmentary information into a coherent picture. A vast spider web of lines, each one a complete universe, each minutely different from all the others; somewhere, a line, or world, in which a device had been developed that enabled a man to move across the lines. Well, why not, I thought. With all those lines to work with, everything was bound to happen in one of them; or was it?

"How about all the other A-lines, Winter," I said at the thought, "where this same discovery must have been made, where there was only some unimportant difference. Why aren't you swarming all over each other, bumping into yourself?"

"That's been a big question to our scientists, old chap, and they haven't yet come up with any definite answers. However, there are a few established points. First, the thing is a fantastically delicate device, as I've explained. The tiniest slip in the initial experimentation, and we'd have ended like some of those other lines you've seen photos of. Apparently the odds were quite fantastically against our escaping the consequences of the discovery; still, we did, and now we know how to control it.

"As to the very close lines, theory now seems to indicate that there is no actual physical separation between lines; those microscopically close to one another actually merge or blend. It's difficult to explain. One actually wanders from one to another, at random, you know. In fact, such is the number of infinitely close lines we're constantly shifting about in. Usually this makes no difference; we don't notice it, any more than we're aware of hopping along from one temporal point to the next as normal entropy progresses."

At my puzzled frown he added, "The lines run both ways, you know, in an infinite number of directions. If we could run straight back along the normal E-line, we'd be travelling into the past. This won't work, for practical reasons involving two bodies occupying the same space, and all that sort of thing. The Maxoni principle enables us to move in a manner which we think of as being at right angles to the normal drift. With it, we can operate through 360 degrees, but always at the same E-level at which we start. Thus, we will arrive at Stockholm Zero Zero at the same moment we departed from B-I Three." Winter laughed. "This detail caused no end of misunderstanding and counter-accusation on the first trials."

"So we're all shifting from one universe to another all the time without knowing it," I said skeptically.

"Not necessarily all of us, not all the time," Winter said. "But emotional stress seems to have the effect of displacing one. Of course with the relative positions of two grains of sand, or even of two atoms within a grain of sand being the only difference between two adjacent lines, you'd not be likely to notice. But at times greater slips occur with most individuals. Perhaps you yourself have noticed some tiny discrepancy at one time or another; some article apparently moved or lost; some sudden change in the character of someone you know; false recollections of past events. The universe isn't all as rigid as one might like to believe."

"You're being awfully plausible, Winter," I said. "Let's pretend I accept your story. Now tell me about this vehicle."

"Just a small mobile MC station, mounted on an auto-propelled chassis. It can move about on level ground or paved areas, and also in calm water. It enables us to do most of our spatial maneuvering on our own ground, so to speak, and avoid the hazards of attempting to conduct ground operations in strange areas."

"Where are the rest of the men in your party?" I asked. "There are at least three more of you."

"They're all at their assigned posts," Winter said. "There's another small room containing the drive mechanism forward of the control compartment."

"What's this stuff for?" I indicated the box on the desk from which I'd gotten the gun.

Winter looked at it, then said ruefully, "So that's where you acquired the weapon. I knew you'd been searched. Damned careless of Doyle— bloody souvenir hunter! I told him to submit everything to me for approval before we returned, so I suppose it's my fault." He touched his aching hand tenderly.

"Don't feel too bad about it. I'm just a clever guy," I said. "However, I'm not very brave. As a matter of fact, I'm scared to death of what's in store for me when we arrive at our destination."

"You'll be well treated, Mr. Bayard," Winter assured me. I let that one pass. Maybe when we arrived, I could come out shooting, making an escape. That line of thought didn't seem very encouraging either. What would I do next, loose in this Imperium of Winter's? What I needed was a return ticket home. I found myself thinking of it as B-I Three, and realized I was beginning to accept Winter's story. I took a drink from the blue bottle.

"Why don't we explode when we pass through one of those empty-space lines, or burn in the hot ones?" I asked suddenly. "Suppose we found ourselves peeking out from inside one of those hunks of rock you were photographing?"

"We don't linger about long enough, old boy," Winter said. "We remain in any one line for no finite length of time, therefore there's no time for us to react physically to our surroundings."

"How can you take pictures and use communicators?"

"The camera remains inside the field. The photo is actually a composite exposure of all the lines we cross during the instant of the exposure. The lines differ hardly at all, of course, and the prints are quite clear. Light, of course, is a condition, not an event. Our communicators employ a sort of grating which spreads the transmission."

"Winter," I said, "this is all extremely interesting, but I get the impression that you have small regard for a man's comfort. I think you might be planning to use me in some sort of colorful experiment, and then throw me away—toss me out into one of those cosmic junk heaps you showed me. And that stuff in the blue bottle isn't quite soothing enough to drive the idea out of my mind."

"Great heavens, old boy!" Winter sat bolt upright. "Nothing of that sort, I can assure you. Why, we're not blasted barbarians! Since you are an object of official interest of the Imperium, you can be assured of humane and honorable treatment."

"I didn't like what you said about concentration points a while back. That sounds like jail to me."

"Not at all," Winter expostulated. "There are a vast number of very pleasant A-lines well outside the Blight which are either completely uninhabited, or are occupied by backward or underdeveloped peoples. One can well nigh select the technological and cultural level in which one would like to live. All interrogation subjects are most scrupulously provided for; they're supplied with everything necessary to live in comfort for the remainder of their normal lives."

"Marooned on a desert island, or parked in a native village? That doesn't sound too jolly to me," I said. "I'd rather be at home."

Winter smiled speculatively. "What would you say to being set up with a fortune in gold, and placed in a society closely resembling that of, say,

England in the seventeenth century with the added advantage that you'd have electricity, plenty of modern literature, supplies for a lifetime, whatever you wished. You must remember that we have all the resources of the universe to draw upon."

"I'd like it better if I had a little more choice," I said.

"Suppose we keep right on going, once we're clear of the Blight," I said. "That reception committee wouldn't be waiting then. You could run this buggy back to B-I Three. I could force you."

"See here, Bayard," Winter said impatiently. "You have a gun. Very well, shoot me; shoot all of us. What would that gain you? The operation of this machine requires a very high technical skill. The controls are set for automatic return to the starting point. It is absolutely against Imperium policy to return a subject to the line from which he was taken. The only thing for you to do is cooperate with us, and you have my assurance as an Imperial officer that you will be treated honorably."

I looked at the gun. "According to the movies," I said, "the fellow with the rod always gets his own way. But you don't seem to care whether I shoot you or not."

Winter smiled. "Aside from the fact that you've had quite a few draughts from my brandy flask and probably couldn't hit the wall with that weapon you're holding, I assure . . . "

"You're always assuring me," I said. I tossed the pistol onto the desk. I put my feet up on the polished top, and leaned back in the chair. "Wake me up when we get there. I'll want to fix my face."

Winter laughed. "Now you're being reasonable,

old boy. It would be damned embarrassing for me to have to warn the personnel at base that you were waving a pistol about."

Chapter 3

I woke up with a start. My neck ached abominably; so did the rest of me, as soon as I moved. I groaned, dragged my feet down off the desk, and sat up. There was something wrong. Winter was gone and the humming had stopped. I jumped up.

"Winter," I shouted. I had a vivid picture of myself marooned in one of those hell-worlds. At that moment I realized I wasn't half as afraid of arriving at Zero Zero as I was of not getting there.

Winter pushed the door open and glanced in. "I'll be with you in a moment, Mr. Bayard," he said. "We've arrived on schedule."

I was nervous. The gun was gone. I told myself it was no worse than going to one of the ambassador's receptions. My best bet was to walk in as though I'd thought of it myself.

The two bouncers came in, followed by Winter. One of the two men pushed the door open, and stood at attention beside it. Beyond the opening I

could see muted sunshine on a level paved
surface, and a group of men in white uniforms,
looking in our direction.

I stepped down through the door and looked
around. We were in a large shed, looking something like a railroad station. A group of men in
white uniforms were waiting.

One of them stepped forward. "By Jove,
Winter," he said. "You've brought it off. Congratulations, old man." The others came up, gathered
around Winter, asking questions, turning to stare
at me. None of them said anything to me. To hell
with them, I thought. I turned and started strolling toward the front of the shed. There was one
door with a sentry box arrangement beside it. I
gave the man on duty a glance and started past.

"You'd better memorize this face," I said coolly.
"You'll be seeing a great deal of it from now on.
I'm your new commander." I looked him up and
down. "Your uniform is in need of attention." I
turned and went on.

Winter appeared at that point, putting an end to
what would have been a very neat escape. But
where the hell would I have gone?

"Here, old man," he said. "Don't go wandering
about. I'm to take you directly to Royal Intelligence, where you'll doubtless find out a bit more
about the reasons for your, ah—" Winter cleared
his throat, "visit."

"I thought it was Imperial Intelligence," I said.
"And for the high level operation this is supposed
to be, this is a remarkably modest reception. I
thought there would be a band, or at least a couple
of cops with handcuffs."

"Royal Swedish Intelligence," Winter explained
briskly. "Sweden will bring tributary to the Em-

peror, of course. Imperial Intelligence chaps will be on hand. As for your reception, we don't believe in making much fuss, you know." Winter waved me into a boxy black staff car which waited at the curb. It swung out at once into light traffic which pulled out of our way as we rode down the center of the broad avenue.

"I thought your scout just travelled crossways," I said, "and stayed in the same spot on the map. This doesn't look like the hilly area of the Old Town."

"You have a suspicious mind and an eye for detail," Winter said. "We maneuvered the scout through the streets to the position of the ramps before going into drive. We're on the north side of the city now."

Our giant car roared across a bridge, and swirled into a long gravel drive leading to a wrought-iron gate before a massive grey granite building. The people I saw looked perfectly ordinary, with the exception of a few oddities of dress and an unusually large number of gaudy uniforms. The guard at the iron gate was wearing a cherry-colored tunic, white trousers, and a black steel helmet surmounted by a gold spike and a deep purple plume. He presented arms—a short and wicked looking nickel-plated machine gun—and as the gate swung wide we eased past him and stopped before broad doors of polished ironbound oak. A brass plate beside the entrance said Kungliga Svenska Spionage.

I said nothing as we walked down a spotless white marble-floored hall, entered a spacious elevator, and rode up to the top floor. We walked along another hall, this one paved with red granite, and paused before a large door at the end.

There was no one else around.

"Just relax, Mr. Bayard. Answer all questions fully, and use the same forms of address as I do."

"I'll try not to fall down," I said. Winter looked as nervous as I felt as he opened the door after a polite tap.

The room was an office, large and handsomely furnished. Across a wide expanse of grey rug three men sat around a broad desk, behind which sat a fourth. Winter closed the door, walked across the room with me trailing behind him, and came to a rigid position of attention ten feet from the desk. His arms swung up in a real elbow-buster of a salute and held it.

"Sir, Chief Captain Winter reports as ordered," he said in a strained voice.

"Very good, Winter," said the man behind the desk, sketching a salute casually. Winter brought his arm down wtih a snap. He rotated rigidly toward the others.

"Kaiserliche Hochheit," he said, bowing stiffly from the waist at one of the seated figures. "Chief Inspector," he greeted the second, while the third, a rather paunchy fellow with a jolly expression and a somehow familiar face, rated just "Sir."

" 'Hochwelgeboren' will do," murmured the lean aristocratic-looking one whom Winter had addressed first. Apparently instead of an imperial highness he was only a high-well-born. Winter turned bright pink. "I beg your Excellency's pardon," he said in a choked voice. The round-faced man grinned broadly.

The man behind the desk had been studying me intently during this exchange. "Please be seated, Mr. Bayard," he said pleasantly, indicating an empty chair directly in front of the desk. Winter

was still standing rigidly. The man glanced at him.
"Stand at ease, Chief Captain," he said in a dry
tone, turning back to me.

"I hope that your being brought here has not
prejudiced you against us unduly, Mr. Bayard," he
said. He had a long gaunt face with a heavy jaw.

"I am General Bernadotte," he went on. "These
gentlemen are the Friherr von Richthofen, Chief
Inspector Bale, and Mr. Goering." I nodded at
them. Bale was a thin broad-shouldered man with
a small bald head. He wore an expression of dis-
approval.

Bernadotte went on. "I would like first to assure
you that our decision to bring you here was not
made lightly. I know that you have many questions, and all will be answered fully. For the
present, I shall tell you frankly that we have called
you here to ask for your help."

I hadn't been prepared for this. I don't know
what I expected, but to have this panel of high-
powered brass asking for my puny assistance left
me opening and closing my mouth without
managing to say anything.

"It's remarkable," commented the paunchy
civilian. I looked at him. Winter had called him
Mr. Goering. I thought of pictures of Hitler's gross
Air Chief.

"Not Hermann Goering?" I said.

The fat man looked surprised, and a smile
spread across his face.

"Yes, my name is Hermann," he said. "How did
you know this?" He had a fairly heavy German
accent.

I found it hard to explain. This was something I
hadn't thought of—actual double or analogs of figures in my own world. Now I knew beyond a doubt

that Winter had not been lying to me.

"Back where I came from, everyone knows your name," I said. "Reichmarshall Goering . . ."

"Reichmarshall!" Goering repeated. "What an intriguing title!" He looked around at the others. "Is this not a most interesting and magnificent information?" He beamed. "I, poor fat Hermann, a Reichmarshall, and known to all." He was delighted.

"Multi-phased reality is, of course, rather a shocking thing to encounter suddenly," the general said, "after a lifetime of living in one's own narrow world. To those of us who have grown up with it, it seems only natural and in keeping with the principles of multiplicity and continuum. The idea of a monolinear casual sequence is seen to be an artificially restrictive conception, an oversimplification of reality growing out of human egotism."

The other four men listened as attentively as I. It was very quiet, with only the occasional faint sounds of traffic from the street below.

"Insofar as we have been able to determine thus far from our studies of the B-I Three line, from which you come, our two lines share a common history up to about the year 1790. They remain parallel in many ways for about another century; thereafter they diverge rather sharply.

"Here in our world, two Italian scientists, Giulio Maxoni and Carlo Cocini, in the year 1893, made a basic discovery, which, after several years of study, they embodied in a device which enabled them to move about at will through a wide range of what we now term Alternative lines, or A-lines.

"Cocini lost his life in an early exploratory test, and Maxoni determined to offer the machine to the Italian government. He was rudely rebuffed.

"After several years of harassment by the Italian press, which ridiculed him unmercifully, Maxoni went to England, and offered his invention to the British government. There was a long and very cautious period of negotiation, but eventually a bargain was struck. Maxoni received a title, estates, and one million pounds in gold. He died a year later.

"The British government now had sole control of the most important basic human discovery since the wheel. The wheel gave man the power to move easily across the surface of his world; the Maxoni principle gave him all the worlds to move about in."

Leather creaked faintly as I moved in my chair. The general leaned back and drew a deep breath. He smiled.

"I hope that I am not overwhelming you with an excess of historical detail, Mr. Bayard."

"Not at all," I replied. "I'm very much interested."

He went on. "At that time the British government was negotiating with the Imperial Germanic government in an effort to establish workable trade agreements, and avoid a fratricidal war, which then appeared to be inevitable if appropriate spheres of influence were not agreed upon.

"The acquisition of the Maxoni papers placed a different complexion on the situation. Rightfully feeling that they now had a considerably more favorable position from which to negotiate, the British suggested an amalgamation of the two empires into the present Anglo-Germanic Imperium, with the House of Hanover-Windsor occupying the Imperial throne. Sweden signed the

Concord shortly thereafter, and after the resolution of a number of differences in detail, the Imperium came into being on January 1, 1900."

I had the feeling the general was over-simplifying things. I wondered how many people had been killed in the process of resolving the minor details. I kept the thought to myself.

"Since its inception," the general continued, "the Imperium has conducted a program of exploration, charting, and study of the A-continuum. It was quickly determined that for a vast distance on all sides of the home line, utter desolation existed; outside that blighted region, however, were the infinite resources of countless lines. Those lines lying just outside the Blight seem uniformly to represent a divergence point at about 400 years in the past; that is to say, our common histories differentiate about the year 1550. As one travels further out, the divergence date recedes. At the limits of our explorations to date the CH dated is about 1,000,000 B.C."

I didn't know what to say, so I said nothing. This seemed to be all right with Bernadotte.

"Then, in 1947, examination of photos made by automatic camera scouts revealed an anomaly; an apparently normal, inhabited world, lying well within the Blight. It took weeks of careful searching to pinpoint the line. For the first time, we were visiting a world closely analogous to our own, in which many of the institutions of our own world should be duplicated.

"We had hopes of a fruitful liaison between the two worlds, but in this we were bitterly disappointed."

The general turned to the bald man whom he had introduced as Chief Inspector Bale.

"Chief Inspector," he said, "will you take up the account at this point?"

Bale sat up in his chair, folded his hands, and began.

"In September 1948 two senior agents of Imperial Intelligence were despatched with temporary rank of Career Minister and full diplomatic accreditation, to negotiate an agreement with the leaders of the National People's State. This political unit actually embraces most of the inhabitable world of the B-1 Two line. A series of frightful wars, employing some sort of radioactive explosives, had destroyed the better part of civilization.

"Europe was a shambles. We found that the NPS headquarters was in North Africa, and had as its nucleus the former French colonial government there. The top man was a ruthless ex-soldier who had established himself as uncontested dictator of what remained of things. His army was made up of units of all the previous combatants, held together by the promise of free looting and top position in a new society based on raw force.

"Our agents approached a military sub-chief, calling himself Colonel-General Yang, in charge of a ragtag mob of ruffians in motley uniforms, and asked to be conducted to the headquarters of the dictator. Yang had them clapped into a cell and beaten insensible in spite of their presentation of diplomatic passports and identity cards.

"He did however send them along to the dictator to have an interview. During the talk, the fellow drew a pistol and shot one of my two chaps through the head, killing him instantly. When this failed to make the other volunteer anything further than that he was an accredited envoy of the Imperial government requesting an *exequatur* and appropriate treatment, prior to negotiating an international agreement, he was turned over to experienced torturers.

"Under torture, the agent gave out just enough to convince his interrogators that he was insane; he was released to starve or die of wounds. We managed to spot him and pick him up in time to get the story before he died."

I still had no comment to make. It didn't sound pretty, but then I wasn't too enthusiastic about the methods employed by the Imperium either. The general resumed the story.

"We resolved to make no attempt at punitive action, but simply to leave this unfortunate line in isolation.

"About a year ago, an event occurred which rendered this policy no longer tenable." Bernadotte turned to the lean-faced man.

"Manfred, I will ask you to cover this part of the briefing."

"Units of our Net Surveillance Service detected activity at a point of some distance within the area called Sector 92," Richthofen began. "This was a contingency against which we had been on guard from the first. A heavily armed MC unit of unknown origin had dropped into identity with one of our most prized industrial lines, one of a group with which we conduct a multi-billion pound trade. The intruder materialized in a population center, and released virulent poisonous gases, killing hundreds. Masked troops then emerged, only a platoon or two of them, and proceeded to strip bodies, loot shops—an orgy of wanton destruction. Our NSS scout arrived some hours after the attackers had departed. The scout, in turn, was subjected to a heavy attack by the justifiably aroused inhabitants of the area before it was able to properly identify itself as an Imperium vessel."

Richthofen had a disdainful frown on his face. "I personally conducted the rescue and salvage operation; over four hundred innocent civilians dead, valuable manufacturing facilities destroyed by fire, production lines disrupted, the population entirely demoralized. A bitter spectacle for us."

"You see, Mr. Bayard," Bernadotte said, "we are well nigh helpless to protect our friends against such forays. Although we have developed extremely effective MC field detection devices, the difficulty of reaching the scene of an attack in time is practically insurmountable. The actual transit takes no time, but locating the precise line among numerous others is an extremely delicate operation. Our homing devices make it possible, but only after we have made a very close approximation manually."

"In quick succession thereafter," Richthofen continued, "we suffered seven similar raids. Then the pattern changed. The raiders began appearing in numbers, with large cargo-carrying units. They also set about rounding up all the young women at each raid, and taking them along into captivity. It became obvious that a major threat to the Imperium had come into existence.

"At last we had the good fortune to detect a raider's field in the close vicinity of one of our armed scouts. It quickly dropped in on a converging course, and located the pirate about twenty minutes after it had launched its attack. The commander of the scout quite properly opened up at once with high explosive cannon and

blew the enemy to rubble. Its crew, although demoralized by the loss of their vessel, nevertheless
resisted capture almost to the last man. We were
able to secure only two prisoners for interrogation."

I wondered how the Imperium's methods of
interrogation compared with those of the dictator
of B-I Two, but I didn't ask. I might find out soon
enough.

"We learned a great deal more than we expected
from our prisoners. They were the talkative,
boastful type. The effectiveness of the raiding
parties depended on their striking unexpectedly
and departing quickly. The number of pirate
vessels was placed at no more than four, each
manned by about fifty men. They boasted of a
great weapon held in reserve, and which would be
used to avenge them. It was apparent from the remarks of the prisoners that they had not had the
MC drive long, and that they knew nothing of the
configuration of the Net, or of the endless ramifi-
cations of simultaneous reality.

"They seemed to think their fellows would find
our base and destroy it with ease. They also had
only a vague idea of the extent and the nature of
the Blight. They mentioned that several of their
ships had disappeared, doubtless into that region.
It appears also, happily for us, that they have only
the most elementary detection devices and that
their controls are erratic in the extreme. But the
information of real importance was the identity of
the raiders."

Richthofen paused for dramatic effect. "It was
our unhappy sister world, B-I Two."

"Somehow," Bernadotte took up the story, "in
spite of their condition of chaotic social disorder

and their destructive wars, they had succeeded in harnessing the MC principle. Their apparatus is even more primitive than that with which we began almost sixty years ago; yet they have escaped disaster.

"The next move came with startling suddenness. Whether by virtue of an astonishingly rapid scientific development, or by sheer persistence and blind luck, one of their scouts succeeded, last month, in locating the Zero Zero line of the Imperium itself. The vessel dropped into identity with our continuum on the outskirts of the city of Berlin, one of the royal capitals.

"The crew had apparently been prepared for their visit. They planted a strange device atop a flimsy tower in a field, and embarked instantly. Within a matter of three minutes, as well as we have been able to determine, the device detonated with unbelievable force. Over a square mile was absolutely desolated; casualties ran into the thousands. And the entire area still remains poisoned with some form of radiation-producing debris which renders the region uninhabitable."

I nodded. "I think I understand," I said.

"Yes," the general said, "you have something of this sort in your B-I Three world also, do you not?"

I assumed the question was rhetorical and said nothing.

Bernadotte continued. "Crude though their methods are, they have succeeded already in flaunting the Imperium. It is only a matter of time, we feel, before they develop adequate controls and detection devices. We will then be faced with the prospect of hordes of ragged but efficient soldiers, armed with the frightful radium bombs with which they destroyed their own culture, descending on the mother world of the Imperium.

"This eventuality is one for which it has been necessary to make preparation. There seemed to be two possibilities, both equally undesirable. We could await further attack, meanwhile readying our defenses, of doubtful value against the fantastic explosives of the enemy; or we could ourselves mount an offensive, launching a massive invasion force against B-I Two. The logistics problems involved in either plan would be unbelievably complex."

I was learning a few things about the Imperium. In the first place, they did not have the atomic bomb, and had no conception of its power. Their consideration of war against an organized military force armed with atomics was proof of that. Also, not having had the harsh lessons of two major wars to assist them, they were naive, almost backward, in some ways. They thought more like Europeans of the nineteenth century than modern westerners.

"About one month ago, Mr. Bayard," Bale took over, "a new factor was introduced, giving us a third possibility. In the heart of the Blight, at only a very little distance from B-I Two, and even closer to us than it, we found a second surviving line. That line was of course your home world, designated Blight-Insular Three.

"Within seventy-two hours one hundred and fifty special agents had been placed at carefully scouted positions in B-I Three. We were determined to make no blunders; too much was at stake. As the information flowed in from our men, all of whom, being top agents, had succeeded in establishing their cover identities without diffi-

culty, it was immediately passed to the General
Staff and to the Imperial Emergency Cabinet for
study. The two bodies remained in constant
session for over a week without developing any
adequate scheme for handling the new factor.

"One committee of the Emergency Cabinet was
assigned the important task of determining as
closely as possible the precise CH relationship of
B-I Three with both B-I Two and the Imperium.
This is an extremely tricky chore as it is quite
possible for an amazing parallelism to exist in one
phase of an A-line while the most fantastic vari-
ants crop up in another.

"One week ago today the committee reported
findings they considered to be ninety-eight per
cent reliable. Your B-I Three line shared history of
the B-I Two until the date 1911, probably early in
the year. At that point, my colleague, Mr. Goering,
of German Intelligence, who had been sitting in on
the meeting, made a brilliant contribution. His
suggestion was immediately adopted. All agents
were alerted at once to drop all other lines of
inquiry and concentrate on picking up a trace
of—" Bale looked at me.

"Mr. Brion Bayard."

They knew I was on the verge of exploding from
pure curiosity, so I just sat and looked back at
Bale. He pursed his lips. He sure as hell didn't like
me.

"We picked you up from records at your university—" Bale frowned at me. "Something like
aluminum alloy . . ."

Bale must be an Oxford man, I thought.

"Illinois," I said.

"At any rate," Bale went on, "it was a relatively
simple matter to follow you up then through your

military service and into your Diplomatic Service.
Our man just missed you at your Legation at Viat-
Kai."

"Consulate General," I corrected.

It annoyed Bale. I was glad; I didn't like him
much either.

"You had left the post the preceding day and
were proceeding to your headquarters via Stockholm. We had a man on the spot; he kept tabs on
you until the shuttle could arrive. The rest you
know."

There was a lengthening silence. I shifted in my
chair, looking from one expressionless face to
another.

"All right," I said. "It seems I'm supposed to
ask, so I'll oblige, just to speed things along. Why
me?"

Almost hesitantly General Bernadotte opened a
drawer of the desk and drew out a flat object
wrapped in brown paper. He removed the paper
very deliberately as he spoke.

"I have here an official portrait of the dictator
of the world of Blight-Insular Two," he said. "One
of the two artifacts we have been able to bring
along from that unhappy region. Copies of this picture are posted everywhere there."

He passed it over to me. It was a crude litho-
graph in color, showing a man in uniform, the
chest as far down as the picture extended covered
with medals. Beneath the portrait was the legend:
His Martial Excellency, Duke of Algiers, Warlord
of the Combined Forces, Marshal General of the
State, Brion The First Bayard, Dictator."

The picture was of me.

Chapter 4

I stared at the garish portrait for a long time. It wasn't registering; I had a feeling of disorientation. There was too much to absorb.

"Now you will understand, Mr. Bayard, why we have brought you here," the general said, as I silently handed the picture back to him. "You represent our hidden ace. But only if you consent to help us of your own free will." He turned to Richthofen again.

"Manfred, you will outline our plan to Mr. Bayard?"

Richthofen cleared his throat. "Quite possibly," he said, "we could succeed in disposing of the Dictator Bayard by bombing his headquarters. This, however, would merely create a temporary diversion until a new leader emerged. The organization of the enemy seems to be such that no more than a very brief respite would be gained, if any at all, before the attacks would be resumed; and we are not prepared to sustain such onslaughts as these.

"No, it is far better for our purpose that Bayard remain the leader of the National People's State—and that we control him." Here he looked intently at me.

"A specially equipped TNL scout, operated by our best pilot technician, could plant a man within the private apartment which occupies the top floor of the dictator's palace at Algiers. We believe that a resolute man introduced into the palace in this manner, armed with the most effective hand weapons at our disposal, could succeed in locating and entering the dictator's sleeping chamber, assassinating him, and disposing of the body.

"If that man were you, Mr. Bayard, fortified by ten days' intensive briefing and carrying a small net-communicator, we believe that you could assume the identity of the dead man and rule as absolute dictator over Bayard's twenty million fighting men."

"Do I have another double here," I said, "in your Imperium?"

Bernadotte shook his head. "No, you have remote cousins here, nothing closer."

They all watched me. I could see that all three of them expected me to act solemn and modest at the honor, and set out to do or die for the fatherland. They were overlooking a few things, though. This wasn't my fatherland; I'd been kidnapped and brought here. And oddly enough, I could not see myself murdering anybody—especially, I had the grotesque thought—myself. I didn't even like the idea of being dropped down in the midst of a pack of torturers.

I was ready to tell them so in very definite

terms, when my eye fell on Bale. He was wearing a supercilious half-smile, and I could see that this is what he expected. His contempt for me was plain. I sensed that he thought of me as the man who had killed his best agent in cold blood, a cowardly blackguard. My mouth was open to speak; but under that sneering expression, different words came out—temporizing words. I wouldn't give Bale the satisfaction of being right.

"And after I'm in charge of B-I Two, what then?" I said.

"You will be in constant touch with Imperial Intelligence via communicator," Richthofen said eagerly. "You'll receive detailed instructions as to each move to make. We should be able to immobilize B-I Two within six months. You'll then be returned here."

"I won't be returned home?"

"Mr. Bayard," Bernadotte said seriously, "you will never be able to return to B-I Three. The Imperium will offer you any reward you wish to name, except that. The consequences of revealing the existence of the Imperium in your line at this time are far too serious to permit consideration of the idea. However—"

All eyes were on Bernadotte. He looked as though what he was about to say was important.

"I have been authorized by the Emergency Cabinet," he said with gravity, "to offer you an Imperial commission in the rank of Major General, Mr. Bayard. If you accept this commission, your first assignment will be as we have outlined." Bernadotte handed a heavy piece of parchment across the table to me. "You should know, Mr. Bayard, that the Imperium does not award commissions, particularly that of General

Officer, lightly."

"It will be most unusual rank," Goering said, smiling. "Normally there is no such rank in the Imperium Service; Lieutenant General, Colonel General, Major General. You will be unique."

"We adopted the rank from your own armed forces, as a special mark of esteem, Mr. Bayard," Bernadotte said. "It is not less authentic for being unusual."

It was a fancy sheet of paper. The Imperium was prepared to pay off well for this job they needed done—anything I wanted. And doubtless, they thought the strange look on my face was greed at the thought of a general's two stars. Well, let them think it. I didn't want to give them any more information which might be used against me.

"I'll think about it," I said. Bale looked disconcerted now. After expecting me to back out, he had apparently then expected me to be dazzled by the reward I was being offered. I'd let him worry about it. Suddenly Bale bored me.

Bernadotte hesitated. "I'm going to take an unprecedented step, Mr. Bayard," he said. "For the present, on my personal initiative as head of State, I'm confirming you as Colonel in the Royal Army of Sweden without condition. I do this to show my personal confidence in you, as well as for more practical reasons." He rose and smiled ruefully, as though unsure of my reaction. "Congratulations, Colonel," he said, holding out his hand.

I stood up too. I noticed everyone had.

"You must have twenty-four hours to consider your decision, Colonel," he said. "I'll leave you in the excellent care of Graf von Richthofen and Mr. Goering until then."

Richthofen turned to Winter, standing silently

by, "Won't you join us, Chief Captain," he said.

"Delighted," Winter said.

"Congratulations, old boy, er, Sir," Winter said as soon as we were in the hall. "You made quite a hit with the general." He seemed quite his jaunty self again.

I eyed him. "You mean King Gustav?" I said.

Winter blinked. "But how did you know?" he said. "I mean dash it, how the devil did you know?"

"But it must be," Goering said with enthusiasm, "that also he in your home world is known, not so?"

"That's right, Mr. Goering," I said, "now you've dispelled my aura of mystery."

Goering chuckled. "Please, Mr. Bayard, you must call me Hermann." He gripped my arm in friendly fashion as we moved down the hall. "Now you must tell us more about this intriguing world of yours."

Richthofen spoke up. "I suggest we go along to my summer villa at Drottningholm and enjoy a dinner and a couple of good vintages while we hear all about your home, Mr. Bayard; and we shall tell you of ours."

Chapter 5

I stood before a long mirror and eyed myself, not without approval. Two tailors had been buzzing around me like bees for half an hour, putting the finishing touches on their handiwork. I had to admit they had done all right.

I now wore narrow-cut riding breeches of fine grey whip-cord, short black boots of meticulously stitched and polished black leather, a white linen shirt without collar or cuffs beneath a mess jacket of royal blue, buttoned to the chin. A gold bordered blue stripe ran down the side of the trousers and heavy loops of gold braid ringed the sleeves from wrist to elbow. A black leather belt with a large square buckle bearing the Royal Swedish crest supported a jeweled scabbard containing a slender rapier with an ornate hilt.

In the proper position on the left side of the chest were, to my astonishment, a perfectly accurate set of my World War II Service medals and the Silver Star. On the shoulder straps, the bright silver eagles of a U.S. Colonel gleamed. I was wearing the full dress uniform of my new position in the Imperium society.

I was glad now I hadn't let myself deteriorate into the flabby ill-health of the average Foreign Service Officer, soft and pale from long hours in offices and late hours of heavy drinking at the interminable diplomatic functions. My shoulders were reasonably broad, my back reasonably straight, no paunch marred the lines of my new finery. This outfit made a man look like a man. How the devil had we gotten into the habit of draping ourselves in shapeless double-breasted suits, in mousy colors, of identical cut?

Goering was sitting in a brocaded armchair in the luxurious suite to which Richthofen had shown me in his villa.

"You cut a martial figure, Brion," he said. "It is plain to see you have, for this new job, a natural aptitude."

"I wouldn't count on it, Hermann," I said. His comment had reminded me of the other side of the coin; the deadly plans the Imperium had in mind for me. Well, I could settle that later. Tonight I was going to enjoy myself.

Over a dinner of pheasant served on a sunny terrace in the longer Swedish summer evening, Richthofen had explained to me that, in Swedish society, to be without a title was an extremely awkward social encumbrance. It was not that one needed an exalted position, he assured me; merely that there must be something for others to call one —Herr Doctor, Herr Professor, Ingenjor, Redaktor. My military status would ease my entry into the world of the Imperium.

Winter came in then, carrying what looked like a crystal ball.

"Your topper, sir," he said with a flourish. What he had was a chrome-plated steel helmet, with a rib running along the top, and a gold-dyed plume growing out of it.

"Good God," I said. "Isn't that overdoing it a little?" I took the helmet; it was feather light, I discovered. The tailor took over, placed the helmet just so, handed me a pair of white leather gloves, and faded out.

"You have to have it, old boy," Winter said. "Dragoons, you know."

"You are complete," Hermann said. "A masterpiece."

He was wearing a dark grey uniform with black trim and white insignia. He had a respectable but not excessive display of ribbons and orders.

"Hermann," I said expansively, "you should have seen yourself when you were all rigged out in your medals back home. They came down to here." I indicated my knees. He laughed.

Together we left the suite and went down to the study on the ground floor. Winter, I noted, had changed from his whites to a pale yellow mess jacket with heavy silver braid and a nickel-plated Luger.

Richthofen showed up moments later; his outfit consisted of what looked like a set of tails, circa 1880, with silver buttons and a white beret.

"We're a cool bunch of cats," I said. I was feeling swell. I caught another glimpse of myself in a mirror. "Sharp, daddy-o," I murmured.

A liveried butler swung the glass door open for us and we descended the steps to a waiting car. This one was a yellow phaeton, with the top down. We slid into our places on the smooth yellow leather seats and it eased off down the drive.

It was a magnificent night, with high clouds and

a brilliant moon. In the distance, the lights of the city glittered. We rolled smoothly along, the engine so silent that the sound of the wind in the tall trees along the way was clearly audible.

Goering had thought to bring along a small flask, and by the time we had each tapped it twice we were passing through the iron gates of the summer palace. Colored flood-lights bathed the gardens and people already filled the terrace on the south and west sides of the building. The car dropped us before the gigantic entry and moved off. We made our way through the crowd, and into the reception hall.

Light from massive crystal chandeliers glittered on gowns and uniforms, polished boots and jewels, silks, brocades and velvets. A straight-backed man in rose-pink bowed over the hand of a lovely blonde in white. A slender black-clad fellow with a gold and white sash escorted a lady in green-gold toward the ballroom. The din of laughter and conversation almost drowned out the strains of the waltz in the background.

"All right, boys," I said. "Where's the punch bowl?"

I don't often set out to get stewed, but when I do, I don't believe in half measures. I was feeling great, and wanted to keep it that way. At the moment, I couldn't feel the bruises from my fall, my indignation over being grabbed was forgotten, and as for tomorrow, I couldn't care less. I was having a wonderful time. I hoped I wouldn't see Bale's sour face.

Everybody talked, asked me eager questions, made introductions. I found myself talking to someone I finally recognized as Douglas Fairbanks, Sr. He was a tough-looking old fellow in a naval uniform. I met counts, dukes, officers of a dozen ranks I'd never heard of, several princes, and finally a short broad-shouldered man with a heavy sun tan and a go-to-hell smile whom I finally realized was the son of the Emperor.

I was still walking and talking like a million dollars, but somewhere along the line I'd lost what little tact I normally had.

"Well, Prince William," I said, weaving just a little, "I understood the House of Hanover-Windsor was the ruling line here. Where I come from the Hanovers and the Windsors are all tall, skinny and glum-looking."

The Prince smiled. "Here, Colonel," he said, "a policy was established which put an end to that unfortunate situation. The Constitution requires that the male heir marry a commoner. This not only makes life more pleasant for the heir, with so many beautiful commoners to choose from, but maintains the vigor of the line. And it incidentally produces short men with happy faces occasionally."

I moved on, meeting people, eating little sandwiches, drinking everything from aquavit to beer, and dancing with one heavenly-looking girl after another. For the first time in my life my ten years of Embassy elbow-bending were standing me in good stead. From the grim experience gained through seven evenings a week of holding a drink in my hand from sundown till midnight while pumping other members of the Diplomatic Corps who thought they were pumping me, I had emerged with a skill; I could hold my liquor.

Somewhere along the line I felt the need for a breath of fresh air and stepped out through the tall French doors onto a dark balustraded gallery overlooking the gardens. I leaned on the heavy stone rail, looked up at the stars visible through tall tree-tops, and waited for the buzzing in my head to die down a little.

The night air moved in a cool torrent over the dark lawn, carrying the scent of flowers. Behind me the orchestra played a tune that was almost, but not quite, a Strauss waltz.

I pulled off the white gloves that Richthofen had told me I should keep on when I left my helmet at the checkroom. I unbuttoned the top button of the tight-fitting jacket.

I'm getting old, I thought, or maybe just tired.

"And why are you tired, Colonel?" a cool feminine voice inquired from behind me.

I turned around. "Ah, there you are," I said. "I'm glad. I'd rather be guilty of talking out loud than of imagining voices."

I worked on focusing my eyes a little better. She had red hair, and wore a pale pink gown that started low and stayed with the subject.

"I'm very glad, as a matter of fact," I added. "I like beautiful redheads who appear out of no-where."

"Not out of nowhere, Colonel," she said. "From in there, where it is so warm and crowded."

She spoke excellent English in a low voice, with just enough Swedish accent to render her tritest speech charming.

"Precisely," I said. "All those people were making me just a little bit drunk, so I came out here to recover." I was wearing a silly smile, and having a thoroughly good time being so eloquent and clever with this delightful young lady.

"My father has told me that you are not born to the Imperium, Colonel," she said. "And that you come from a world where all is the same, yet different. It should be so interesting to hear about it."

"Why talk about that place?" I said. "We've forgotten how to have fun back there. We take ourselves very seriously, and we figure out the most elaborate excuses for doing the rottenest things to each other . . ."

I shook my head. I didn't like that train of thought. "See," I said, "I always talk like that with my gloves off." I pulled them on again. "And now," I said grandly, "may I have the pleasure of this dance?"

It was half an hour before we went back inside to visit the punchbowl. The orchestra had just begun a waltz when a shattering blast rocked the floor, and the tall glass doors along the east side of the ballroom blew in. Through the cloud of dust which followed up the explosion, a swarm of men in motley remnants of uniforms leaped into the room. The leader, a black-bearded giant wearing a faded and patched U.S. Army-type battle jacket and baggy Wehrmacht trousers, jacked the lever on the side of a short drum-fed machine gun, and squeezed a long burst into the thick of the crowd.

Men and women alike fell under the murdering attack, but every man who remained on his feet rushed the nearest attacker without hesitation. Standing in the rubble, a bristle-faced redhead wearing an undersized British sergeant's blouse pumped eight shots from the hip, knocking down an on-coming officer of the Imperium with every shot; when he stepped back to jam a new clip into the M-1, the ninth man ran him through the throat with a jewel-encrusted rapier.

I still stood frozen, holding my girl's hand. I whirled, started to shout to her to get back, to run; but the calm look I saw in her eyes stopped me.

She'd rather be decently dead than flee this rabble.

I jerked my toy sword from its scabbard, dashed to the wall, and moved along it to the edge of the gaping opening. As the next man pushed through the cloud of dust and smoke, peering ahead, gripping a shot-gun, I jammed the point of sword into his neck, hard, and jerked it back before it was wrenched from my hands. He stumbled on, choking, shotgun falling with a clatter. I reached out, raked it in, as another man appeared. He carried a Colt .45 in his left hand, and he saw me as I saw him. He swivelled to fire, and as he did I brought the poised blade down on his arm. The shot went into the floor and the pistol bounced out of the loose hand. He fell back into the trampling crowd.

Another fellow lunged out of the dust, cutting across the room, and saw me. He levelled a heavy rifle on its side across his left forearm. He moved slowly and clumsily. I saw that his left hand was hanging by a thread. I grabbed up the shotgun and blew his face off. It had been about two minutes since the explosion.

I waited a moment, but no more came through the blasted window. I saw a wiry ruffian with long yellow hair falling back toward me as he pushed another magazine into a Browning automatic rifle. I jumped two steps, set the point of the sword just about where the kidneys should be, and rammed with both hands. No very elegant style, I thought, but I'm just a beginner.

I saw Goering then, arms around a tall fellow who cursed and struggled to raise his battered sub-machine gun. A gun roared in my ear and the back of my neck burned. I realize my jump had literally saved my neck. I ran around to the side of the grappling pair, and shoved the blade into the man's ribs. It grated and stuck, but he wilted. I'm not much of a sport, I thought, but I guess guns against pig-stickers makes it even.

Hermann stepped back, spat disgustedly, and leaped on the nearest bandit. I wrenched at my sword, but it was wedged tight. I left it and grabbed up the tommy gun. A long-legged villain was just closing the chamber of his revolver as I pumped a burst into his stomach. I saw dust fly from the shabby cloth of his coat as the slugs smacked home.

I glanced around. Several of the men of the Imperium were firing captured guns now, and the remnant of the invading mob had fallen back toward the shattered wall. Bullets cut them down as they stood at bay, still pouring out a ragged fire. None of them tried to flee.

I ran forward, sensing something wrong. I raised my gun and cut down a bloody-faced man as he stood firing two .45 automatics. My last round nicked a heavy-set carbine man, and the drum was empty. I picked up another weapon from the floor, as one lone thug standing pounded the bolt of his rifle with his palm.

"Take him alive," someone shouted. The firing stopped and a dozen men seized the struggling man. The crowd milled, women bending over those who lay on the floor, men staggering from their exertions. I ran toward the billowing drapes.

"Come on," I shouted. "Outside . . ." I didn't have time or breath to say more, or to see if anyone came. I leaped across the rubble, out onto the blasted terrace, leaped the rail, and landed in the garden, sprawled a little, but still moving. In the light of the colored floods a grey-painted van,

ponderously bulky, sat askew across flower beds.
Beside it, three tattered crewmen struggled with a
bulky load. A small tripod stood on the lawn,
awaiting the momentary mental vision of what a
fission bomb would do to the summer palace and
its occupants, before I dashed at them with a yell.
I fired the pistol I had grabbed, as fast as I could
pull the trigger, and the three men hesitated,
pulled against each other, cursed, and started
back toward the open door of their van with the
bomb. One of them fell, and I realized someone behind me was firing accurately. Another of the men
yelped and ran off a few yards to crumple on the
grass. The third jumped for the open door, and a
moment later a rush of air threw dust against my
face as the van flicked out of existence. The sound
was like a pool of gasoline igniting.

The bulky package lay on the ground now,
ominous. I felt sure it was not yet armed. I turned
to the others. "Don't touch this thing," I called.
"I'm sure it's some kind of atomic bomb."

"Nice work, old boy," a familiar voice said. It
was Winter, blood spattered on the pale yellow of
his tunic. "Might have known those chaps were
fighting a delaying action for a reason. Are you all
right?"

"Yeah," I said, breathless. "Let's go back inside.
They'll need tourniquets and men to twist them."

We picked our way through the broken glass,
fragments of flagstones, and splinters of framing,
past the flapping drapes, into the brightly lit dust-
rolled ballroom.

Dead and wounded lay in rough semicircle
around the broken wall. I recognized a pretty
brunette in a blue dress whom I had danced with
earlier, lying on the floor, face waxen. Everyone

was splattered with crimson. I looked around frantically for my redhead, and saw her kneeling beside a wounded man, binding his head.

There was a shout. Winter and I whirled. One of the wounded intruders moved, threw something, then collapsed as shots struck him. I heard the thump and the rattle as the object fell, and as in a dream I watched the grenade roll over and over, clattering, stop ten feet away and spin and turn. I stood frozen. Finished, I thought. And I never even learned her name.

From behind me I heard a gasp as Winter leaped past me and threw himself forward. He landed spread-eagled over the grenade as it exploded with a muffled thump, throwing Winter two feet into the air.

I staggered, and turned away, dizzy. Poor Winter. Poor damned Winter.

I felt myself passing out, and went to my knees. The floor was tilting.

She was bending over me, face pale, but still steady.

I reached up and touched her hand. "What's your name?" I said.

"My name?" she said. "Barbro Lundane. I thought you knew my name." She seemed a bit dazed. I sat up. "Better lend a hand to someone who's worse off than I am, Barbro," I said. "I just have a weak constitution."

"No," she said. "You've bled much."

Richthofen appeared, looking grim. He helped me up. My neck and head ached. "Thank God you are alive," he said.

"Thank Winter I'm alive," I replied. "I don't suppose there's a chance . . . ?"

"Killed instantly," Richthofen said. "He knew

his duty."

"Poor guy," I said. "It should have been me."

"We're fortunate it wasn't you," Richthofen said. "It was close. As it is, you've lost considerable blood. You must come along and rest now."

"I want to stay here," I said. "Maybe I can do something useful."

Goering had appeared from somewhere, and he laid an arm across my shoulders, leading me away.

"Calmly, now, my friend," he said. "There is no need to feel it so strongly; he died in performance of his duty, as he would have wished."

Hermann knew what was bothering me. I could have blanked out that grenade as easily as Winter, but the thought hadn't even occurred to me. If I hadn't been paralyzed, I'd have run.

I didn't struggle; I felt washed out, suddenly suffering a premature hangover. Manfred joined us at the car, and we drove home in near silence. I asked about the bomb and Goering said that Bale's men had taken it over. "Tell them to dump it at sea," I said.

At the villa, someone waited on the steps as we drove up. I recognized Bale's rangy figure with the undersized head. I ignored him as he collared Hermann.

I went into the dining room, poured a stiff drink at the sideboard, sat down.

The others came behind me, talking. I wondered where Bale had been all evening.

Bale sat down, eyeing me. He wanted to hear all about the attack. He seemed to take news calmly but sourly.

He looked at me, pursing his lips. "Mr. Goering has told me that you conducted yourself quite well, Mr. Bayard, during the fight. Perhaps I was hasty in my judgment of you."

"Who the hell cares what you think, Bale?" I said. "Where were you when the lead was flying? Under the rug?"

Bale turned white, stood up glaring and stalked out of the room. Goering cleared his throat and Manfred cast an odd look at me as he rose to perform his hostly duty of conducting a guest to the door.

"Inspector Bale is not a man easy to associate with," Hermann said. "I understand your feeling." He rose and came around the table.

"I feel you should know," he went on, "that he is among the most skillful with sabre and epee. Make no hasty decision now—"

"What decision?" I asked.

"Already you have a painful wound," he said. "We must not allow you to be laid up at this critical time. Are you sure of your skill with a pistol?"

"What wound?" I said. "You mean my neck?" I put my hand up to touch it. I winced; there was a deep gouge, caked with blood. Suddenly I was aware that the back of my jacket was soggy. That near-miss was a little nearer than I had thought.

"I hope you will accord Manfred and myself the honor of seconding you," Hermann continued, "and perhaps of advising you . . ."

"What's this all about, Hermann?" I said. "What do you mean—seconding me?"

"Why," he seemed confused, "we wish to stand with you in your meeting with Bale."

"Meeting with Bale?" I repeated. I knew I didn't sound very bright. I was beginning to realize how lousy I felt.

Goering stopped and looked at me. "Inspector Bale is a man most sensitive of personal dignity," he said. "You have given him a tongue-lashing before witnesses, and a well deserved one it was; however, it remains a certainty that he will demand satisfaction." He saw that I was still groping. "Bale will challenge you, Brion," he said. "You must fight him."

Chapter 6

I was cold, chilled to the bone. I was still half asleep, and I carried my head tilted forward and a little to the side in a hopeless attempt to minimize the vast throbbing ache from the furrow across the back of my neck.

Richthofen, Goering and I stood together under spreading linden trees at the lower end of the Royal Game Park. It was a few minutes before dawn and I was wondering how a slug in the knee-cap would feel.

There was the faint sound of an engine approaching, and a long car loomed up in the gloom on the road above, lights gleaming through morning mist.

The sound of doors opening and slamming was muffled and indistinct. Three figures were dimly visible, approaching down the gentle slope. My seconds moved away to meet them. One of the three detached itself from the group and stood alone, as I did. That would be Bale.

Another car pulled in behind the first. The doctor, I thought. In the dim glow from the second car's small square cowl lights I saw another figure emerge. I watched; it looked like a woman.

I heard a murmur of voices, a low chuckle. They were very palsy, I thought. Everything on a very high plane.

I thought over what Goering had told me on the way to the field of honor, as he called it.

Bale had offered his challenge under the Toth convention. This meant that the duelists must not try to kill each other; the object of the game was to inflict painful wounds, to humiliate one's opponent.

This could be a pretty tricky business. In the excitement of the fight, it wasn't easy to inflict wounds that were thoroughly humiliating but definitely not fatal.

Richthofen had lent me a pair of black trousers and a white shirt for the performance, and a light overcoat against the pre-dawn chill. I wished it had been a heavy one. The only warm part of me was my neck, swathed in bandages.

The little group broke up now. My two backers approached, smiled encouragingly, and in low voices invited me to come along. Goering took my coat. I missed it.

Bale and his men were walking toward a spot in the clear, where the early light was slightly better. We moved up to join them.

"I think we have light enough now, eh, Baron?" said Hallendorf.

I could see better now; the light was increasing rapidly. Long pink streamers flew in the east; the trees were still dark in silhouettes.

Hallendorf stepped up to me, and offered the pistol box. I picked one of the pistols, without looking at it. Bale took the other, methodically worked the action, snapped the trigger, examined the rifling. Richthofen handed each of us a magazine.

"Five rounds," he said. I had no comment.

Bale stepped over to the place indicated by Hallendorf and turned his back. I could see the cars outlined against the sky now. The big one looked like a '30 Packard, I thought. At Goering's gesture, I took my post, back to Bale.

"At the signal, gentlemen," Hallendorf said, "step forward ten paces and pause; at the command turn and fire. Gentlemen, in the name of the Emperor and of honor!"

The white handkerchief in his hand fluttered to the ground. I started walking. One, two, three . . .

There was someone standing by the smaller car. I wondered who it was . . . eight, nine, ten. I stopped, waiting. Hallendorf's voice was calm. "Turn and fire."

I turned, holding the pistol at my side. Bale pumped a cartridge into the chamber, set his feet apart, body sideways to me, left arm behind his back, and raised his pistol. We were seventy feet apart across the wet field.

I started walking toward him. Nobody had said I had to stay in one spot. Bale lowered his pistol slightly and I saw his pale face, eyes staring. The pistol came up again, and almost instantly jumped as a flat crack rang out. The spent cartridge popped up over Bale's head and dropped on the wet grass, catching the light. A miss.

I walked on. I had no intention of standing in the

half dark, firing wildly at a half-seen target. I
didn't intend to be forced into killing a man by
accident, even if it was his idea. And I didn't intend to be pushed into solemnly playing Bale's
game with him.

Bale held the automatic at arm's length, following me as I approached. He could have killed me
easily, but that was against the code. The weapon
wavered; he couldn't decide on a target. My
moving was bothering him.

The pistol steadied and jumped again, the shot
sounding faint on the foggy air. I realized he was
trying for the legs; I was close enough now to see
the depressed angle of the barrel.

He stepped back a pace, set himself again, and
raised the Mauser higher. He was going to try to
break a rib, I guessed. A tricky shot, easy to miss—
either way. My stomach muscles tensed with
anticipation.

I didn't hear the next one; the sensation was exactly like a baseball bat slammed against my side.
I felt that I was stumbling, air knocked from my
lungs, but I kept my feet. A great warm ache
spread from just above the hip. Only twenty feet
away now. I fought a draw of breath.

Bale's expression was visible, a stiff shocked
look, mouth squeezed shut. He aimed at my feet
and fired in rapid succession; I think by error. One
shot went through my boot between the toes of my
right foot, the other in the dirt. I walked up to him.
I sucked air in painfully. I wanted to say something, but I couldn't. It was all I could do to keep
from gasping. Abruptly, Bale backed a step, aimed
the pistol at my chest and pulled the trigger; it
clicked. He looked down at the gun.

I dropped the Mauser at his feet, doubled my

fist, and hit him hard on the jaw. He reeled back as I turned away.

I walked over to Goering and Richthofen as the doctor hurried up. They came forward to meet me.

"Lieber Gott," Hermann breathed as he seized my hand and pumped it. "This story they will never believe."

"If your object was to make a fool of Inspector Bale," Richthofen said with a gleam in his eye, "you have scored an unqualified success. I think you have taught him respect."

The doctor pressed forward. "Gentlemen, I must take a look at the wound." A stool was produced, and I gratefully sank down on it.

I stuck my foot out. "Better take a look at this too," I said, "it feels a little tender."

The doctor muttered and exclaimed as he began snipping at the cloth and leather. He was enjoying every minute of it. The doc, I saw, was a romantic.

A thought was trying to form itself in my mind. I opened my eyes. Barbro was coming toward me across the grass, dawn light gleaming in her red hair. I realized what it was I had to say.

"Hermann," I said. "Manfred. I need a long nap, but before I start I think I ought to tell you; I've had so much fun tonight that I've decided to take the job."

"Easy, Brion," Manfred said. "There's no need to think of it now."

"No trouble at all," I said.

Barbro bent over. "Brion," she said. "You are not badly hurt?" She looked worried.

I smiled at her and reached for her hand. "I'll bet you think I'm accident prone; but actually I sometimes go for days at a time without so much as a bad fall."

She took my hand in both of hers as she knelt down. "You must be suffering great pain, Brion, to talk so foolishly," she said. "I thought he would lose his head and kill you." She turned to the doctor. "Help him, Dr. Blum."

"You are fortunate, Colonel," the doctor said, sticking a finger into the furrow on my side. "The rib is not fractured. In a few days you will have only a little scar and a big bruise to remind you."

I squeezed Barbro's hand. "Help me up, Barbro," I said.

Goering gave me his shoulder to lean on. "For you now, a long nap," he said. I was ready for it.

Chapter 7

I tried to relax in my chair in the cramped shuttle. Just in front of me the operator sat tensed over a tiny illuminated board, peering at instrument faces and tapping the keys of what looked like a miniature calculating machine. A soundless hum filled the air, penetrating my bones.

I twisted, seeking a more comfortable position. My half-healed neck and side were stiffening up again. Bits and fragments of the last ten days' incessant briefing ran through my mind. Imperial Intelligence hadn't been able to gather as much material as they wanted on Marshal of the State Bayard, but it was more than I was able to assimilate consciously. I hoped the hypnotic sessions I had had every night for a week in place of real sleep had taken at a level where the data would pop up when I needed it.

Bayard was a man of mystery, even to his own people. He was rarely seen, except via what the puzzled Intelligence men said seemed to be a sort of electric picture apparatus. I had tried to explain that TV was commonplace in my world, but they never really understood it.

They had given me a good night's sleep the last three nights, and a tough hour of cleverly planned calisthenics every day. My wounds had healed well, so that now I was physically ready for the adventure; mentally, however, I was fagged. The result was an eagerness to get on with the thing and find out the worst of what I was faced with. I had enough of words; now I wanted the relief of action.

I checked over my equipment. I wore a military tunic duplicating that shown in the official portrait of Bayard. Since there was no information on what he wore below the chest, I had suggested olive drab trousers, matching what I recognized as the French regulation jacket.

At my advice, we'd skipped the ribbons and orders shown in the photo; I didn't think he would wear them around his private apartment in an informal situation. For the same reason, my collar was unbuttoned and my tie loosened.

They had kept me on a diet of lean beefsteak, to try to thin my face a bit. A hair specialist had given me vigorous scalp massages every morning and evening, and insisted that I not wash my head. This was intended to stimulate rapid growth and achieve the unclipped continental look of the dictator's picture.

Snapped to my belt was a small web pouch containing my communication transmitter. We had decided to let it show rather than seek with doubtful success to conceal it. The microphone was woven into the heavy braid on my lapels. I had a thick stack of NPS currency in my wallet.

I moved my right hand carefully, feeling for the pressure of the release spring that would throw the palm-sized slug-gun into my hand with the proper flexing of the wrist.

The little weapon was a marvel of compact deadliness. In shape it resembled a water-washed stone, grey and smooth. It could lie unnoticed on the ground, a feature which might be of great importance to me in an emergency.

Inside the gun a hair-sized channel spiralled down into the grip. A compressed gas, filling the tiny hole, served as both propellant and projectile. At a pressure on the right spot, unmarked, a minute globule of the liquefied gas was fired with tremendous velocity. Once free of the confining walls of the tough alloy barrel, the bead expanded explosively to a volume of a cubic foot. The result was an almost soundless blow, capable of shattering one-quarter inch armor, instantly fatal within a range of ten feet.

It was the kind of weapon I needed—inconspicuous, quiet, and deadly at short range. The spring arrangement made it almost a part of the hand, if the hand were expert.

I had practiced the motion for hours, while listening to lectures, eating, even lying in bed. I was very conscientious about that piece of training; it was my insurance. I tried not to think about my other insurance, set in the hollowed-out bridge replacing a back tooth.

Each evening, after the day's hard routine, I had relaxed with new friends, exploring the Imperial Ballet, theatres, opera and a lively variety show. With Barbro, I had dined sumptuously at half a dozen fabulous restaurants and afterwards walked in moonlit gardens, sipped coffee as the sun rose, and talked. When the day came to leave, I had more than a casual desire to return. The sooner I got started, the quicker I would get back.

The operator turned. "Colonel," he said, "brace yourself, sir. There's something here I don't understand."

I tensed, but said nothing. I figured he would tell me more as soon as he knew more. I moved my hand tentatively against the slug-gun release. I already had the habit.

"I've detected a moving body in the Net," he said. "It seems to be trying to match our course. My spatial fix on it indicates it's very near."

The Imperium was decades behind my world in nuclear physics, television, aerodynamics, etc., but when it came to the instrumentation of these Maxoni devices, they were fantastic. After all, they had devoted their best scientific efforts to the task for almost sixty years.

Now the operator hovered over his panel controls like a nervous organist.

"I get a mass of about fifteen hundred kilos," he said. "That's about right for a light scout, but it can't be one of ours . . ."

There was a tense silence for several minutes.

"He's pacing us, Colonel," the operator said. "Either they've got better instrumentation than we thought, or this chap has had a stroke of blind luck. He was lying in wait."

Both of us were assuming the stranger could be nothing but a B-I Two vessel.

The operator tensed up suddenly, hands frozen. "He's coming in on us, Colonel," he said. "He's going to ram. We'll blow sky-high if he crosses our fix."

My thoughts ran like lightning over my slug-gun —the hollow tooth; I wondered what would happen when he hit. Somehow, I hadn't expected it to end here. The impossible tension lasted only a few seconds. The operator relaxed.

"Missed," he said. "Apparently his spatial maneuvering isn't as good as his Net mobility. But he'll be back; he's after blood."

I had a thought. "Our maximum rate is controlled by the energy of normal entropy, isn't it?" I asked.

He nodded.

"What about going slower," I said. "Maybe he'll overshoot."

I could see the sweat start on the back of his neck from here.

"A bit risky in the Blight, sir," he said, "but we'll have a go at it."

I knew how hard that was for an operator to say. This young fellow had had six years of intensive training, and not a day of it had passed without a warning against any unnecessary control changes in the Blight.

The sound of the generators changed, the pitch of the whine descending into the audible range, dropping lower.

"He's still with us, Colonel," the operator said.

The pitch fell lower. I didn't know what critical point would be reached when we would lose our artificial orientation and rotate into normal entropy. We sat rigid, waiting. The sound dropped down, almost baritone now. The operator tapped again and again at a key, glancing at a dial.

The drive hum was a harsh droning now; we couldn't expect to go much further without disaster. But then neither could the enemy.

"He's right with us, Colonel, only—" Suddenly the operator shouted.

"We lost him, Colonel! His controls aren't as good as ours in that line, anyway; he dropped into identity."

I sank back, as the whine of our MC generator built up again. My palms were wet. I wondered into which of the hells of the Blight they had gone. But I had another problem to face in a few minutes. This was not the time for shaken nerves.

"Good work, operator," I said at last. "How much longer?"

"About—good God—ten minutes, sir," he answered. "That little business took longer than I thought."

I started a last minute check. My mouth was dry. Everything seemed to be in place. I pressed the button on my communicator.

"Hello, Talisman," I said, "here is Wolfhound Red. How do you hear me? Over."

"Wolfhound Red, Talisman here, you're coming in right and bright, over." The tiny voice spoke almost in my ear from the speaker in a button on my shoulder strap.

I liked the instant response; I felt a little less lonesome.

I looked at the trip mechanism for the escape door. I was to wait for the operator to say, "Crash out," and hit the lever. I had exactly two seconds then to pull my arm back and kick the slug-gun into my palm before the seat would automatically dump me, standing, out the exit. The shuttle would be gone before my feet hit the floor.

I had been so wrapped up in the business at hand for the past ten days that I had not really thought about the moment of my arrival in the B-I

Two world. The smoothly professional handling of my hasty training had given the job an air of practicality and realism. Now, about to be propelled into the innermost midst of the enemy, I began to realize the suicidal aspects of the mission. But it was too late now for second thoughts—and in a way I was glad. I was involved now in this world of the Imperium; it was a part of my life worth risking something for.

I was a card the Imperium held, and it was my turn to be played. I was valuable property, but that value could only be realized by putting me into the scene in just this way, and the sooner the better. I had no assurance that the dictator was in residence at the palace now; I might find myself hiding in his quarters awaiting his return, for God knows how long—and maybe lucky at that, to get that far. I hoped our placement of the suite was correct, based on information gotten from the captive taken at the ballroom, under deep narcohypnosis. Otherwise, I might find myself treading air, 150 feet up.

There was a slamming of switches, and the operator twisted in his chair.

"Crash out, Wolfhound," he cried, "and good hunting."

Reach out and slam the lever; arm at the side, snap the gun into place in my hand; with a metallic whack and a rush of air the exit popped and a giant hand palmed me out into dimness. One awful instant of vertigo, of a step missed in the dark, and then my feet slammed against carpeted floor. Air whipped about my face, and the echoes of the departing boom of the shuttle still hung in the corridor.

I remembered my instructions. I stood still,

turning casually to check behind me. There was no one in sight. The hall was dark except for the faint light from a ceiling fixture at the next intersection. I had arrived.

I slipped the gun back into its latch under my cuff. No point in standing here; I started off at a leisurely pace toward the light. The doors lining the hall were identical, unmarked. I paused and tried one. Locked. So was the next. The third one opened, and I looked cautiously into a sitting room. I went on. What I wanted was the sleeping room of the dictator, if possible. If he were in, I knew what to do; if not, presumably he would return if I waited long enough. Meanwhile, I wanted very much not to meet anyone.

There was the sound of an elevator door opening, just around the corner ahead. I stopped. I eased back to the last door I had checked, opened it and stepped inside, closing it almost all the way behind me. My heart was thudding painfully. I didn't feel daring; I felt like a sneak thief. Faintly, I heard steps coming my way.

I silently closed the door, taking care not to let the latch click. I stood behind it for a moment before deciding it would be better to conceal myself, just in case. I glanced around, moving into the center of the room. I could barely make out outlines in the gloom. There was a tall shape against the wall—a wardrobe, I thought. I hurried across to it, opened the door, and stepped in among hanging clothes.

I stood for a moment, feeling foolish, then froze as the door to the hall opened and closed again softly. There were no footsteps, and then a light went on. My closet door was open just enough to catch a glimpse of a man's back as he turned away from the lamp. I heard the soft sound of a chair being pulled out, and then the tiny jingle of keys. There were faint metallic sounds, a pause, more faint metallic sounds. The man was apparently trying keys in the lock of a table or desk.

I stood absolutely rigid. I breathed shallowly, tried not to think about a sudden itch on my cheek. I could see the shoulder of the coat hanging to my left. I turned my eyes to it. It was almost identical with the one I was wearing. The lapels were adorned with heavy braid. I had a small moment of relief; I had found the right apartment, at least. But my victim must be the man in the room; and I had never felt less like killing anyone in my life.

The little sounds went on. I could hear the man's heavy breathing. All at once I wondered what he would look like, this double of mine. Would he really resemble me, or more to the point, did I look enough like him to take his place?

I wondered why he took so long finding the right key; then another thought struck me. Didn't this sound a little more like someone trying to open someone else's desk? I moved my head a fraction of an inch. The clothes moved silently, and I edged a little farther. Now I could see him. He sat hunched in the chair, working impatiently on the lock. He was short and had thin hair, and resembled me not in the least. It was not the dictator.

This was a new factor for me to think over, and in a hurry. The dictator was obviously not around, or this fellow would not be here attempting to rifle his desk. And the dictator had people around him who were not above prying. That fact might be useful to me.

It took him five minutes to find a key that fit. I

stood with muscles aching from the awkward
pose, trying not to think of the lint that might
cause a sneeze. I could hear the shuffling of
papers and faint muttering as the man looked over
his finds. At length there was the sound of the
drawer closing, the click of the lock. Now the man
was on his feet, the chair pushed back, and then
silence for a few moments. Steps came toward me.
I froze, my wrist twitching, ready to cover him and
fire if necessary the instant he pulled the door
open. I wasn't ready to start my imposture just
yet, skulking in a closet.

I let out a soundless sigh as he passed the opening and disappeared. More sounds as he ran
through the drawers of a bureau or chest.

Suddenly the hall door opened again, and
another set of steps entered the room. I heard my
man freeze. Then he spoke, in guttural French.

"Oh, it's you, is it, Maurice."

There was a pause. Maurice's tone was insinu-
ating.

"Yes, I thought I saw a light in the chief's study.
I thought that was a bit odd, what with him away
tonight."

The first man sauntered back toward the center
of the room. "I just thought I'd have a look to see
that everything was OK here."

Maurice tittered. "Don't try to rob a thief,
Georges; I know why you came here—for the same
reason as I."

"What are you up to?" the first man hissed.
"What do you want?"

"Sit down, Flic. Oh, don't get excited; they call
you that." Maurice was enjoying himself. I listened carefully for half an hour while he goaded
and cajoled, and pressured the other. The first

man, I learned, was Georges Pinay, the chief of the dictator's security force. The other man was a civilian military adviser to the Bureau of Propaganda and Education. Pinay, it seemed, had been less clever than he thought in planning a *coup* that was to unseat Bayard. Maurice knew all about it, and had bided his time; and now he was taking over. Pinay didn't like it, but he accepted it after Maurice mentioned a few things nobody was supposed to know about a hidden airplane and a deposit of gold coins buried a few miles outside the city.

I listened carefully, without moving, and after a while even the itch went away. Pinay had been looking for lists of names, he admitted; he planned to enlist a few more supporters by showing them their names in the dictator's own hand on the purge schedule. He hadn't planned to mention that he himself had nominated them for the list.

I made the mistake of over-confidence; I was just waiting for them to finish up when a sudden silence fell. I didn't know what I had done wrong, but I knew at once what was coming. The steps were very quiet and there was just a moment's pause before the door was flung open. I hoped my make-up was on straight.

I stepped out, casting a cool glance at Pinay.

"Well, Georges," I said, "it's nice to know you keep yourself occupied when I'm away." I used the same French dialect they had used, and my wrist was against the little lever.

"The devil," Maurice burst out. He stared at me with wide eyes. For a moment I thought I was going to get away with it. Then Pinay lunged at me. I whirled, side-stepped; and the slug-gun slapped my palm.

"Hold it," I barked.

Pinay ignored the order and charged again. I squeezed the tiny weapon, bracing myself against the recoil. There was a solid thump and Pinay bounced aside, landed on his back, loose-limbed, and lay still. Then Maurice hit me from the side. I stumbled across the room, tripped and fell, and he was on top of me. I still had my gun, and tried to bring it into play, but I was dazed, and Maurice was fast and strong as a bull. He flipped me and held me in a one-handed judo hold that pinned both arms behind me. He was astride me, breathing heavily.

"Who are you?" he hissed.

"I thought you'd know me, Maurice," I said. With infinite care I groped, tucked the slug-gun into my cuff. I heard it click home and I relaxed.

"So you thought that, eh?" Maurice laughed. His face was pink and moist. He pulled a heavy blackjack from his pocket as he slid off me.

"Get up," he said. He looked me over.

"My God," he said. "Fantastic. Who sent you?"

I didn't answer. It seemed I wasn't fooling him for a minute. I wondered what was wrong. Still, he seemed to find my appearance interesting. He stepped forward and slammed the sap against my neck, with a controlled motion. He could have broken my neck with it, but what he did was more painful. I felt the blood start from my half-healed neck wound. He saw it, and looked puzzled for a moment. Then his face cleared.

"Excuse me," he said grinning. "I'll try for a fresh spot next time. And answer when spoken to." There was a viciousness in his voice that reminded me of the attack at the palace. These men had seen hell on earth and they were no longer fully human.

He looked at me appraisingly, slapping his palm with the blackjack. "I think we'll have a little talk downstairs," he said. "Keep the hands in sight." His eyes darted about, apparently looking for my gun. He was very sure of himself; he didn't let it worry him when he didn't see it. He didn't want to take his eyes off me long enough to really make a search.

"Stay close, Baby," he said. "Just like that, come along now, nice and easy."

I kept my hands away from my sides, and followed him over to the phone. He wasn't as good as he thought; I could have taken him any time. I had a hunch, though, that it might be better to string along a little, to find out something more.

Maurice picked up the phone, spoke softly into it and dropped it back in the cradle. His eyes stayed on me.

"How long before they get here?" I asked.

Maurice narrowed his eyes, not answering.

"Maybe we have just time enough to make a deal," I said.

His mouth curved in what might have been a smile. "We'll make a deal all right, Baby," he said. "You sing loud and clear, and maybe I'll tell the boys to make it a fast finish."

"You've got an ace up your sleeve here, Maurice," I urged. "Don't let that rabble in on it."

He slapped his palm again. "What have you got in mind, Baby?"

"I'm on my own," I said. I was thinking fast. "I'll bet you never knew Brion had a twin brother. He cut me out, though, so I thought I'd cut myself in."

Maurice was interested. "The devil," he said. "You haven't seen your loving twin in a long time, I see." He grinned. I wondered what the joke was.

"Let's get out of here," I said. "Let's keep it between us two."

Maurice glanced at Pinay.

"Forget him," I said. "He's dead."

"You'd like that, wouldn't you, Baby?" Maurice said. "Just the two of us, and maybe then a chance to narrow it back down to one." His sardonic expression turned suddenly to a snarl, with nostrils flaring. "By God," he said, "you, you'd plan to kill me, you little man of straw—" He was leaning toward me now, arm loosening for a swing. I realized he was insane, ready to kill in an instantaneous fury.

"You'll see who is the killer between us," he said. His eyes gleamed as he swung the blackjack loosely in his hand.

I couldn't wait any longer. The gun popped into my hand, aimed at Maurice. I felt myself beginning to respond to his murder lust. I hated everything he stood for.

"You're stupid, Maurice," I said. "Stupid and slow, and in just a minute, dead. But first you're going to tell me how you knew I wasn't Bayard."

It was a nice try, but wasted.

Maurice leaped and the slug-gun slapped him aside. He hit and lay limp. My arm ached from the recoil. Handling the tiny weapon was tricky. It was good for about fifty shots on a charge; at this rate it wouldn't last a day.

I had to get out fast now. I reached up and smashed the ceiling light, then the table lamp. That might slow them up for a few moments. I eased out into the hall and started for the dark end. Behind me I heard the elevator opening. They were here already. I pushed at the glass door, and it swung open quietly. I didn't wait around to see what their reaction would be when they found Maurice and Georges. I went down the stairs two at a time, as softly as I could. I thought of my communicator and decided against it. I didn't have anything good to report.

I passed three landings before I emerged into a hall. This would be the old roof level. I tried to remember where the stair had come out in the analogous spot at Zero Zero. I spotted a small door in an alcove; it seemed to be in about the right place.

A man came out of a room across the hall and glanced toward me. I rubbed my mouth thoughtfully, while heading for the little door. The resemblance was more of a hindrance than a help now. He went on, and I tried the door. It was locked, but it didn't look very strong. I put my hip against it and pushed. It gave way with no more than a mild splintering sound. The stairs were there, and I headed down.

I had no plan other than to get in the clear. It was obvious that the impersonation was a complete flop. All I could do was get to a safe place and ask for further instructions. I had gone down two flights when I heard the alarm bell start.

I stopped dead. I had to get rid of the fancy uniform. I pulled off the jacket, then settled for tearing the braid off the wrists, and removing the shoulder tabs. I couldn't ditch the lapel braid; my microphone was woven into it. I couldn't do much else about my appearance.

This unused stair was probably as good a way out as any. I kept going. I checked the door at each floor. They were all locked. That was a good sign, I thought. The stair ended in a cul-de-sac filled with barrels and mildewed paper cartons. I went back up to the next landing and listened. Beyond the door there were loud voices and the clatter of feet. I remembered that the entry to the stair was near the main entrance to the old mansion. It looked like I was trapped.

I went down again, pulled one of the barrels aside. I peered behind it at the wall. The edge of a door frame was visible. I maneuvered another barrel out of place and found the knob. It was frozen. I wondered how much noise I could make without being heard. Not much, I decided.

I needed something to pry with. The paper cartons looked like a possibility; I tore the flaps loose on one and looked in. It was filled with musty ledger books; no help.

The next was better. Old silverware, pots and pans. I dug out a heavy cleaver and slipped it into the crack. The thing was as solid as a bank vault. I tried again; it couldn't be that strong, but it didn't budge.

I stepped back. Maybe the only thing to do was forget caution and chop through the middle. I leaned over to pick the best spot to swing at—then jumped back flat against the wall, slug-gun in my hand. The door knob was turning.

Chapter 8

I was close to panic; being cornered had that effect on me. I didn't know what to do. I had plenty of instructions on how to handle the job of taking over after I had succeeded in killing the dictator, but none to cover retreat after failure.

There was a creak, and dust sifted down from the top of the door. I stood as far back as I could get, waiting. I had an impulse to start shooting, but restrained it. Wait and see.

The door edged open a crack. I really didn't like this; I was being looked over, and could see nothing myself. At least I had the appearance of being unarmed; the tiny gun was concealed in my hand. Or was that an advantage? I couldn't decide.

I didn't like suspense. "All right," I said. "You're making a draft. In or out." I spoke in the gutter Parisian I had heard upstairs.

The door opened farther, and a grimy-faced fel-

low was visible beyond it. He blinked in the dim
light, peered up the stairs. He gestured.

"This way, come on," he said in a hoarse whisper. I didn't see any reason to refuse under the
circumstances. I stepped past the barrels and
ducked through the low doorway. As the man
closed the door, I slipped the gun back into its
clip. I was standing in a damp stone-lined tunnel,
lit by an electric lantern sitting on the floor. I
stood with my back to it. I didn't want him to see
my face yet, not in a good light.

"Who are you?" I asked.

The fellow pushed past me and picked up his
lantern. He hardly glanced at me.

"I'm just a dumb guy," he said. "I don't ask no
questions, I don't answer none. Come on."

I couldn't afford to argue that point so I followed him. We made our way along the hand-hewn
corridor, then down a twisting flight of steps, to
emerge into a dark windowless chamber. Two
men and a dark-haired girl sat around a battered
table where a candle spluttered.

"Call them in, Miche," my guide said. "Here's
the pigeon."

Miche lolled back in his chair and motioned me
toward him. He picked up what looked like a
letter-knife from the table and probed between
two back teeth while he squinted at me. I made a
point not to get too close.

"One of the kennel dogs, by the uniform," he
said. "What's the matter, you bit the hand that fed
you?" He laughed humorously.

I said nothing. I thought I'd give him a chance to
tell me something first if he felt like it.

"A ranker, too, by the braid," he said. "Well,
they'll wonder where you got to." His tone

changed. "Let's have the story," he said. "Why are you on the run?"

"Don't let the suit bother you," I said. "I borrowed it. But it seemed like the people up there disliked me on sight."

"Come on over here," the other man said. "Into the light."

I couldn't put it off forever. I moved forward, right up to the table. Just to be sure they got the idea, I picked up the candle and held it by my face.

Miche froze, knife point in his teeth. The girl started violently and crossed herself. The other man stared, fascinated. I'd gone over pretty big. I put the candle back on the table and sat down casually in the empty chair.

"Maybe you can tell me," I said, "why they didn't buy it."

The second man spoke. "You just walked in like that, sprung it on them?"

I nodded.

He and Miche looked at each other.

"You've got a very valuable property here, my friend," the man said. "But you need a little help. Chica, bring wine for our new friend here."

The girl, still wide-eyed, scuttled to a dingy cupboard and fumbled for a bottle, looking at me over her shoulder.

"Look at him sitting there, Gros," Miche said. "Now that's something."

"You're right that's something," Gros said. "If it isn't already loused up." He leaned across the table. "Now just what happened upstairs?" he said. "How long have you been in the palace? How many have seen you?"

I gave them a brief outline, leaving out my mode of arrival. They seemed satisfied.

"Only two seen his face, Gros," Miche said, "and they're out of the picture." He turned to me. "That was a nice bit of work, mister, knocking off Souvet; and nobody ain't going to miss Pinay neither. By the way, where's the gun? Better let me have it." He held out his hand.

"I had to leave it," I said. "Tripped and dropped it in the dark."

Miche grunted.

"The Boss will be interested in this," Gros said. "He'll want to see him."

Someone else panted up the stairs into the room. "Say, Chief," he began, "we make it trouble in the tower—" He stopped dead as he caught sight of me, and dropped into a crouch, utter astonishment on his face. His hand clawed for a gun at his hip, found none, as his eyes darted from face to face.

"What—what—"

Gros and Miche burst into raucous laughter, slapping the table and howling. "At ease, Spider," Miche managed. "Bayard's throwed in with us." At this even Chica snickered.

Spider still crouched. "OK, what's the deal?" he gasped. "I don't get it." He glared around the room, face white. He was scared stiff. Miche wiped his face, whooped a last time, hawked and spat on the floor.

"OK, Spider, as you were," he said. "This here's a ringer. Now you better go bring in the boys. Beat it."

Spider scuttled away. I was puzzled. Why did some of them take one startled look and relax, while this fellow was apparently completely taken in? I had to find out. There was something I was doing wrong.

"Do you mind telling me," I said, "what's wrong with the get-up?" Miche and Gros exchanged glances again.

"Well, my friend," Gros said, "it's nothing we can't take care of. Just take it easy, and we'll set you right. You wanted to step in and take out the Old Man, and sit in for him, right? Well, with the Organization behind you you're as good as in."

"What's the Organization?" I asked.

Miche broke in. "For now we'll ask the questions," he said. "What's your name? What's your play here?"

I looked from Miche to Gros. I wondered which one was the boss. "My name's Bayard," I said.

Miche narrowed his eyes as he rose and walked around the table. He was a big fellow with small eyes.

"I asked you what's your name, mister?" he said. "I don't usually ask twice."

"Hold it, Miche," Gros said. "He's right. He's got to stay in this part, if he's going to be good; and he better be plenty good. Let's leave it at that; he's Bayard."

Miche looked at me. "Yeah," he said, "you got a point." I had a feeling Miche and I weren't going to get along.

"Who's backing you, uh, Bayard?" Gros said.

"I play a lone hand," I said. "Up to now, anyway. But it seems I missed something. If your Organization can get me in, I'll go along."

"We'll get you in, all right," Miche said.

I didn't like the looks of this pair of hoodlums, but I could hardly expect high-toned company here. As far as I could guess, the Organization was an underground anti-Bayard party. The room seemed to be hollowed out of the walls of the palace. Apparently they ran a spying operation all through the building, using hidden passages.

More men entered the room now, some via the stair, others through a door in the far corner. Apparently the word had gone out. They gathered around, staring curiously, commenting to each other, but not surprised.

"These are the boys," Gros said, looking around at them. "The rats in the walls."

I looked them over, about a dozen piratical-looking toughs; Gros had described them well. I looked back at him. "All right," I said. "Where do we start?" These weren't the kind of companions I would have chosen, but if they could fill in the gaps in my disguise for me, and help me take over in Bayard's place, I could only be grateful for my good luck.

"Not so fast," Miche said. "This thing is going to take time. We got to get you to a layout we got out of town. We got a lot of work ahead of us."

"I'm here now," I said. "Why not go ahead today? Why leave here?"

"We got a little work to do on your disguise," Gros said, "and there's plans to make. How do we get the most out of this break and how do we make sure there's no wires on this?"

"And no double-cross," Miche added.

A hairy lout listening in the crowd spoke up.

"I don't like the looks of this stool, Miche. I don't like funny stuff. I say under the floor with him." He wore a worn commando knife in a sheath fixed horizontally to his belt buckle. I was pretty sure he was eager to use it.

Miche looked at me. "Not for now, Gaston," he said.

Gros rubbed his chin. "Don't get worried about

Mr. Bayard, boys," he said. "We'll have our eyes on him." He glanced up at Gaston. "You might make a special effort along those lines, Gaston; but don't get ahead of yourself. Let's say if he has any kind of accident, you'll have a worse one."

The feel of the spring under my wrist was comforting. I felt that Gaston wasn't the only one in this crew who didn't like strangers.

"I figure time is important," I said. "Let's get moving."

Miche stepped over to me. He prodded my leg with his boot. "You've got a flappy mouth, mister," he said. "Gros and me gives the orders around here."

"OK," Gros said. "Our friend has got a lot to learn, but he's right about the time. Bayard's due back here sometime tomorrow, so that means we get out today, if we don't want the Ducals all over the place on top of the regulars. Miche, get the boys moving. I want things folded fast and quiet, and good men on the stand-by crew."

He turned to me as Miche bawled orders to the men.

"Maybe you better have a little food now," he said. "It's going to be a long day."

I was startled. I had been thinking of it as night. I looked at my watch. It had been one hour and ten minutes since I had entered the palace. Doesn't time go fast, I thought to myself, when everyone's having fun.

Chica brought over a loaf of bread and a wedge of brown cheese from the cupboard, and placed them on the table with a knife. I was cautious.

"OK if I pick up the knife?" I asked.

"Sure," Gros said. "Go ahead." He reached under the table and laid a short-nosed revolver before him.

Miche came back to the table as I chewed on a slice of tough bread. It was good bread. I tried the wine. It wasn't bad. The cheese was good, too.

"You eat well," I said. "This is good."

Chica threw me a grateful smile. "We do all right," Gros said.

"Better get Mouth here out of that fancy suit," Miche said, jerking his head at me. "Somebody might just take a shot at that without thinking. The boys have got kind of nervous about them kind of suits."

Gros looked at me. "That's right," he said. "Miche will give you some other clothes. That uniform doesn't go over so big here."

I didn't like this development at all. My communicator was built into the scrambled eggs on my lapels. I had to say no and make it stick.

"Sorry," I said. "I keep this outfit. It's part of the act. I'll put a coat over it if necessary."

Miche put his foot against my chair and shoved; I saw it coming and managed to scramble to my feet instead of going over with the chair. Miche faced me.

"Strip, mister," he said. "You heard the man."

The men still in the room fell silent, watching. I looked at Miche. I hoped Gros would speak up. I couldn't see anything to be gained by this.

Nobody spoke. I glanced over at Gros. He was just looking at us.

Miche reached behind, brought out a knife. The blade snickered out. "Or do I have to cut it off you," he growled.

"Put the knife away, Miche," Gros said mildly. "You don't want to cut up our secret weapon here; and we want the uniform off all in one piece."

"Yeah," Miche said. "You got a point." He dropped the knife on the table and moved in on me. From his practiced crouch and easy shuffling step, I saw that he had been a professional.

I decided not to wait for him. I threw myself forward with my weight behind a straight left to the jaw. It caught Miche by surprise, slammed against his chin and rocked him back. I tried to follow up, catch him again while he was still off balance, but he was a veteran of too many fights. He covered up, back-pedalled, shook his head, and then flicked out with a right that exploded against my temple. I was almost out, staggering. He hit me again, square on the nose. Blood flowed.

I wouldn't last long against this bruiser. The crowd was still bunched at the far end of the room, moving this way, now, watching delightedly, calling encouragement to Miche. Gros still sat, and Chica stared from her place by the wall.

I moved back, dazed, dodging blows. I had only one chance and I needed a dark corner to try it. Miche was right after me. He was mad; he didn't like that smack on the jaw in front of the boys. That helped me. He forgot boxing and threw one haymaker after another. He wanted to floor me with one punch to retrieve his dignity. I dodged and retreated.

I moved back toward the deep shadows at the end of the room, beyond Chica's pantry. I had to get there quickly, before the watching crowd closed up the space.

Miche swung again, left, right. I heard the air whistle as his hamlike fist grazed me. I backed another step; almost far enough. Now to get between him and the rest of the room. I jumped in behind a wild swing, popped a stinging right off his ear, and kept going. I whirled, snapped the slug-gun into my hand, and as Miche lunged, I shot him in the stomach, faked a wild swinging attack as he bounced off the wall and fell full length at my feet. I slipped the gun back into my cuff and turned.

"I can't see," a man shouted. "Get some light down here." The mob pushed forward, forming a wide ring. They stopped as they saw that only I was on my feet.

"Miche is down," a man called. "The new guy took him."

Gros pushed his way through, hesitated, then walked over to the sprawled body of Miche. He squatted, beckoned to the man with the candle.

He pulled Miche over on his back, then looked closer, feeling for the heartbeat. He looked up abruptly, got to his feet.

"He's dead," he said. "Miche is dead." He looked at me with a strange expression. "It's quite a punch you got, mister," he said.

"I tried not to use it," I said. "But I'll use it again if I have to."

"Search him, boys," Gros said. They prodded and slapped, everywhere but my wrist. "He's clean, Gros," a man said. Gros looked the body over carefully, searching for signs of a wound. Men crowded around him.

"No marks," he said at last. "Broken ribs, and it feels like something funny inside; all messed up." He looked at me. "He did it barehanded."

I hoped they would go on believing that. It was my best insurance against a repetition. I wanted them scared of me, and the ethics of it didn't bother me at all.

"All right," Gros called to the men. "Back on the job. Miche asked for it. He called our new man 'Mouth.' I'm naming him 'Hammer-hand.'"

I thought this was as good a time as any to push a little farther.

"You'd better tell them I'm taking over Miche's spot, here, Gros," I said. "We'll work together, fifty-fifty."

Gros squinted at me. "Yeah, that figures," he said. I had a feeling he had mental reservations.

"And by the way," I added, "I keep the uniform."

"Yeah," Gros said. "He keeps the uniform." He turned back to the men. "We pull out of here in thirty minutes. Get moving."

There was a ragged streak of light showing at the end of the dark tunnel. Gros signalled a halt. The men bunched up, filling the cramped passage.

"Most of you never came this way before," he said. "So listen. We push out of here into the Street of the Olive Trees; it's a little side street under the palace wall. There's a dummy stall in front; ignore the old dame in it.

"Ease out one at a time, and move off east; that's to the right. You all got good papers. If the guy on the gate asks for them, show them. Don't get eager and volunteer. If there's any excitement behind, just keep going. We rendezvous at the Thieves' Market. OK—and duck the hardware."

He motioned the first man out, blinking in the glare as the ragged tarpaulin was pushed aside. After half a minute, the second followed. I moved close to Gros.

"Why bring this whole mob along?" I asked in a low voice. "Wouldn't it be a lot easier for just a few of us?"

Gros shook his head. "I want to keep my eye on these slobs," he said. "I don't know what ideas they might get if I left them alone a few days; and I can't afford to have this set-up poisoned. And I'm going to need them out at the country place. There's nothing they can do here while I'm not around to tell them."

It sounded fishy to me, but I let it drop. All the men passed by us and disappeared. There was no alarm.

"OK," Gros said. "Stay with me." He slipped under the mouldy hanging and I followed as he stepped past a broken-down table laden with pottery. An old crone huddled on a stool ignored us. Gros glanced out into the narrow dusty street, then pushed off into the crowd. We threaded our way through loud-talking, gesticulating customers, petty merchants crouched over fly-covered displays of food or dog-eared magazines, tottering beggars, grimy urchins. The dirt street was littered with refuse; starving dogs wandered listlessly through the crowd. No one paid the least attention to us. It appeared we'd get through without trouble.

Under a heavy cloak Gros had given me, I was sweating. Flies buzzed about my swollen face. A whining beggar thrust a gaunt hand at me. Gros ducked between two fat men engaged in an argument. As they moved, I had to sidestep and push past them. Gros was almost out of sight in the mob.

I saw a uniform suddenly, a hard-faced fellow in yellowish khaki pushing roughly through the press ahead. A chicken fluttered up, squawking in my face. There was a shout; people began milling, thrusting against me. I caught a glimpse of Gros, face turned toward the soldier, eyes wide in a pale face. He started to run. In two jumps the uniformed man had him by the shoulder, spun him around, shouting. A dog yelped, banged against my legs, scuttled away. The soldier's arm rose and fell, clubbing at Gros with a heavy riot stick.

Far ahead I heard a shot, and almost instantly another, close. Gros was free and running, blood on his head, as the soldier fell among the crowd. I darted along the wall, trying to overtake Gros, or at least keep him in sight. The crowd was opening, making way as he ran, pistol in hand. He fired again, the shot a faint pop in the mob noise.

Another uniform jumped in front of me, club raised; I shied, threw up an arm, as the man jumped back, saluted.

I caught the words, "Pardon, sir," as I went past him at a run. He must have caught a glimpse of the uniform I wore.

Ahead, Gros fell in the dust, scrambled to his knees, head down. A soldier stepped out of an alley, aimed, and shot him through the head. Gros lurched, collapsed, rolled on his back. The dust caked in the blood on his face. The crowd closed in. From the moment they spotted him, he didn't have a chance.

I stopped. I was trying to remember what Gros had told the men. I had made the bad mistake of assuming too much, thinking I would have Gros to lead me out of this. There was something about a gate; everyone had papers, Gros said. All but me. That was why they had had to come out in daylight, I realized suddenly. The gate probably closed at sundown.

I moved on, not wanting to attract attention by

standing still. I tried to keep the cloak around me
to conceal the uniform. I didn't want any more soldiers noticing it; the next one might not be in such
a hurry.

Gros had told the men to rendezvous at the
Thieves' Market. I tried to remember Algiers from
a three-day visit years before; all I could recall
was the Casbah and the well-lit streets of the Euro-
pean shopping section.

I passed the spot where a jostling throng craned
to see the body of the soldier, kept going. Another
ring surrounded the spot where Gros lay dead.
Now there were soldiers everywhere, swinging
their sticks carelessly, breaking up the mob. I
shuffled, head down, dodged a backhanded swipe,
found myself in the open. The street sloped up,
curving to the left. There were still a few cobbles
on this part, fewer shops and stalls. Wash hung
from railings around tiny balconies above the
street.

I saw the gate ahead. A press of people packed
against it, while a soldier examined papers. Three
more uniformed men stood by, looking toward the
scene of the excitement.

I went on toward the gate. I couldn't turn back
now. There was a new wooden watch tower
scabbed onto the side of the ancient brick wall
where the sewer drained under it. A carbon arc
searchlight and a man with a burp gun slung over
his shoulder were on top of it. I thought I saw one
of the Organization men ahead in the crowd at the
gate.

One of the soldiers was staring at me. He
straighened, glanced at the man next to him. The
other soldier was looking, too, now. I decided a
bold front was the only chance. I beckoned to one

of the men, allowing the cloak to uncover the front of the uniform briefly. He moved toward me, still in doubt. I hoped my battered face didn't look familiar.

"Snap it up, soldier," I said in my best *Ecole Militaire* tone; he halted before me, saluted. I didn't give him a chance to take the initiative.

"The best part of the catch made it through the gate before you fools closed the net," I snapped. "Get me through there fast, and don't call any more attention to me. I'm not wearing this flea-circus for fun." I flipped the cloak.

He turned and pushed through the gate, and said a word to the other soldier, gestured toward me. The other man, wearing sergeant's stripes, looked at me.

I glared at him as I approached. "Ignore me," I hissed. "You foul this up and I'll see you shot."

I brushed past him, thrust through the gate as the first soldier opened it. I walked on, listening for a sound of a round snapping into the chamber of that burp gun on the tower. A goat darted out of an alley, stared at me. Sweat rolled down my cheek. There was a tree ahead, with a black shadow under it. I wondered if I'd ever get that far.

I made it, and breathed a little easier.

I still had problems, plenty of them. Right now I had to find the Thieves' Market. I had a vague memory of such a thing from the past, but I had no idea where it was. I moved along the road, past a weathered stuccoed building with a slatternly tavern downstairs and sagging rooms above, bombed out at the far end. The gate was out of sight now.

Ahead were more bomb-scarred tenements,

ruins, and beyond open fields. There was a river in sight to the right. A few people were in view, moving listlessly in the morning heat. They seemed to ignore the hubbub within the walled town. I couldn't risk asking any of them for the place I sought; I didn't know who might be a police informer, or a cop, for that matter. They had been ready for us, I realized.

Gros wasn't as well-hidden as he had thought. Probably a police could have cleared his outfit from the palace at any time; I suspected they had tolerated them against such a time as now. The ambush had been neat. I wondered if any of the boys had made it through the gate.

Apparently word had not gone out to be on the alert for a man impersonating an officer; I didn't know how much Maurice had said when he telephoned for his men, but my bluff at the gate indicated no one had been warned of my disguise.

I paused. Maybe my best bet would be to try the tavern, order a drink, try to pick up something. I saw nothing ahead that looked encouraging.

I walked back fifty feet to the doorless entrance to the bistro. There was no one in sight. I walked in, barely able to make out the positions of the tables and chairs in the gloom. The glassless windows were shuttered. I blinked, made out the shape of the bar. Outside the door, the dusty road glared white.

A hoarse-breathing fellow loomed up behind the bar. He didn't say anything.

"Red wine," I said.

He put a water glass on the bar and filled it from a tin dipper. I tasted it. It was horrible. I had a feeling good manners would be out of place here, so I turned and spat it on the floor.

I pushed the glass across the bar. "I want wine," I said. "Not what you wring out of the bar rag." I dropped a worn thousand franc note on the bar.

He muttered as he turned away, and was still muttering when he shuffled back with a sealed bottle and a wine glass. He drew the cork, poured my glass half full, and put the thousand francs in his pocket. He didn't offer me any change.

I tried it; it wasn't too bad. I stood sipping, and waited for my eyes to get used to the dim light. The bartender moved away and began pulling a pile of boxes, grunting hard.

I didn't have a clear idea of what to do if I did find the survivors of the Organization. At best I might find out what was wrong with the disguise, and use their channels to get back into the palace. I could always call for help on my communicator, and have myself set back inside via shuttle, but I didn't like the idea of risking that again. I had almost been caught arriving last time. The scheme couldn't possibly work if any suspicion was aroused.

A man appeared in the doorway, silhouetted against the light. He stepped in and came over to the bar. The bartender ignored him.

Two more came through the door, walked past me and leaned on the bar below me. The bartender continued to shuffle boxes, paying no attention to his customers. I started to wonder why.

The man nearer me moved closer. "Hey, you," he said. He jerked his head toward the gate. "You hear the shooting back there?"

That was a leading question. I wondered if the sound of the shots had been audible outside the walls of the fortified town. I grunted.

"Who they after?" he said.

I tried to see his face, but it was shadowed. He was a thin broad fellow, leaning on one elbow. Here we go again, I thought.

"How would I know?" I said.

"Kind of warm for that burnoose, ain't it?" he said. He stretched out a hand as if to touch the tattered cape. I stepped back, and two pairs of arms wrapped around me in a double bear-hug from behind.

The man facing me twitched the cape open. He looked at me.

"Lousy Ducal," he said, and hit me across the mouth with the back of his hand. I tasted blood.

"Hold on to them arms," another man said, coming around from behind me. This was one I hadn't seen. I wondered how many more men were in the room. The new man took the old military cape in his hands and ripped it off me.

"Look at that," he said. "We got us a lousy general." He dug his finger under the top of the braided lapel of my blouse and yanked. The lapel tore but stayed put. I started to struggle then; that was my communicator they were about to loot for the gold wire on it. I didn't have much hope of getting loose that way, but maybe it would distract them if I kicked a little. I swung a boot and caught the rangy one under the kneecap. He yelped and jumped back, then swung at my face. I twisted away, and the blow grazed my cheek. I threw myself backward, jerking hard, trying to throw someone off balance.

"Hold him," a man hissed. They were trying not to make too much noise. The thin man moved in close, watched his chance and slammed a fist into my stomach. The pain was agonizing; I crammed up, retching.

The men holding me dragged me to a wall, flung me upright against it, arms outspread. The fellow who wanted the braid stepped up with a knife in his hand. I was trying to breathe, wheezing and twisting. He grabbed my hair, and for a moment I thought he was going to slit my throat. Instead, he sawed away at lapels, cursing as the blade scraped wire.

"Get the buttons, too, Beau Joe," a husky voice suggested.

The pain was fading a little now, but I sagged, acting weaker than I actually was. The communicator was gone, at least the sending end. All I could try to salvage now was my life.

The buttons took only a moment. The man with the knife stepped back, slipping it into a sheath at his hip. He favored the leg I had kicked. I could see his face now. He had straight fine features.

"OK, let him go," he said. I slumped to the floor. For the first time my hands were free. Now maybe I had a chance; I still had the gun. I got shakily to hands and knees, watching him. He aimed a kick at my ribs.

"On your feet, General," he said. "I'll teach you to kick your betters."

The others laughed, called out advice, shuffled around us in a circle. There was an odor of dust and sour wine.

"That General's a real fighter, ain't he?" somebody called. "Fights sittin' down." That went over big. Lots of happy laughter.

I grabbed the foot as it came to me, twisted it hard, and threw the man to the floor. He swore loudly, lunged at me, but was up again, backing away. The ring opened and somebody pushed me. I let myself stumble and gained a few more feet toward the shadowed corner. I could see better now, enough to see pistols and knives in every belt. If they had any idea I was armed, they'd use them. I had to wait.

Beau Joe was after me again, throwing a round-house left. I ducked it, then caught a couple of short ones. I stepped back two paces, glanced at the audience; they were as far away as I'd get them. It was time to make my play. The man shielded me as the slug-gun popped into my hand, but at that instant he swung a savage kick. It was just luck; he hadn't seen the tiny weapon, but the gun spun into a dark corner. Now I wasn't acting any more.

I went after him, slammed a hard left to his face, followed with a right to the stomach, then straightened him out with another left. He was a lousy boxer.

The others didn't like it; they closed in and grabbed me. Knuckles bounced off my jaw as a fist rammed into my back. Two of them ran me back-wards and sent me crashing against the wall. My head rang; I was stunned. I fell down and they let me lie. I needed the rest.

To hell with secrecy, I thought. I got to my knees and started crawling toward the corner. The men laughed and shouted, forgetting about being quiet now.

"Crawl, General," one shouted. "Crawl, you lousy spy."

"Hup, two, soldier," another sallied. "By the numbers, crawl."

That was a good one; they roared, slapped each other. Where the hell was that guy?

He grabbed my jacket, hauled me to my feet as I groped for him. My head spun; I must have a con-cussion, I thought. He jabbed at me, but I leaned on him, and he couldn't get a good swing. The others laughed at him, now, enjoying the farce.

"Watch him, Beau Joe," someone called. "He's liable to wake up, with you shakin' him that way."

Beau Joe stepped back, and aimed a straight right at my chin, but I dropped and headed for the corner again; that was where the gun went. He kicked me again, sent me sprawling into the wall—and my hand fell on the gun.

I rolled over, and Beau Joe yanked me up, spun me around, and stepped back. I stood, slumped in the corner, watching him. He was enjoying it now. He mouthed words silently, grinning in spite of his bleeding mouth. He intended to keep me propped there in the corner and beat me to death. As he came to me, I raised the gun and shot him in the face.

I wished I hadn't; he did a back-flip, landed head first, but not before I caught a glimpse of the smashed face. Joe was not beau any more.

I held my hand loosely at my side, waiting for the next comer. The same fellow who had grabbed me before rushed up. He jumped the body and twisted to deliver a skull-crusher. I raised the gun a few inches as he leaped and I fired at his belly. The shot made a hollow whop, as the man's feet left the floor. He smashed into the wall as I side-stepped.

The other three fanned out. It was too dark to see clearly here, and they didn't yet realize what had happened. They thought I had downed the two men with my fists. They were going to jump me to-gether and finish it off.

"Freeze, bunnies!" a voice said from the door. We all looked. A hulking brute stood outlined there, and the gun in his hand was visible.

"I can see you rats," he said. "I'm used to the dark. Don't try nothing." He beckoned a man behind him forward. One of the three in the room edged toward the rear, and the gun coughed, firing through a silencer. The man slammed sideways, and sprawled.

"Come on, Hammer-hand," the big man said. "Let's get out of here." He spat into the room. "These pigeons don't want to play no more."

I recognized the voice of Gaston, the big fellow who had wanted to bury me under the floor. Gros had appointed him my body guard, but he was a little late. I had taken a terrible beating. I tucked the gun away clumsily and lurched forward.

"Cripes, Hammer-hand," Gaston said, stepping forward to steady me. "I didn't know them bunnies had got to you; I thought you were stringing them. I was wondering when you was going to make music with that punch."

He paused to stare at Beau Joe.

"You pushed his mush right in," he said admiringly. "Hey, Touhey, get Hammer-hand's wraparound, and let's move." He glanced once more around the room.

"So long, bunnies," he said. The two men didn't answer.

Chapter 9

I don't remember much about my trip to the Organization's hide-out in the country. I recall walking endlessly, and later being carried over Gaston's shoulder. I remember terrific heat, and agonizing pain from my battered face, my half-healed gunshot wounds, and innumerable bruises. And I remember at last a cool room, and a soft bed.

I awoke slowly, dreams blending with memories, none of them pleasant. I lay on my back, propped up on enormous fluffy feather bolsters, with a late afternoon sun lighting the room through partly-drawn drapes over a wide dormer window. For a while I struggled to decide where I was. Gradually, I recalled my last conscious thought.

This was the place in the country Gros had been headed for. Gaston had taken his charge seriously, in spite of his own suggestion that I be disposed of and although Miche and Gros were dead.

I moved tentatively, and caught my breath. That hurt, too. My chest, ribs and stomach were one great ache. I pushed the quilt down and tried to examine the damage. Under the edges of a broad tape wrapping, purple bruises showed all around my right side.

Bending my neck had been a mistake; now the bullet wound that Maurice had re-opened with the blackjack began to throb. I was a mess. I didn't risk moving my face; I knew what it must look like.

As a secret-service type, I was a complete bust, I thought. My carefully prepared disguise had fooled no one, except maybe Spider. I had been subjected to more kicks, blows, and threats of death in the few hours I had been in the dictator's realm than in all my previous 42 years, and I had accomplished exactly nothing. I had lost my communicator, and now my slug-gun too; the comforting pressure under my wrist had gone. It wouldn't have helped me much anyway; I was dizzy from the little effort I had just expended.

Maybe I had made some progress, though, in a negative way. I knew that walking in and striking a pose wasn't good enough to get by as the Dictator Bayard, in spite of the face. And I had also learned that the dictator's regime was riddled with subversives and malcontents. Perhaps we could somehow use the latter to our advantage.

If, I thought, I can get back with the information. I thought that over. How would I get back? I had no way of communicating. I was completely on my own now.

Always before I had had the knowledge that in

the end I could send out a call of help, and count on rescue within an hour. Richthofen had arranged for a 24-hour monitoring of my communications band, alert for my call. Now that was out. If I was to return to the Imperium, I would have to stall one of the crude shuttles of this world, or better, commandeer one as dictator. I had to get back into the palace, with a correct disguise, or end my days in this nightmare world.

I heard voices approaching outside the room. I closed my eyes as the door opened. I might learn a little by playing possum, if I could get away with it.

The voices were lower now, and I sensed several people coming over to stand by the bed.

"How long has he been asleep?" a new voice asked. Or was it new? It seemed familiar somehow, but I connected it with some other place.

"Doc gave him some shots," someone answered. "We brought him this time yesterday."

There was a pause. Then the half-familiar voice again. "I don't like his being alive. However— perhaps we can make use of him."

"Gros wanted him alive," another voice said. I recognized Gaston. He sounded sullen. "He had big plans for him."

The other voice grunted. There was a silence for a few moments.

"He's no good to us until the face is healed. Keep him here until I send along further instructions."

I hadn't liked what I heard, but for the present I had no choice but to lie here and try to regain my strength. At least, I was comfortably set up in this huge bed. I drifted off to sleep again.

I awoke with Gaston sitting by the bed, smoking.

He sat up when I opened my eyes, crushed out his cigarette in an ash tray on the table, and leaned forward.

"How are you feeling, Hammer-hand?" he said.

"Rested," I said. My voice came out in a faint whisper. I was surprised at its weakness.

"Yeah, them pigeons give you a pretty rough time, Hammer-hand. I don't know why you didn't lay the punch on them sooner.

"I got some chow here for you," Gaston said. He put a tray from the bedside table on his lap and offered me a spoonful of soup. I was hungry; I opened my mouth for it. I never expected to have a gorilla for a nursemaid, I thought.

Gaston was good at his work, though. For the next three days he fed me regularly, changed my bedding, and performed all the duties of a trained nurse with skill, if not with grace. I steadily gained strength, but I was careful to conceal the extent of my progress from Gaston and the others who occasionally came in. I didn't know what might be coming up and I wanted something in reserve.

Gaston told me a lot about the Organization during the next few days. I learned that the group led by Gros and Miche was only one of several such cells; there were hundreds of members, in half a dozen scattered locations in Algeria, each keeping surveillance over some vital installation of the regime. Their ultimate objective was the overthrow of Bayard's rule, enabling them to get a share in the loot.

Each group had two leaders, all of whom reported to the Big Boss, a stranger about whom Gaston knew little. He appeared irregularly, and no one knew his name or where he had his headquarters. I sensed that Gaston didn't like him.

On the third day I asked Gaston to help me get up and walk a bit. I faked extreme weakness, but was pleased to discover that I was feeling better than I had hoped. After Gaston helped me back into bed and left the room, I got up again, and practiced walking. It made me dizzy and nauseous but I leaned on the bed post and waited for my stomach to settle down, and went on. I stayed on my feet for fifteen minutes, and slept soundly afterwards. Thereafter, whenever I awoke, day or night, I rose and walked, jumping back into bed when I heard footsteps approaching.

When Gaston insisted on walking me after that, I continued to feign all the symptoms I had felt the first time. The doctor was called back once, but he assured me that my reactions were quite normal, and that I could not expect to show much improvement for another week, considering the amount of blood I had lost. This suited me perfectly. I needed time to learn more.

I tried to pump Gaston about my disguise, subtly; I didn't want to put him on his guard, or give him any inkling of what I had in mind. But I was too subtle; Gaston avoided the subject.

I searched for my clothes, but the closet was locked and I couldn't risk forcing the door.

A week after my arrival, I allowed myself enough improvement to permit a walk through the house, and down into a pleasant garden behind it. The layout of the house was simple. From the garden I had seen no signs of guards. It looked as though I could walk out any time, but I restrained the impulse.

By the time ten days had passed, I was getting very restless. I couldn't fake my role of invalid much longer without arousing suspicion. The inactivity was getting on my nerves; I had spent the night lying awake, thinking, and getting up occasionally to walk up and down the room. By dawn, I had succeeded in fatiguing myself, but I hadn't slept at all.

I had to be doing something. I got out my canes, and reconnoitred the house after Gaston had taken away my breakfast tray. From the upstairs windows I had a wide view of the surrounding country. The front of the house faced a paved highway, in good repair. I assumed it was a main route into Algiers. Behind the house, tilled fields stretched a quarter of a mile to a row of trees. Perhaps there was a river there. There were no other houses near.

I thought about leaving. It looked to me as though my best bet would be to go over the wall after dark and head for the cover of the trees. I had the impression that the line of trees and the road converged to the west, so perhaps I could re-gain the road at a distance from the house, and follow it into the city. I went back to my room to wait.

It was almost dinner time when I heard some-one approaching my door. I was lying down, so I stayed where I was and waited. Gaston entered with the doctor. The doctor was pale, and per-spiring heavily. He avoided my eyes as he drew out a chair, sat down and started his examination. He said nothing to me, ignoring the questions I asked him. I gave up and lay silently while he prodded and poked. After a while he rose suddenly, packed up his kit, and walked out.

"What's the matter with doc, Gaston?" I asked.

"He's got something on his mind," Gaston said. Even Gaston seemed subdued. Something was up;

something that worried me.

"Come on, Gaston," I said. "What's going on?"

At first I thought he wasn't going to answer me.

"They're going to do like you wanted," he said. "They're getting ready to put you in for Bayard."

"That's fine," I said. That was why I had come here for. This way was as good as any. But there was something about it.

"Why all the secrecy?" I asked. "Why doesn't the Big Boss show himself? I'd like to talk to him."

Gaston hesitated. I had the feeling he wanted to say more, but couldn't.

"They got a few details to fix yet," he said. He didn't look at me. I let it go at that.

After Gaston left the room, I went out into the hall. Through the open back windows I heard the sound of conversation. I moved over to eavesdrop.

There were three men, strolling out into the garden with their backs to me. One was the doctor; I didn't recognize the other two. I wished I could see their faces.

"It was not for this I was trained," the doctor was saying. He waved his hands in an agitated way. "I'm not a butcher, to cut up a side of mutton for you."

I couldn't make out the reply.

I went down to the landing and listened. All was quiet. I descended to the hall on the ground floor, listened again. Somewhere a clock was ticking.

I went into the main dining room; the table was set for three, but no food was in sight. I tried the other dining room; nothing. I went across and eased the parlor door open. There was no one there; it looked as unused as ever.

I passed the door I had found locked once before and noticed light under it. I stepped back and tried it. It was probably a broom closet, I thought as I turned the knob. It opened.

I stood staring. There was a padded white table in the center of the room. At one end stood two floodlamps on tall tripods. Glittering instruments were laid out on a small table. On a stand beside the operating table lay scalpels, sutures, heavy curved needles. There was a finely made saw, like a big hacksaw, and heavy snippers. On the floor beneath the table was a large galvanized steel wash tub.

I didn't understand this; I turned to the door— and heard footsteps approaching.

I looked around, saw a door, jumped to it and jerked it open. When the two men entered the room, I was standing rigid in the darkness of the storeroom, with the door open half an inch.

The floodlights flicked on, then off again. There was a rattle of metal against metal.

"Lay off that," a nasal voice said. "This is all set. I checked it over myself."

"They're nuts," Nasal-voice said. "Why don't they wait until morning, when they got plenty sunlight for this? No, they gotta work under the lights."

"I don't get this deal," a thin voice said. "I didn't get what was supposed to be wrong with this guy's legs, they got to take them off. How come if he's—"

"You ain't clued in, are you, Mac?" Nasal-voice said harshly. "This is a big deal; they're going to ring this mug in when they knock off the Old Man."

"Yeah, that's what I mean," Thin-voice cut in. "So what's the idea they take off the legs?"

"You don't know much, do you, small-timer?"

Nasal-voice said. "Well, listen; I got news for you."
There was a pause.

"Bayard's got no pins, from the knees down."
Nasal spoke in a hushed tone. "You didn't know
that, did you? That's why you never seen him
walking around on the video; he's always sitting
back of a desk.

"There ain't very many people know about
that," he added. "Keep it to yourself."

"Cripes," Thin-voiced said. His voice was thinner than ever. "Got no legs?"

"That's right. I was with him a year before the
landing. I was in his outfit when he got it. Machine
gun slug, through both knees. Now forget about it.
But maybe now you get the set-up."

"Cripes," Thin-voice said. "Where did they get a
guy crazy enough to go into a deal like this?"

"How do I know?" the other said. He sounded as
though he regretted having told the secret. "These
revolutionist types is all nuts anyway."

I stood there feeling sick. My legs tingled. I
knew now why nobody mistook me for the dictator, as I walked into the room; and why Spider
had been taken in, when he saw me sitting.

I was leaving now. Not tomorrow, not tonight;
now. I had no gun, no papers, no map, no plans,
but I was leaving.

It was almost dark; I went to the back of the
house. Through a window I could see the men in
the garden standing under a small cherry tree in
the gloom, still talking. I found a door, and examined it in the failing light. It was the type that
opens in two sections. The upper one was locked,
but the lower half swung silently open—below the
line of vision of the men outside. I bent over and
stepped through.

A short path led off to the drive beside the house; I ignored it and crept along beside the wall, through weed-grown flower beds.

I turned to start out across the plowed field and a dark form rose up before me. I recoiled, my wrist twitching in a gesture that had become automatic; but no slug-gun snapped into my hand. I was unarmed, weak, and shaken, and the man loomed over me, hulking.

"Let's go, Hammer-hand," he whispered. It was Gaston.

"I'm leaving, Gaston," I said. "Just don't try to stop me." Vague ideas of a bluff were in my mind. After all, he called me Hammer-hand.

He came after me. "Hold it down to a roar," he said. "I wondered when you was going to make your break. You been getting pretty restless these last few days."

"Yeah," I said. "Who wouldn't?" I was just stalling; I had no plan.

"You got more nerve than me, Hammer-hand," Gaston said. "I would of took off a week ago. You must of wanted to get a look at the Big Boss real bad to stick as long as you did."

"I saw enough today," I said. "I don't want to see any more."

"Do you make him?" Gaston asked. He sounded interested.

"No," I said. "I didn't see his face. But I've lost my curiosity."

Gaston laughed. "OK, chief," he said. He handed me a soiled card, with something scribbled on it. "Maybe this will do you some good. It's the Big Boss's address out of town. I swiped it; it was all I could find. Now let's blow out of here."

I stuck the card in my pocket. I was a little confused.

"Wait a minute, Gaston; you mean you're helping me get away?"

"Gros said I was supposed to keep an eye on you, look out you didn't have no accident," Gaston said. "I always done all right doing what my brother told me; I don't see no reason to stop now just because they killed him."

"Your brother," I said.

"Gros was my brother," Gaston said. "I ain't smart like Gros, but he always took care of me. I always done what he said. He told me to look out for you, Hammer-hand."

"What about them?" I asked, nodding toward the house. "They won't like it when they find us both missing."

Gaston spat. "To hell with them monkeys," he said. "They gimme the willies."

I was beginning to feel jolly all of a sudden, by reaction.

"Listen, Gaston; can you go back in there and get the clothes I had on when I got here?"

Gaston fumbled in the dark at a sack slung over his shoulder. "I thought you might want that suit, Hammer-hand," he said. "You was real particular about that with Miche." He handed me a bundle. I knew the feel of it. It was the uniform.

"Gaston," I said. "You're a wonder. I don't suppose you brought along the little gimmick I had on my wrist?"

"I think I stuck it in the pocket," he said. "Somebody swiped the fancy gloves you had in the belt, though. I'm sorry about the gloves."

I fumbled over the blouse, and felt the lump in the pocket. With that slug-gun in my hand I was ready to lick the world.

"That's OK about the gloves, Gaston," I said. I strapped the clip to my wrist and tucked the gun away. I pulled off the old coat I wore and slipped the blouse on. This was more like it.

I looked at the house. All was peaceful. It was dark enough now that we wouldn't be seen crossing the field. It was time to go.

"Come on," I said. I took a sight on a bright star and struck out across the soft ground.

In fifty steps the house was completely lost to view. The wall and high foliage obscured the lights on the first floor; upstairs the house was in darkness. I kept the star before me and stumbled on. I never knew how hard it was to walk in a plowed field in the dark.

It was fifteen minutes before I made out a deeper darkness against the faintly lighter sky ahead. That would be the line of trees along the river; I was still assuming there was a river.

Then we were among the trees, feeling our way slowly. The ground sloped and the next moment I was sliding down a muddy bank into shallow water.

"Yes," I said, "it's a river all right." I scrambled out, and stood peering toward the west. I could see nothing. If we had to pick our way through trees all night, without a moon, we wouldn't be a mile away by dawn.

"Which way does this river flow, Gaston?" I asked.

"That way," he said. "To Algiers—into the city."

"Can you swim?" I asked.

"Sure," Gaston replied. "I can swim good."

"OK," I said, "strip and make a bundle of your clothes. Put whatever you don't want to get wet in the middle; strap the bundle to your shoulders with your belt."

We grunted and fumbled in the darkness.

I finished my packing and stepped down into the water. It was warm weather; that was a break. I still had the slug-gun on my wrist. I wanted it close to me.

I stepped out into the stream, pushed off as the bottom shelved. I paddled a few strokes to get clear of the reeds growing near the shore. All around was inky blackness, with only the brilliant stars overhead to relieve the emptiness.

"OK, Gaston?" I called.

I heard him splashing quietly.

"Sure," he said.

"Let's go out a little farther and then take it easy," I said. "Let the river do the work."

Chapter 10

The current was gentle. Far across the river I saw a tiny light now. We drifted slowly past it. I moved my hands just enough to keep my nose above the water. The surface was calm. I yawned; I could have slept tonight, I thought, remembering the sleepless hours of the night before. But it would be a long time between beds for me.

I saw a glinting reflection on a ripple ahead, and glanced back. There were lights on in the second story of the house we had left.

I called to Gaston, pointing out the lights.

"Yeah," he said. "I been watching them. I don't think we got nothing to worry about."

They could follow our trail to the water's edge easily enough, I knew, with nothing more than a flashlight. As if in response to my thought, a tiny gleam appeared at ground level, wavering, blinking as the trees passed between us. It moved, bobbing toward the river. I watched until it emerged from the trees. I saw the yellow gleam dancing across the water where we had started. Other lights were following now, two, three.

The whole household must have joined the chase. They must be expecting to find me huddled on the ground nearby, exhausted, ready for the table they had prepared for me in the presence of my enemies.

The lights fanned out, moving along the shore. I saw that we were safely ahead of them.

"Gaston," I said, "have they got a boat back there?"

"Nah," he replied. "We're in the clear."

The little lights were pitiful, bobbing along the shore, falling behind.

We floated along then in silence for an hour or more. It was still, almost restful. Only a gentle fluttering of the hands was required to keep our heads above water.

Suddenly lights flashed ahead, over the river.

"Cripes," Gaston hissed, backing water. "I forgot about the Salan bridge. Them bunnies is on there waitin' for us."

I could see the bridge, now, as the lights flashed across the pilings. It was about a hundred yards ahead.

"Head for the far shore, Gaston," I said. "Fast and quiet."

I couldn't risk the splash of a crawl stroke, so I dog-paddled frantically, my hands under the surface. They would have had us neatly, if they hadn't shown the lights when they did, I thought. They wouldn't see us without them, though, so it was just a chance they had to take. They must have estimated the speed of the river's flow, and tried to pin-point us. They didn't miss by much; in fact, they might not have missed at all. I concentrated on putting every ounce of energy into my strokes. My knees hit mud, and reeds brushed my face. I rolled over and sat up, breathing hard. Gaston floundered a few feet away.

"Here," I hissed. "Keep it quiet."

The light on the bridge blinked out suddenly. I wondered what they'd do next. If they headed along the banks, flashing lights, we'd have to take to the water again; and if one man stayed on the bridge, and flashed his light down just about the right moment—

"Let's get going," I said.

I started up the slope, crouching low. The lights appeared again, down at the water's edge now, flashing on the tall grass and cattails. Another appeared on the opposite bank. I stopped to listen. Feet made sloshing sounds in the mud, a hundred feet away. Good; that would cover our noise. My wet shoes dangled by the strings, thumping in my chest.

The ground was firmer now, the grass not so tall. I stopped again, Gaston right behind me, looking back. They'd find our tracks any minute. We had no time to waste. The bundle of clothing was a nuisance, but we couldn't stop to dress now.

"Come on," I whispered, and broke into a run.

Fifty feet from the top we dropped and started crawling. I didn't want to be seen in silhouette against the sky as we topped the rise.

We pulled ourselves along, puffing and grunting. Crawling is hard work for a grown man. Just over the top we paused to look over the situation. The road leading to the bridge wound away toward a distant glow in the sky.

"That's an army supply depot out that way,"

Gaston said. "No town."

I raised up to look back toward the river. Two lights bobbed together, then started slowly away from the water's edge. I heard a faint shout.

"They've spotted the trail," I said. I jumped up and ran down the slope, trying to breathe deep in for four strides, out for four. A man could run for a long time if he didn't get winded. Stones bruised my bare feet.

I ankled over toward the highway, with some idea of making better time. Gaston was beside me.

"Nix," he said, puffing hard. "Them bunnies got a machine."

For a moment I didn't know what he meant; then I heard the sound of an engine starting up, and headlights lanced into the darkness, beams aimed at the distant treetops as the car headed up the slope of the approach to the bridge from the other side. We had only a few seconds before the car would slant down on this side, and illuminate the road and a wide strip on either side; we'd be spotlighted.

Ahead, I saw a fence, just a glint from a wire. That finished it; we were stopped. I slid to a halt. Then I saw that the fence lined a cross road, joining the road we were paralleling twenty feet away. Maybe a culvert . . . I dived for shelter.

A corrugated steel pipe eighteen inches in diameter ran beside the main road where the other joined it. I scrambled over pebbles and twigs and into the mouth. The sounds I made echoed hollowly inside. I kept going to the far end, Gaston wheezing behind me. I stopped and looked over my shoulder. Gaston had backed in and lay a few feet inside his end. The glow of the headlights gave me a glimpse of a heavy automatic in his hand.

"Good boy," I hissed. "Don't shoot unless you have to."

The lights of the car flickered over trees, highlighting rocks. Through the open end of the pipe I saw a rabbit sitting up in the glare, a few feet away. He turned and bounded off.

The car came slowly along, passed, moved on down the road. I breathed a little easier.

I was on the point of turning to say something to Gaston when a small stone rolled down into the ditch before me. I stiffened. A faint scuff of shoes on gravel, another stone dislodged—and then a flashlight beam darted across the gulley, played on the grass opposite, came to rest on the open end of the drain pipe. I held my breath. Then the steps came nearer, and the light probed, found my shoulder. There was a frozen instant of silence, then the sharp slap of the slug-gun hitting my palm. I caught a glimpse of the car a hundred feet away now, still edging along, heard a sharp intake of breath as the man with the light readied a shout. I pointed the gun to the right of the flash and the recoil slammed my arm back. The flashlight skidded across the rocky ground and went out as the man's body crashed heavily and lay still. I groped for the man's feet, hauled him back toward the pipe.

"Gaston," I whispered. The sound was hollow in the dark tunnel. "Give me a hand." I pulled at the feet. I was glad it wasn't the doctor; he wouldn't have fitted.

I crawled out of the pipe and Gaston came up beside me.

"After the car," I said. I had what I hoped was an idea. I was tired of being chased; the hunted would become the hunter.

I headed up the ditch at a trot, head down, Gaston at my heels. The car had stopped a hundred yards away. I counted three flashlights moving in the edge of the field.

"Close enough," I hissed. "Let's split up now. I'll cross the road and come up the other side. There's only one man over there. You get up in the tall grass and sneak in as close to the car as you can. Watch me and take your cue."

I darted across the road, a grotesque figure, naked, my bundle dangling by its strap from my shoulder. The car's headlights were still on. No one could see us from beyond them, looking into the glare. I dropped down into the ditch, wincing as sharp sticks jabbed my bare feet. The man on my side was casting about in wide circles, fifty feet from the road. A cricket sawed away insistently.

The car started backing, swung to one side of the road, then went forward; the driver was in the car, all right, he was turning around. They must have come up the road to cut us off, planning to move back to the river, searching foot by foot until they flushed us. No one seemed to have missed the man who now lay quietly in the steel pipe.

The car swung around and moved along at a snail's pace, headlights flooding the road I had just crossed. I dropped down to the bottom of the ditch as the lights passed over me. The car came on, and stopped just above me. I could see the driver, staring out through the windshield. He leaned forward, peering. I wondered if he was looking for the man who had been coming along on foot, checking the ditch; he'd be a long time seeing him from here.

He opened the door, stepped out, one foot on the

running board. The car was long and top-heavy
with flaring fenders. Dust roiled and gnats danced
in the beams from the great bowl-shaped headlights.

I picked up a heavy stone, rose silently to hands
and knees, and crept up out of the ditch. The
chauffeur stood with a hand on the top of the door,
looking over it. I came up behind him and hit him
as hard as I could on the top of the head. He folded
into the seat. I shoved him over, jumped in, and
closed the door. It was hard to get the coat off him
in the dark, while trying to stay down behind the
door, but I managed it. I put it on and sat up.
There was no alarm. The three flashlights continued to bob around in the fields. The engine was
running quietly.

I looked over the controls. The steering wheel
was in the center, and there were three pedals on
the floor. I let the center pedal in; the car moved
off slowly. I steered to the right side of the road,
crept along the edge. Gaston must be about here, I
thought. I stared out into the darkness; I could see
practically nothing.

I eased to a stop. The flashlight nearest me
swung back and forth, moving toward the bridge. I
reached out to the dash, and pushed in a lever that
projected from it. The headlights died.

I could see better now. The flashlights to my
right stopped moving, turned toward me. I waved
cheerfully. I didn't think they could make out my
face in the dim beam at that distance. One of the
lights seemed satisfied, resumed its search; the
other hesitated, flashing over the car.

There was a shout then, and I saw Gaston up and
running toward me. The flashlights converged on
him as he leaped across the ditch ahead, coming

into the road. The lights came bounding toward him and someone was yelling. Gaston stopped, whirled toward the nearest light, aiming the pistol. There was a sharp sound. Both lights on his side dropped. Not a bad shooting for a .45, I thought. Behind there was a faint shout from the remaining man on the other side of the road, and the crack of a gun. The slug made a solid thunk as it hit the heavy steel of the car. I floorboarded the center and left pedals; the car jumped ahead, then coasted. Another slug starred the glass beside me, scattering glass chips in my hair. I let my foot off, tried again. The car surged forward. I flipped the lights on. The car shifted up, tires squealing. Ahead, a figure stumbled down into the ditch, scrambled up the other side into the road, waving its arms. I saw the open mouth in the taut white face for an instant in the flare of the lights before it was slammed down out of sight, with a shock that bounced us in our seats.

The bridge loomed ahead, narrow and highly arched. We took it wide open, crushed down in the seat as we mounted the slope, floating as we dropped on the other side. The road curved off to the left, tall trees lining it. The tires howled as we rounded the turn and hit the straightaway.

"This is great, Hammer-hand," Gaston shouted. "I never rode in one of these here machines before."

"Neither did I," I yelled back.

Chapter 11

The night was black, with no moon. The next problem was to get into the walled town. The road led
along the river's edge into the heart of the city,
according to Gaston. The dictator's stronghold lay
at the edge of the city north of the highway we
were on. He had fortified the area, enclosing shops
and houses within an encircling wall like a
medieval town, creating a self-sufficient com-
munity to support the castle and its occupants,
easily patrolled and policed. It was no defense
against an army, but practical as a safeguard
against assassins and rioters.

"That's us," I said aloud. "Assassins and
rioters."

"Sure, chief," Gaston said.

Twenty minutes of driving brought us to the
bombed-out edge of the city. The rubble stretched
ahead, with here and there a shack or a tiny patch
of garden. To the right the mass of the castle

loomed up, faintly visible in the glow from the streets below it, unseen behind the wall. To the original massive old country house, Bayard had added rambling outbuildings, great mismatched wings, and the squat tower.

I pulled over, cut the headlights. Gaston and I looked silently at the lights in the tower. He lit a cigarette.

"How are we going to get in there, Gaston?" I said. "How do we get over the wall?"

Gaston stared at the walls, thinking. "Listen, Hammer-hand," he said. "You wait here, while I check around a little. I'm pretty good at casing a layout, and I know this one from the inside; I'll find a spot if there is one. Keep an eye peeled for the street gangs."

I sat and waited. I rolled up the windows and locked the doors. I couldn't see any signs of life about the broken walls around me. Somewhere a cat yowled.

I checked my clothes over. Both lapels were missing; the tiny set was still clipped to my belt, but without speaker or mike, it was useless. I ran my tongue over the tooth with the cyanide sealed in it. I might need it yet.

The door rattled. I had dozed off. Gaston's face pressed against the glass. I unlocked it and he slid in beside me.

"OK, Hammer-hand," he said. "I think I got us a spot. We go along the edge of the drainage ditch over there to where it goes under the wall. Then we got to get down inside it and ease under the guard tower. It comes out in the clear on the other side."

I got out and followed Gaston over broken stones to the ditch. It was almost a creek, and the smell of it was terrible.

Gaston led me along its edge for a hundred yards, until the wall hung over us just beyond the circle of light from the guard tower. I could see a fellow with a burp gun leaning against a post on top of the tower, looking down onto the street inside the wall. There were two large floodlights beside him, unlit.

Gaston leaned close to my ear. "It kind of stinks," he said, "but the wall is pretty rough, so I think we can make it OK."

He slid over the edge, found a foothold, and disappeared. I slid down after him, groping with my foot for a ledge. The wall was crudely laid, with plenty of cracks and projecting stones, but slimy with moss. I groped along, one precarious foot at a time. We passed the place where the light gleamed on the black water below, hugging the shadow. Then we were under the wall, which arched massively over us. The sound of trickling water was louder here.

I tried to see what was going on ahead. Gaston had stopped and was descending. I could barely make out his figure, knee-deep in the malodorous stream. I moved closer. Then I saw the grating. It was made of iron bars, and completely blocked the passage.

I climbed over to the grating, leaned against the rusty iron to ease my arms. The defense system didn't have quite the hole in it we thought it had. Gaston moved around below me, reaching under the surface to try to find a bottom edge. Maybe we could duck under the barrier.

Suddenly I felt myself slipping.

Below me, Gaston hissed a curse, scrabbled upward. My grip was firm, I realized in an instant; it was the grating that was slipping. It dropped another eight inches with a muffled scraping and clank, then stopped. The rusty metal had given under our weight. The corroded ends of the bars had broken off at the left side. There wasn't room to pass, but maybe we could force it a little further.

Gaston braced himself against the wall and heaved. I got into position behind him and added my weight. The frame shifted a little, then stuck.

"Gaston," I said. "Maybe I can get under it now, and heave from the other side." Gaston moved back, and I let myself down into the reeking water. I worked an arm through, then dropped down waist deep, chest deep, pushing. The rough metal scraped my face, caught at my clothing; but I was through.

I crawled back up, dripping, and rested. From the darkness behind Gaston I heard a meshing of oiled metal parts and then the cavern echoed with the thunder of machine gun fire. In the flashing light I saw Gaston stiffen against the grating and fall. He hung by one hand, caught in the grating. There were shouts, and men dropped onto the stone coping at the culvert mouth. Gaston jerked, fumbled his pistol from his blouse.

"Gaston," I said. "Quick, under the bars . . ." I was helpless. I knew he was too big.

A man appeared, clinging to the coping with one hand, climbing down to enter the dark opening. He flashed a light at us and Gaston, still dangling by the left hand, fired. The man fell over into the stream with a tremendous splash.

Gaston gasped. "That's . . . all . . ." The gun fell from his hand into the black water.

I moved fast now, from one hand-hold to the

next, slipping and clutching, but not quite falling somehow. I managed to get a look back as I reached the open air. Two men were tugging at the body wedged in the opening. Even in death, Gaston guarded my retreat.

I came up over the side, flattened against the wall, slug-gun in my hand; the street was empty. They must have thought they had us trapped; this side was deserted. I was directly under the tower, I eased out a few feet, and craned my neck; a shadow moved at the top of the tower. There was still one man on duty there. He must have heard the grating fall and called for reinforcements.

I looked down the street ahead. I recognized the Street of the Olive Trees, the same one I had come through on my way out with Gros, ten days earlier. It slanted down, curving to the right. That was where I had to go, into the naked street, under the guns. I liked it here in the shadow of the tower, but I couldn't stay. I leaped forward, running for my life. The searchlight snapped on, swung, found me, burning my leaping shadow against the dusty walls and the loose-cobbled street. Instinct told me to leap aside. As I did, the gun clattered and slugs whined off the stones to my left. I was out of the light now, and dashing for the protection of the curving wall ahead. The light was still groping as I rounded the turn. No lights came on above me; I ran in utter silence. The dwellers in these scarred tenements had learned to sit silent behind barred windows when guns talked in the narrow streets.

I passed the spot where Gros had died, dashed on. In the distance a whistle blew again and again. A shot rang out, kicking up dust ahead. I kept going.

I heard running feet behind me now. I scanned
the shabby stalls ahead, empty and dark, trying to
find the one we had used the day we left the
palace, where the old woman huddled over her
table of clay ware. It had been tiny, with a ragged
gray awning sagging over the front and broken
pots scattered before it.

I almost passed it, caught myself, skidded, and
dived for the back. I fought the stiff tarpaulin,
found the opening and squeezed through.

I panted in complete darkness now. Outside, I
heard voices as the men shouted to each other,
searching. I had a moment's respite; they didn't
know this entry.

I looked at my watch. Things happened fast in
this war world; it was not yet half past nine. I had
left the house at seven. I had killed three men in
those two hours, and a man had died for me. I
thought how easily a man slips back to his ancient
role as nature's most deadly hunter.

I felt the fatigue suddenly. I yawned, sat on the
floor. I had an impulse to lie back and go to sleep,
but instead I got up and began feeling my way
toward the passage. I wasn't finished yet; I was in
the palace, unwounded, armed. I had all I had any
right to hope for—a fighting chance.

I was no longer the eager neophyte, ignorant of
the realities; I came now, steeled by necessity, a
hardened fighter, a practical killer. I was armed
and I was desperate, and I bore the scars of
combat. I did not intend to fail.

Half an hour later, I eased a door open and
looked down the length of the same hall into
which the shuttle had pitched me headlong two
weeks before. It hadn't changed. I stepped into the

hall, tried the first door. It opened, and I saw that it was a bedroom. I went in, and by the faint light shining through the curtains from below, looked over a wide bed, a large desk against the far wall, a closet door, an easy chair, and through a partly open door, a roomy bathroom to the right. I closed the door behind me, and crossed to the windows. There were steel shutters, painted light green to match the walls, folded back behind the draperies. I closed them, and went to the desk and flipped on the lamp. I had had enough of groping through the dark for one night.

The room was very handsome, spacious, with a deep pile grey-green rug and a pair of bold water-colors on the wall. Suddenly I was aware of my own neck. The clothes seemed to crawl on my back. I had lain in mud, waded a sewer, crept through the ancient dust. Without considering further, I pulled the encrusted tunic off, tossed my clothes in a heap by the door, and headed for the bath.

I took half an hour soaping myself, and then climbed out and got my uniform. I had nothing else to put on, and I wouldn't wear it as it was. I soaped it up, rinsed it out, and draped it over the side of the tub. There was a vast white bathrobe behind the door, and I wrapped myself in it and went back into the bedroom.

The thought penetrated to my dulled mind that I was behaving dangerously. I tried again to shake myself alert. But alarm wouldn't come. I felt perfectly safe, secure, comfortable. This won't do, I thought; I'm going to go to sleep on my feet. I yawned again.

I sat down in the chair opposite the door, and prepared to wait it out. I got up, as an afterthought, and turned the light out. I don't remember sitting down again.

Chapter 12

I dreamt. I was at the seashore, and the sun reflected from the glassy water. It flashed in my eyes, and I turned away. I twisted in the chair, opened my eyes. My head was thick.

I stared at the pale green walls of the room, across the grey-green rug. It was silent in the room and I didn't move. The door stood open.

I remembered turning the light off, nothing more. Someone had turned it on; someone had opened the door. I had come as a killer in the night; and someone had found me here sleeping, betrayed by my own exhaustion.

I sat up, and in that instant realized I was not alone. I turned my head, and looked at the man who sat quietly in the chair on my left, leaning back with his legs thrust out stiffly before him, his hands lightly gripping the arms of a rosewood chair upholstered in black leather. He smiled, and leaned forward. It was like looking into a mirror.

I didn't move. I stared at him. His face was thinner than mine, more lined. The skin was burned dark, the hair bleached lighter by the African sun; but it was me I looked at. Not a twin, not a double, not a clever actor; it was myself sitting in a chair, looking at me.

"You have been sleeping soundly," he said. I thought of hearing my voice on a tape recorder, except this voice spoke in flawless French.

I moved my hand slightly; my gun was still there, and the man I had come to kill sat not ten feet away, alone, unprotected. But I didn't move. I wasn't ready, not yet. Maybe not ever.

"Are you rested enough," he said, "or will you sleep longer before we talk?"

"I'm rested," I said.

"I do not know how you came here," he said, "but that you are here is enough. I did not know what gift the tide of fortune would bring me, but there could be no finer thing than this—a brother."

I didn't know what I had expected the Dictator Bayard to be—a sullen ruffian, a wild-eyed megalomaniac, a sly-eyed schemer. But I had not expected a breathing image of myself, with a warm smile, and a poetic manner of speech, a man who called me brother.

He looked at me with an expression of intense interest.

"You speak excellent French, but with an English accent," he said. "Or is it perhaps American?" He smiled. "You must forgive my curiosity. Linguistics, accents, they are a hobby of mine and, in your case, I am doubly intrigued."

"American," I said.

"Amazing," he said. "I might have been born an

American myself . . . but that is a long dull tale to tell another time."

No need, I thought. My father told it to me often, when I was a boy.

He went on, his voice intense, but gentle, friendly. "They told me, when I returned to Algiers ten days ago, that a man resembling myself had been seen here in the apartment. There were two men found in my study, quite dead. There was a great deal of excitement, a garbled report. But I was struck by the talk of a man who looked like me. I wanted to see him, talk to him; I have been so very much alone here. It was a thing that caught my imagination. Of course, I did not know what brought this man here; they even talked of danger . . ." He spread his hands in a Gallic gesture.

"But when I came into this room and found you here, sleeping, I knew at once that you could not have come but in friendship. I was touched, my friend, to see that you came here on your own, entrusting yourself to my hands."

I couldn't say anything. I didn't try.

"When I lit the lamp and saw your face, I knew at once that this was more than some shallow impersonation; I saw my own face there, not so worn by war as my own, the lines not so deeply etched. But there was the call of blood to blood; I know you for my brother."

I licked my lips, swallowed. He leaned forward, placed his hand over mine, gripped it hard, then leaned back in his chair with a sigh.

"Forgive me again, brother. I fall easily into oratory, I fear; a habit I should do well to break. There is time enough for plans later. But now, will you tell me of yourself? I know you have in you the blood of the Bayards."

"Yes, my name is Bayard."

"You must have wanted very much to come to me, to have made your way here alone and unarmed. No one has ever passed the wall before, without an escort and many papers."

I couldn't sit here silent, but neither could I tell this man anything of my real purpose in coming. I reminded myself of the treatment the Imperial ambassadors had received at his hands, of all that Bale had told me that first morning in the meeting with Bernadotte. But I saw nothing here of the ruthless tyrant I expected. Instead, I found myself responding to his spontaneous welcome.

I had to tell him something. My years of diplomatic experience came to my assistance once again. I found myself lying smoothly.

"You're right in thinking I can help you, Brion," I said. I was startled to hear myself calling him by his first name so easily, but it seemed the natural thing to do.

"But you're wrong in assuming that your state is the only surviving center of civilization. There is another, a strong, dynamic, and friendly power which would like to establish amicable relations with you. I am the emissary of that government."

"But why did you not come to me openly? The course you chose, while daring, was of extreme danger; but it must be that you were aware of the treachery all about me, and feared that my enemies would keep you from me."

He seemed so eager to understand that he supplied most of his own answers. This seemed an opportune moment to broach the subject of the Bale's two agents who had carried full diplomatic credentials, and who had been subjected to beating, torture, and death. It was a contradiction in the dictator's character I wanted to shed a little light on.

"I recall that two men sent to you a year ago were not well received," I said. "I was unsure of my reception. I wanted to see you privately, face to face."

Bayard's face tensed. "Two men?" he said. "I have heard nothing of ambassadors."

"They were met first by a Colonel-General Yang." I said, "and afterward were interviewed by you personally."

Bayard's face went red. "There is a dog of a broken officer who leads a crew of cut-throats in raids on what pitiful commerce I have been able to encourage. His name is Yang. If he has molested a legation sent to me from your country, I promise you his head."

"It was said that you yourself shot one of them," I said, pressing the point.

Bayard gripped the arm of the chair, his eyes on my face.

"I swear to you by the honor of the House of Bayard that I have never heard until this moment of your Embassy, and that no harm came to them through any act of mine."

I believed him. I was starting to wonder about a lot of things. He seemed sincere in welcoming the idea of an alliance with a civilized power. And yet, I myself had seen the carnage done by his raiders at the palace, and the atom bomb they had tried to detonate there.

"Very well," I said. "On behalf of my government, I accept your statement; but if we treaty with you now, what assurance will be given to use that there will be no repetition of the bombing raids?"

"Bombing raids!" He stared at me. There was a silence.

"Thank God you came to me by night, in secret," he said. "It is plain to me now that control of affairs has slipped from me farther even than I had feared."

"There have been seven raids, four of them accompanied by atomic bombs, in the past year," I said. "The most recent was less than one month ago."

His voice was deadly now. "By my order, every gram of fissionable material known to me to exist was dumped into the sea on the day that I established this state. That there were traitors in my service, I knew; but that there were madmen who would begin the horror again, I did not suspect."

He turned and stared across the room at a painting of sunlight shining through leaves onto a weathered wall. "I fought them when they burned the libraries, melted down the Cellini altar pieces, trampled the Mona Lisa in the ruins of the Louvre. I could save only a fragment here, a remnant there, always telling myself that it was not too late. But the years passed and they have brought no change.

"There has been an end to industry, farming, family life. Even with the plenty that lies about us for the taking, men fight over three things: gold, liquor, and women.

"I have tried to arouse a spirit of rebuilding against the day when even the broken storehouses run dry; but it's useless. Only my rigid martial rule holds them in check.

"I will confess. I had lost hope. There was too

much decay all around me. In my own house, among my closest advisors, I heard nothing but talk of armament, expeditionary forces, domination, renewed war against the ruins outside our little island of order. Empty war, meaningless overlordship of dead nations. They hoped to spend our slender resources in stamping out whatever traces might remain of human achievement, unless it bowed to our supremacy."

When he looked at me I thought of the expression, "Blazing eyes."

"Now my hole springs up renewed," he said. "With a brother at my side, we will prevail."

I thought about it. The Imperium had given me full powers. I might as well use them.

"I think I can assure you," I said, "that the worst is over. My government has resources; you may ask for whatever you need—men, supplies, equipment. We ask only one thing of you—friendship and justice between us."

He leaned back, closed his eyes. "The long night is over," he said.

There were still major points to be covered, but I felt sure that Bayard had been grossly misrepresented to me, and to the Imperial government. I wondered how Imperial Intelligence had been so completely taken in and why. Bale had spoken of having a team of his best men here, sending a stream of data back to him.

There was also the problem of my transportation back to Zero Zero world of the Imperium. Bayard hadn't mentioned the MC shuttles. In fact, thinking over what he had said, he talked as though they didn't exist. Perhaps he was holding out on me, in spite of his apparent candor.

Bayard opened his eyes. "There has been

enough of gravity for now," he said. "I think that a
little rejoicing between us would be appropriate. I
wonder if you share my liking for an impromptu
feast on such occasion?"

"I love to eat in the middle of the night," I said,
"especially when I've missed my dinner."

"You are a true Bayard," he said. He reached to
the table beside me and pressed a button. He
leaned back and placed his finger tips together.

"And so now we must think about the menu."
He pursed his lips, looking thoughtful. "Tonight,
permit me to select the menu," he said. "We will
see if our tastes are as similar as ourselves."

"Fine," I said.

There was a tap on the door. At Brion's call, it
opened and a sour-faced fiftyish little man came
in. He saw me, started; then his face blanked. He
crossed to the dictator's chair, drew himself up,
and said, "I came as quick as I could, Major."

"Fine, fine, Luc," he said. "At ease. My brother
and I are hungry. We have a very special hunger,
and I want you, Luc, to see to it that our dinner
does the kitchen credit."

Luc glanced at me from the corner of his eyes. "I
see the gentleman resembles the Major some-
what," he said.

"An amazing likeness. Now—" he stared at the
ceiling. "We will begin with a very dry Madeira, I
think; Secrial, the 1875. Then we will whet our
appetites with *Les Huitres de Whitstable*, with a
white Burgundy; Chablis Vaudesir. I think there is
still a bit of the '29."

I leaned forward. This sounded like something
special indeed. I had eaten oysters Whitstable before, but the wines were vintages of which I had
only heard.

"The soup, *Consomme Double aux Cepes*; then *Le Supreme de Brochet au Beurre Blanc*, and for our first red Burgundy, Romanee-Conti, 1904."

Brion ran through the remainder of a sumptuous menu. Luc went away quietly. If he could carry that in his head, he was the kind of waiter I'd always wanted to find.

"Luc has been with me for many years," Brion said. "A faithful friend. You noticed that he called me 'Major.' That was the last official rank I held in the Army of France-in-Exile, before the collapse. I was later elected as Colonel over a regiment of survivors of the Battle of Gibraltar when we had realized that we were on our own. Later still, when I saw what had to be done, and took into my hands the task of rebuiling, other titles were given me by my followers, and I confess I conferred one or two myself; it was just necessary psychological measure, I felt. But to Luc I have always remained 'Major.' He himself was a sous-officer, my regimental Sergeant-Major."

"I know little about events of the last few years in Europe," I said. "Can you tell me something about them?"

He sat thoughtfully for a moment. "The course was steadily downhill," he said, "from the day of the unhappy Peace of Munich in 1919. America faced the Central Powers alone, and the end was inevitable. When America fell under the massive onslaught in '32, it seemed that the Kaiser's dream of a German-dominated world was at hand. Then came the uprisings. I held a Second Lieutenant's commission in the Army of France-in-Exile. We spearheaded the organized resistance, and the movement spread like wild-fire. Men, it seemed, would not live as slaves. We had high hopes in those days.

"But the years passed, and stalemate wore away at us. At last the Kaiser was overthrown by a palace coup, and we chose that chance to make our last assault. I led my battalion on Gibraltar, and took a steel-jacketed bullet through both knees almost before we were ashore.

"I will never forget the hours of agony while I lay conscious in the surgeons' tent. There was no more morphine, and the medical officers worked over the minor cases, trying to get men back into the fight; I was out of it and therefore took last priority. It was reasonable, but at the time I did not understand."

I listened, rapt. "When," I asked, "were you hit?"

"That day I will not soon forget," he said. "April 15, 1945."

I stared. I had been hit by a German machine gun slug at Jena and had waited in the aid station for the doctors to get to me—on April 15, 1945. There was a strange affinity that linked this other Bayard's life with mine, even across the unimaginable void of the Net.

We finished the 1855 brandy, and still we sat, talking through the African night. We laid ambitious plans for the rebuilding of civilization. We enjoyed each other's company, and all stiffness had long since gone. I closed my eyes, and I think I must have dozed off. Something awakened me.

Dawn was lightening the sky. Brion sat silent, frowning. He tilted his head.

"Listen."

I listened. I thought I caught a faint shout and something banged in the distance. I looked inquiringly at my host. His face was grim.

"All is not well," he said. He gripped the chair arms, rose, got his canes, started around the table.

I got up and stepped forward through the glass doors into the room. I was dizzy from the wine and brandy. There was a louder shout outside in the hall and a muffled thump. Then the door shook, splintered and crashed inward.

Thin in a tight black uniform, Chief Inspector Bale stood in the opening, his face white with excitement. He carried a long-barrelled Mauser automatic pistol in his right hand. He stared at me, stepped back, then with a sudden grimace raised the gun and fired.

In the instant before the gun slammed, I caught a blur of motion from my right, and then Brion was there, half in front of me, falling as the shot echoed. I grabbed for him, caught him by the shoulders as he went down, limp. Blood welled from under his collar, spreading; too much blood, a life's blood. He was looking into my face as the light died from his eyes.

Chapter 13

"Get back, Bayard," Bale snarled. "Rotten luck, that; I needed the swine alive for hanging." I stood up slowly. He stared at me, gnawing his lip. "It was you I wanted dead; and this fool traded lives with you."

He seemed to be talking to himself. I recognized the voice now, a little late. Bale was the Big Boss. It was the fact that he spoke in French here that had fooled me.

"All right," he said in abrupt decision. "He can trade deaths with you too. You'll do to hang in his place. I'll give the mob their circus. You wanted to take his place, here's your chance."

He stepped farther into the room, motioned others in. Evil-looking thugs came through the door, peering about, glancing at Bale for orders.

"Put him in a cell," Bale said. "And I'm warning you, Cassu, keep your bloody hands off him. I want him strong for the surgeon."

Cassu grunted, twisted my arm until the joint creaked, and pushed me past the dead body of the man I had come in one night to think of as a brother.

They marched me off down the corridor, pushed me into an elevator, led me out again through a mob of noisy toughs armed to the teeth, down stone stairs, along a damp tunnel in the rock, and at the end of the line, sent me spinning with a kick into the pitch black of a cell.

My stunned mind worked, trying to assimilate what had happened. Bale! And not a double; he had known who I was. It was Bale of the Imperium, a traitor. That answered a lot of questions. It explained the perfect timing and placement of the attack at the palace, and why Bale had been too busy to attend the gala affair that night. I realized now why he had sought me out afterward; he was hoping that I'd been killed, of course. That would have simplified matters for him. And the duel—I had never quite been able to understand why the Intelligence chief had been willing to risk killing me, when I was essential to the scheme for controlling the dictator. And all the lies about the viciousness of the Bayard of B-I Two were Bale's fabrications designed to prevent establishment of friendly relations between the Imperium and this unhappy world.

Why? I asked myself. Did Bale plan to rule this hellworld himself, making it his private domain? It seemed so.

And I saw that Bale did not intend to content himself with this world alone; this would be merely a base of operations, a source of fighting men and weapons—including atomic bombs. Bale himself was the author of the raids on the

Imperium. He had stolen shuttles, or components thereof, and had manned them here in B-I Two, and set out on a career of piracy. The next step would be the assault on the Imperium itself, a full-scale attack, strewing atomic death. The men of the Imperium would wear gay uniforms and dress sabres into battle against atomic cannon.

I wondered why I hadn't realized it sooner. The fantastic unlikeliness of the development of the MC drive independently by the war-ruined world of B-I Two seemed obvious now.

While we had sat in solemn conference, planning moves against the raiders, their prime mover had sat with us. No wonder an enemy scout had lain in wait for me as I came in on my mission.

When he found me at the hideout, Bale must have immediately set to work planning how best to make use of the unexpected stroke of luck. And when I had escaped, he had had to move fast.

I could only assume that the State was now in his hands; that a show execution of Bayard in the morning had been scheduled to impress the populace with the reality of the change in regimes.

Now I would hang in the dictator's place. And I remembered what Bale had said; he wanted me strong for the surgeon. The wash tub would be useful after all. There were enough who knew the dictator's secret to make a corpse with legs embarrassing.

They would shoot me full of dope, perform the operation, bind up the stumps, dress my unconscious body in a uniform and hang me. A dead body wouldn't fool the public. They would be able to see the color of life in my face, even if I were still out, as the noose tightened.

I heard someone coming, and saw a bobbing

light in the passage through the barred opening in the door. I braced myself. Maybe this was the man with the saws and the heavy snippers already.

Two men stopped at the cell door, opened it, came in. I squinted at the glare of the flashlight. One of the two dropped something on the floor.

"Put it on," he said. "The boss said he wanted you should wear this here for the hanging."

I saw my old costume, the one I had washed. At least it was clean, I thought. It was strange, I considered, how inconsequentials still had importance.

A foot nudged me. "Put it on, like I said."

"Yeah," I said. I took off the robe and pulled on the light wool jacket and trousers, buckled the belt. There were no shoes; I guessed Bale figured I wouldn't be needing them.

"OK," the man said. "Let's go, Hiem."

I saw and listened as the door clanked again; the light receded. It was very dark.

I fingered the torn lapels of my jacket. The communicator hadn't helped me much. I could feel the broken wires, tiny filaments projecting from the cut edge of the cloth. Beau Joe had cursed as he slashed at them!

I looked down. Tiny blue sparks jumped against the utter black as the wires touched.

I sat perfectly still. Sweat broke out on my forehead. I didn't dare move; the pain of hope awakening against all hope was worse than the blank acceptance of certain death.

My hands shook. I fumbled for the wires, tapped them together. A spark; another.

I tried to think. The communicator was clipped to my belt still; the speaker and mike were gone but the power source was there. Was there a possibility that touching the wires together would transmit a signal? I didn't know. I could only try.

I didn't know Morse Code, or any other code; but I knew S.O.S. Three dots, three dashes, three dots. Over and over, while I suffered the agony of hope.

A long time passed. I tapped the wires, and waited. I almost fell off the bunk as I dozed for an instant. I couldn't stop. I had to try until time ran out for me.

I heard them coming from far off, the first faint grate of leather on dusty stone, a clink of metal. My mouth was dry, and my legs began to tingle. I thought of the hollow tooth and ran my tongue over it. The time for it had come. I wondered how it would taste, if it would be painful. I wondered if Bale had forgotten it, or if he hadn't known.

There were more sounds in the passage now, sounds of men and loud voices; a clank of something heavy, a ponderous grinding. They must be planning on setting the table up here in the cell, I thought. I went to the tiny opening in the door and looked through. I could see nothing but almost total darkness. Suddenly light flared brilliantly, and I jumped, blinded.

There was more noise, then someone yelled. They must be having a hell of a time getting the stuff through the narrow hall, I thought. My eyeballs ached, my legs were trembling, my stomach suddenly felt bad. I gagged. I hoped I wouldn't go to pieces. Time for the tooth now. I thought of how disappointed Bale would be when he found me dead in my cell. It helped a little; but still I hesitated. I didn't want to die. I had a lot of living I wanted to do first.

Then someone called out, nearby.

"Wolfhound!"

My head came up. My code name. I tried to shout, choked. "Yes," I croaked. I jumped to the bars, yelled.

"Wolfhound, where in the hell . . ."

"Here!" I yelled. "Here!"

"Get back, Colonel," someone said. "Get in the corner and cover up."

I moved back and crouched, arms over my head. There was a sharp hissing sound, and a mighty blast that jarred the floor under me. Tiny particles bit and stung, and grit was in my mouth. With a drawn-out clang, the door fell into the room.

Arms grabbed me, pulled me through the boiling dust, out into the glare. I stumbled, felt broken things underfoot.

Men milled around a mass blocking the passage. Canted against the wall a great box sat with a door hanging wide, light streaming out. Arms helped me through the door, and I saw wires, coils, junction boxes, stapled to bare new wood, with angle-irons here and there. White-uniformed men crowded into the tiny space; a limp figure was hauled through the door.

"Full count," someone yelled. "Button up!" Wood splintered as a bullet came through.

The door banged shut, and the box trembled while a rumble built up into a whine, then passed on up out of audibility.

Someone grabbed my arm. "My God, Brion, you must have had a terrible time of it."

It was Richthofen, in a grey uniform, a cut on his face, staring at me.

"No hard feelings," I said. "Your timing . . . was good."

"We've had a monitor on your band day and

night, hoping for something," he said. "We'd given you up, but couldn't bring ourselves to abandon hope; then four hours ago the tapping started coming through. They went after it with locators, and fixed it here in the wine cellars.

"The patrol scouts couldn't get in here; no room. We pitched this box together and came in."

"Fast work," I said. I thought of the trip through the dreaded Blight, in a jury-rig made of pine boards. I felt a certain pride in the men of the Imperium.

"Make a place for Colonel Bayard, men," someone said. A space was cleared on the floor, jackets laid out on it. Richthofen was holding me up and I made a mighty effort, got to the pallet and collapsed. Richthofen said something but I didn't hear it. I wondered what had held the meat cutters up so long, and then let it go. I had to say something, warn them. I couldn't remember . . .

Chapter 14

I was lying in a clean bed in a sunny room, propped up on pillows. It was a little like another room I had awakened in not so long before, but there was one important difference. Barbro sat beside my bed, knitting a ski stocking from red wool. Her hair was piled high on her head, and the sun shone through it, coppery red. Her eyes were hazel, and her features were perfect, and I liked lying there looking at her. She had come every day since my return to the Imperium, and read to me, talked to me, fed me soup and fluffed my pillow. I was enjoying my convalescence.

"If you are good, Brion," Barbro said, "and eat all of your soup today, perhaps by tomorrow evening you will be strong enough to accept the king's invitation."

"OK," I said. "It's a deal."

"The Emperor Ball," Barbro said, "is the most brilliant affair of the year and all the three kings and the Emperor with their ladies will be there to-gether."

I didn't answer; I was thinking. There seemed to be something I wasn't figuring out. I had been leaving all the problems to the Intelligence men, but I knew more than they did about Bale.

I thought of the last big affair, and the brutal attack. I suspected that this time every man would wear a slug-gun under his braided cuff. But the fight on the floor had been merely a diversion, de-signed to allow the crew to set up an atomic bomb.

I sat bolt upright. The bomb had been turned over to Bale. There would be no chance of surprise attack from the shuttle this time, with alert crew watching around the clock for traces of unscheduled MC activity; but there was no need to bring a bomb in. Bale had one here.

"What is it, Brion?" Barbro asked, leaning for-ward.

"What did Bale do with that bomb?" I said. "The one they tried to set off at the dance. Where is it now?"

"I don't know. It was turned over to Inspector Bale . . ."

"When do the royal parties arrive for the Emp-eror Ball?" I asked.

"They are already in the city," Barbro said, "at Drottningholm."

I felt my heart start to beat a little faster. Bale wouldn't let this opportunity pass. With the three kings here in the city, and an atomic bomb hidden somewhere, he had to act. At one stroke he could wipe out the leadership of the Imperium, and follow-up with a full-scale assault; and against his atomic weapons, the fight would be hopeless.

"Call Manfred, Barbro," I said. "Tell him that

bomb's got to be found fast. The kings will have to be evacuated from the city; the ball will have to be cancelled . . ."

Barbro spoke into the phone, looked back at me. "He has left the building, Brion," she said. "Shall I try to reach Herr Goering?"

"Yes," I said. I started to tell her to hurry, but she was already speaking rapidly to someone at Goering's office. Barbro was quick to catch on.

"He also is out," Barbro said. "Is there anyone else?"

I thought furiously. Manfred or Hermann would listen to anything I might say, but with their staffs it would be a different matter. To call off the day of celebration, disturb the royal parties, alarm the city, were serious measures. No one would act on my vague suspicions alone. I had to find my friends in a hurry—or find Bale.

Imperial Intelligence had made a search, found nothing. His apartment was deserted, as well as his small house at the edge of the city. And the monitors had detected no shuttle not known to be an Imperium vessel moving in the Net recently.

There were several possibilities; one was that Bale had returned almost at the same time as I had, slipping in before the situation was known, while some of his own men still manned the alert stations. A second was that he planned to come in prepared to hold off attackers until he could detonate the bomb. Or possibly an accomplice would act for him.

Somehow I liked the first thought best. It seemed more in keeping with what I knew of Bale; shrewder, less dangerous. If I were right, Bale was here now, somewhere in Stockholm, waiting for the hour to blow the city sky-high.

As for the hour, he would wait for the arrival of the Emperor, not longer.

"Barbro," I said, "when does the Emperor arrive?"

"I'm not sure, Brion," she said. "Possibly tonight, but perhaps this afternoon."

That didn't give me much time. I jumped out of bed, and staggered.

"Here I come, ready or not," I said. "I can't just lie here, Barbro. Do you have a car?"

"Yes, my car is downstairs, Brion. Sit down and let me help you." She went to the closet and I sank down. I seemed always to be recuperating lately. I had been through this shaky-legs business just a few days ago, and here I was starting in again. Barbro turned, holding a brown suit in her hands.

"This is all there is, Brion," she said. "It is the uniform of the dictator, that you wore when you came here to the hospital."

"It will have to do," I said. Barbro helped me dress, and we left the room as fast as I could walk. A passing nurse stared, but went on. I was dizzy and panting already.

The elevator helped. I sank down on the stool, head spinning.

I felt something stiff in my chest pocket, and suddenly I had a vivid recollection of Gaston giving me a card as we crouched in the dusk behind the hideout near Algiers, telling me that he thought it was the address of the Big Boss's out-of-town headquarters. I grabbed for the card, squinted at it in the dim light of the ceiling lamp as the car jolted to a stop.

"Ostermalmsgatan 71" was scrawled across the card in blurred pencil. I remembered how I had dismissed it from my mind as of no interest when

Gaston had handed it to me; I had hoped for something more useful. Now this might be the little key that could save an empire.

"What is it, Brion?" Barbro asked. "Have you found something?"

"I don't know," I said. "Maybe just a dead end, but maybe not." I handed her the card. "Do you know where this is?"

She read the address. "I think I know the street," she said. "It is not far from the docks, in the warehouse district."

"Let's go," I said, with a fervent hope that we were right, and not too late.

We squealed around a corner, slowed in a street of gloomy warehouses, blind glass windows in looming brick-red facades, with yard-high letters identifying the shipping lines which owned them.

"This is the street," Barbro said. "And the number was seventy-one?"

"That's right," I said. "This is seventy-three; stop here."

We stepped out onto a gritty sidewalk, shaded by the bulk of the buildings, silent. There was a smell of tar and hemp in the air and a hint of sea water.

I stared at the building before me. There was a small door set in the front beside a leading platform. I went up to it, tried it. Locked. I leaned against it and rested.

"Barbro," I said. "Get me a jack handle or tire tool from your car." I hated to drag Barbro into this, but I had no choice. I couldn't do it alone.

She came back with a flat piece of steel eighteen inches long. I jammed it into the wide crack at the edge of the door and pulled. Something snapped, and with a jerk the door popped open. A stair ran up into gloom above. Barbro gave me an arm, and we started up. The hard work helped to keep my mind off the second sun that might light the Stockholm sky at any moment.

Five flights up, we reached a landing. The door we faced was of red-stained wood, solid and with a new lock. I looked at the hinge pins. They didn't look as good as the lock.

It took fifteen minutes, every one of which took a year off my life, but after a final wrench with the steel bar, the last pin clattered to the floor. The door pivoted out and fell against the wall.

"Wait here," I said. I started forward, into the papered hall.

"I'm going with you, Brion," Barbro said. I didn't argue.

We were in a handsome apartment, a little too lavishly furnished. Persian rugs graced the floor, and in the bars of dusty sunlight that slanted through shuttered windows, mellow old teak furniture gleamed and polished ivory figurines stood on dark shelves under silk scrolls from Japan. An ornate screen stood in the center of the room. I walked around a brocaded ottoman over to the screen and looked behind it. On a light tripod of aluminium rods rested the bomb.

Two heavy castings, bolted together around a central flange, with a few wires running along to a small metal box on the underside. Midway up the curve of the side, four small holes, arranged in a square. That was all there was; but it could make a mighty crater where a city had been.

I had no way of knowing whether it was armed or not. I leaned toward the thing, listening. I could hear no sound of a timing device. I thought of cutting the exposed wires, which looked like some sort of jury-rig, but I couldn't risk it; that might set it off.

"Here it is," I said, "but when does it go up?" I had an odd sensation of intangibility, as though I were already a puff of incandescent gas. I tried to think.

"Start searching the place, Barbro," I said. "You might come across something that will give us a hint. I'll phone Manfred's office and get a squad up here to see if we can move the thing without blowing it."

I dialed Imperial Intelligence. Manfred wasn't in, and the fellow on the phone was uncertain what he should do.

"Get a crew here on the double," I yelled. "Somebody who can at least make a guess as to whether this thing can be disturbed."

He said he would confer with General Somebody.

"When does the Emperor arrive?" I asked him. He was sorry, but he was not at liberty to discuss the Emperor's movements. I slammed the receiver down.

"Brion," Barbro called. "Look what's here."

I went to the door which opened onto the next room. A two-man shuttle filled the space. Its door stood open. I looked inside. It was fitted out in luxury; Bale provided well for himself even for short trips. This was what he used to travel from the home line to B-I Two, and the fact that it was here should indicate that Bale was here also; and that he would return to it before the bomb went off.

But then again, perhaps the bomb was even now

ticking away its last seconds, and Bale might be far away, safe from the blast. If the latter were true, there was nothing I could do about it; but if he did plan to return here, arm the bomb, set a timer and leave via the shuttle in the bedroom—then maybe I could stop him.

"Barbro," I said, "you've got to find Manfred or Hermann. I'm going to stay here and wait for Bale to come back. If you can find them, tell them to get men here fast who can make a try at disarming this thing. I don't dare move it, and it will take at least two to handle it. If we can move it, we can shove it in the shuttle and send it off; I'll keep phoning. I don't know where you should look but do your best."

Barbro looked at me. "I would rather stay here with you, Brion," she said. "But I understand that I must not."

"You're quite a girl, Barbro," I said.

Chapter 15

I was alone now, except for the ominous sphere behind the screen. I hoped for a caller, though. I went to the door which leaned aslant against the rough brick wall outside and unlatched it, maneuvered it into place and dropped the pins back in the hinges, then closed and relatched it.

I went back to the over-stuffed room, started looking through drawers, riffling through papers on the desk. I hoped for something—something that might give me a hint of what Bale planned. I didn't find any hints, but I did find a long-barrelled twenty-two revolver, loaded. That helped. I hadn't given much thought to what I would do when Bale got here. I was in no condition to grapple with him; now I had a reasonable chance.

I picked out a hiding place to duck into when and if I heard him coming, a storeroom in the hall, between the bomb and the door. I found a small

liquor cabinet and poured myself two fingers of
sherry.

I sat in one of the fancy chairs, and tried to let
myself go limp. I was using up too much energy in
tension. My stomach was a hard knot. I could see
the edge of the bomb behind its screen from where
I sat. I wondered if there would be any warning before it detonated. My ears were cocked for a click
or a rumble from the silent grey city-killer.

The sound I heard was not a click; it was the
scrape of shoes on wood, beyond the door. I sat
paralyzed for a moment, then got to my feet,
stepped to the storeroom and eased behind the
door. I loosened the revolver in my pocket and
waited.

The sounds were closer now, gratingly loud in
the dead silence. Then a key scraped in the lock,
and a moment later the tall thin figure of Chief
Inspector Bale, traitor, shuffled into view. His
small bald head was drawn down between his
shoulders, and he looked around the room almost
furtively. He pulled off his coat, and for one
startled instant I thought he would come to my
storeroom to hang it up; but he threw it over the
back of a chair.

He went to the screen, peered at the bomb. I
could easily have shot him, but that wouldn't
have helped me. I wanted Bale to let me know
whether the bomb was armed, if it could be
moved. He was the only man in the Imperium who
knew how to handle this device.

He leaned over the bomb, took a small box from
his pocket and stared at it. He looked at his watch,
went to the phone. I could barely hear his mutter
as he exchanged a few words with someone. He
went into the next room, and as I was about to

follow to prevent his using the shuttle, he came back. He looked at his watch again, sat in a chair, and opened a small tool kit which lay on the table. He started to work on the metal box with a slender screwdriver. This, then, was the arming device. I tried not to breathe too loud, or to think about how my legs ached.

Shocking in the stillness, the phone rang. Bale looked up, startled, laid the screwdriver and box on the table, and went over to the phone. He looked down at it, chewing his lip. After five rings it stopped. I wondered who it was.

Bale went back to his work. Now he was replacing the cover on the box, frowning over the job. He got up, went to the bomb, licked his lips and leaned over it. He was ready now to arm the bomb. I couldn't wait any longer.

I pushed the door open, and Bale leaped upright, grabbing for his chest, then jumped for the coat on the chair.

"Stand where you are, Bale," I said. "I'd get a real kick out of shooting you."

Bale's eyes were almost popping from his head, his head was tilted back, his mouth opened and closed. I got the impression that I had startled him.

"Sit down," I said. "There." I motioned with the pistol as I came out into the room.

"Bayard," Bale said hoarsely. I didn't say anything. I felt sure now that the bomb was safe. All I had to do was wait until the crew arrived, and turn Bale over to them. Then we could carry the bomb to the shuttle, and send it off into the Blight. But I was feeling very bad now.

I went to a chair, and sank down. I tried not to let Bale see how weak I was. I leaned back, and tried breathing deep through my nose again. If I started to pass out I would have to shoot Bale; he couldn't be left free to threaten the Imperium again.

It was little better now. Bale stood rigid, staring at me.

"Look, Bayard," he said. "I'll bring you in on this with me. I swear I'll give you a full half share. I'll let you keep B-I Two as your own, and I shall take the home line; there's plenty for all. Just put that gun aside . . ." He licked his lips, started towards me.

I started to motion with the gun, squeezed the trigger instead. A bullet slapped Bale's shirt sleeve, smacked the wall. He dropped down into the chair behind him. That was close, I thought. That could have killed him. I've got to hold on.

I might as well impress him a little, I thought. "I know how to use this pop gun, you see," I said. "Just a quarter of an inch from the arm, firing from the hip; not bad, don't you agree? Don't try anything else."

"You've got to listen to me, Bayard," Bale said. "Why should you care what happens to these popinjays? We can rule as absolute monarchs."

Bale went on, but I wasn't listening. I was concentrating on staying conscious, waiting for the sounds of help arriving.

" . . . take one moment, and we're off. What about it?"

Bale was looking at me, with a look of naked greed. I didn't know what he had been saying. He must have interpreted my silence as weakness; he got up again, moved toward me. It was darker in the room; I rubbed my eyes. I was feeling very bad now, very weak. My heart thumped in my throat, my stomach quivered. I was in no shape to be trying to hold this situation in check alone.

Bale stopped, and I saw that he suddenly realized that I was blacking out. He crouched, and with a snarl jumped at me. I would have to kill him. I fired the pistol twice, and Bale reeled away, startled, but still standing.

"Hold on, Bayard, for the love of God," he squealed. I was still alive enough to kill him. I raised the pistol, aimed and fired. I saw a picture jump on the wall. Bale leaped aside. I didn't know if I had hit him yet or not. I was losing my hold, but I wouldn't let him get away. I fired twice more, peering from my chair, and I knew it was the light in my mind fading, not the room. Bale yelled; I saw that he didn't dare to try for the door to the hall or the room where the shuttle waited. He would have to pass me. He screamed as I aimed the pistol with wavering hands, and dived for the other door. I fired and heard the sound echo through a dream of blackness.

I wasn't out for more than a few minutes; I came to myself, sitting in the chair, the pistol lying on my lap. The screen had fallen over, and lay across the bomb. I sat up, panicky; maybe Bale had armed it. And where was Bale? I remembered only that he had dashed for the next room. I got up, grabbed for the chair again, then got my balance, made my way to the door. There was a strange sound, a keening, like a cat in the distant alley. I looked into the room, half expecting to see Bale lying on the floor. There was nothing. The light streamed through an open window, a curtain flapped. Bale must have panicked and jumped, I thought. I went to the window, and the keening started up again.

Bale hung by his hands from the eave of the building across the alley, fifteen feet away. The sound came from him. The left leg of his trousers had a long stain of blackish red on it, and drops fell from the toe of his shoe, five stories to the brick payment below.

"Good God, Bale," I said. "What have you done?" I was horrified. I had been ready to shoot him down, but to see him hanging there was something else again.

"Bayard," he croaked. "I can't hold on much longer. For the love of God . . ."

What could I do? I was far too weak for any heroics. I looked around the room frantically for an inspiration; I needed a plan or a piece of rope. There was nothing. I pulled a sheet off the bed; it was far too short. Even two or three would never make it. And I couldn't hold it even if I could throw it and Bale caught it. I ran to the phone.

"Operator," I called. "There's a man about to fall from a roof. Get the fire department here with ladders, fast; seventy-one Ostermalmsgatan, fifth floor."

I dropped the phone, ran back to the window. "Hold on, Bale," I said. "Help's on the way." He must have tried to leap to the next roof, thinking that I was at his heels; and with that hole in his leg he hadn't quite made it.

I thought of Bale, sending me off on a suicide mission, knowing that my imposture was hopeless as long as I stood on my own legs; I thought of the killer shuttle that had lain in wait to smash us as we went in; of the operating room at the hideout, where Bale had planned to carve me into a shape more suitable for his purpose. I remembered Bale shooting down my new-found brother, and the night I had lain in the cold cell, waiting for the butcher; and still I didn't want to see him die this way.

He started to scream suddenly, kicking desperately. He got one foot up on the eave beside his white straining hands; it slipped off. Then he was quiet again. I had been standing here now for five minutes. I wondered how long I had been unconscious. Bale had been there longer now than I would have thought possible. He couldn't last much longer.

"Hold on, Bale," I called. "Only a little while. Don't struggle."

He hung, silent. Blood dripped from his shoe. I looked down at the alley below and shuddered.

I heard a distant sound, a siren, howling. I dashed to the door, opened it, listened. Heavy footsteps sounded below.

"Here," I shouted, "all the way up."

I turned and ran back to the window. Bale was as I had left him. Then one hand slipped off, and he hung by one arm, swinging slightly.

"They're here, Bale," I said. "A few seconds . . ."

He didn't try to get a new hold. He made no sound. Feet pounded on the stairs outside and I yelled again.

I turned back to the window as Bale slipped down, silent. I didn't watch. I heard him hit— twice.

I staggered back, and the burly man called, looked out the window, milled about. I made my way back to the chair, slumped down. I was empty of emotion. There was a noise all around me, people coming and going. I was hardly conscious of it. After a long time I saw Hermann, and then Barbro was leaning over me. I reached for her hand, hungrily.

"Take me home, Barbro," I said.

I saw Manfred.

"The bomb," I said. "It's safe. Put it in the shuttle and get rid of it."

"My crew is moving it now, Brion," he said.

"You spoke of home, just now," Goering put in. "Speaking for myself, and I am sure also for Manfred, I will make the strongest recommendation that in view of your extraordinary services to the Imperium you be dispatched back to your home as soon as you are well enough to go, if that is your wish. I hope that you will stay with us. But it must be for you to make that decision."

"I don't have to decide," I said. "My choice is made. I like it here, for many reasons. For one thing, I can use all the old cliches from B-I Three, and they sound brand new; and as for home . . ." I looked at Barbro:

"Home is where the heart is."

THE WAR AGAINST THE YUKKS

Professor Peter Elton swung his machete half-heartedly at a hanging vine as thick as his wrist; the blade rebounded with a dull clunk. He lowered the black pigskin suitcase in his left hand to the spongy layer of rotted vegetation that covered the ground, took out a large handkerchief with a faded machine-stitched monogram belonging to a fellow customer of the Collegiate Laundry and Cleaners, and mopped at his face.

"Constable Boyle," he called to the stocky, khaki-clad man whacking at the dense verdure ahead. "Are you sure you know where we're going?"

Boyle turned, flicked the sweat from the end of his nose.

"Absolutely, sir," he called cheerily. "Chased that ruddy great jaguar right through this same ruddy thicket. Lost him at the river's edge—the Choluteca, that is. That would be about five miles ahead."

Elton groaned. He hobbled to a convenient log, sat, pulled off his brand-new hiking boots and began massaging his foot.

"But *we* don't have to go all that way, sir," Constable Boyle reassured him. "It was on the way back I stumbled over it; it can't be far from where we are at this moment."

"I can't help recalling my last ill-advised venture into the brush," Elton said. "An unspoiled Aztec site just twenty miles south of Texaco. We reached it after a fourteen-hour burro ride. After clearing away the greenery, I uncovered a Dr. Pepper sign, several hundred beer bottles, and the principle chassis members of a Model T Ford."

"This is the real thing, sir," Boyle said heartily. "Just this column, like, sticking up; bloody great slab o' rock the size of a Bentley Tourer."

"And you're sure it shows signs of human handicraft?"

"Oh, that I can guarantee, sir." Boyle got out a well-worn hip flask, passed it across to Elton, who uncapped it and took a healing draught. "I hope you're not thinking of packing it home as a souvenir," Boyle went on. "You'd need a ruddy derrick."

"Nothing like that, constable," the professor said. "I've already told you I merely wish to examine it; make a few tests."

"I understand; that's what that bloody great case is in aid of . . ." He nodded at the heavy piece of expensive-looking luggage at Elton's feet. "I wish you'd let me carry it for you for a bit."

"No, no, I'll see to this, constable." Elton put a protective hand on the case. "The device I have here—which I developed myself—may well revolutionize the whole art of archaeological dating."

"That's a bit over my head, sir," the constable said.

Elton took another swig from the flask and handed it back. "With the chronalyzer—" he patted the case—"I'll be able to establish the ages of stone artifacts which have hitherto defied analysis. You see, the incidence of naturally occurring high-velocity particles on exposed rock surfaces induces submicroscopic changes in the internal crystal-line structure of the material; naturally, when a cut is made in a stone surface by man—"

"Who cares how old a blinking rock is?" Boyle cut in. "Now, *my* idea is, you can vet this thing, say whether it's worth the trouble of doing a bit of digging; then if we turn up anything—say a few solid-gold chamber pots—"

"Now, constable, I'm not interested in visionary schemes to defraud the authorities."

"Defraud, sir? That's rather a rash term. As for myself, my salary as a blooming game warden is—"

"Is none of my business," Elton pulled his boots on and got to his feet. "I suggest we resume while the sunlight is good."

"As you say, sir. But it seems a shame, considering the fact that we're a good fifty miles from Tegucigalpa and there's boats on the river to be had for a song."

"I don't sing very well," Elton said severely. "I have an adequate position with a reasonably good, small university and a full professorship in the offing if my chronalyzer proves out. That is the sole purpose of this expedition."

Boyle squinted at the sun. "We'd best be moving if we want to be back to Yuscaran tonight."

Late sunlight was filtering through high treetops where green parrots had set up a raucous evening serenade among the orchids when Boyle stumbled into a tiny clearing, yelled "Ha!" and pointed.

Elton came up beside him, his once natty bush jacket hanging damply, his solar topi on backward, his shins scratched. Before him, a two-yard thick cylinder thrust up from a tangle of flowering vines, its weathered surface almost obscured by a growth of grayish moss.

"Well, it appears to be artificial, just as you said," Elton commented. He gazed at the ten-foot high monument, circled it, studying the surface.

"Not much over a thousand years old, I'd guess," he said. "The Mayan stone workers—"

"Why not try your apparatus on it and find out for sure?" Boyle suggested. "Then perhaps we might do just a bit of digging."

"No digging," Elton said firmly. He squatted by the case containing the chronalyzer, noting the scars and scratches in the once-splendid leather. He remembered the dinner the previous spring at which the luggage had been presented to him, along with a nice little check, on the occasion of his award-winning paper on *Some Evidences of an Advanced Technology Among Pre-Columbian Central Americans*. What would his colleagues say, he wondered, opening the case, if he returned from this trip with proof of the chronalyzer's success?

"Crikey," Boyle said, leaning over to peer into the case. "Looks like the insides of a reddy telly set."

"Oh, it's quite simple, really," Elton said, erecting the folding tripod he had taken from the case. "I merely expose the surface in question to radiation of specific wavelength, and the resultant refraction patterns are interpreted by the sensor unit; the results are read directly from the screen here. Later, of course, it would be a simple matter to devise a direct-reading scale."

He lifted the chronalyzer from the case, settled it in position on the tripod, then flipped a switch and checked indicator dials. Power was flowing at the correct levels. He sighted through an eye piece, fine-focused the crystal-guided light source, then flipped down the toggle switch which bombarded the target with high-range ultraviolet. A beam of pale light made a gray spot on the curve of mossy rock. The constable stood at Elton's shoulder, staring at the wavering green glow of the four-inch square indicator screen, watching the wave-forms dance.

"What's that wiggly line mean?" he inquired.

"Hmmm." Elton studied the pattern, compared it with the scale taped to the panel above the glass. "Curious; the surface seems to date about eight thousand years back. That is, it was exposed to the open air at about that date."

There was a harsh, grating sound, a sense of vibration deep underfoot. Elton stepped back, looking startled. Before him, the stone seemed to tremble . . .

"Here, what's that?" the constable's voice had a note of surprise. "You feel that, sir?"

The vibration was very perceptible now. The

stone was quivering visibly. Elton hastily
switched off the chronalyzer with a loud *click!* A
hairline crack became visible running from top to
bottom of the looming cylinder. The crack
widened; curved panels were opening out, sliding
silently on oiled bearings. A bluish light winked
on, revealing an interior chamber lined with fittings of an incomprehensible complexity.

"It's not . . . not one of these missiles, sir?"

A loud beep! came from the interior of the appa-
rition. Elton jumped.

"Ascrabilik ahubarata" an inhuman, metallic
voice said from inside the capsule.

"That's not Rooshian, is it, sir?"

"Definitely not Russian," Elton said, backing
away.

"You had me fooled, sir," Boyle said. "Nice bit
o' camouflage it was, too." He chuckled. "I'd of
wagered you'd never been here before; a jolly good
act you put on."

"Thank you, constable," Elton said in a squeaky
voice, mentally picturing squads of armed security men pounding through the jungle to take
him into custody. *"But how,"* he pictured himself
asking, *"was I to know that there was a secret
minuteman silo under this old rock . . . ?"*

"You scientist blokes," the cop said. "You're
full of surprises." He shook his head admiringly.

"Yes," Elton mumbled, going into motion suddenly. "Well, thanks for your cooperation, constable. We may as well be running along now."
He lifted the chronalyzer from its tripod, lowered
it into the case.

"You're going to leave it like this, sir?" The constable's eyebrows went up.

"We're pressed for time," Elton said hurriedly.

"We don't want to be caught out in the jungle after dark . . ."

"Ascrabilik ahubarata," the voice said again.

"Here sir, where's the voice coming from?" The constable poked his head inside the blue-glowing interior, his voice taking on an echoic quality. "What's—" A sharp buzz cut him off in mid-sentence. He stiffened, his arms jerking out from his sides; a dazed look spread over his face. A pair of bright metal clamps had extended from a receptacle, locked into the constable's head. Elton jumped forward, grabbed his arm and hauled at him. The buzz stopped abruptly, the clamps retracted. The constable staggered back, his hands to his head.

"Wh-what happened?" he choked. "Felt like my ruddy brains was being wrung out like a bar rag!"

"Mobile Command Center Ten Ninety-four, standing by for instructions," a harsh, high-pitched voice with a Middlesex accent said from inside the capsule.

"You might've warned me, sir," the constable said in a hurt tone.

"Uh . . . well, after all, these secret installations . . ." Elton improvised. "But I'll explain it all as we hike out."

"MCC Ten Ninety-four, awaiting instructions," the voice said again. "On five minute standby alert, counting . . ."

"Where's the chap manning this show, anyway?" the constable asked. "They oughtn't to go off and leave it like this."

"Probably they just stepped out for coffee. No

concern of ours, constable. Now, if you'll just give me a hand with the bag."

"Abandoned their post? Very strange, I'd call that, sir. Un-British. But then I suppose they're Wogs."

"MCC Ten Ninety-four awaiting instructions. Battle status, active."

"You hear that, sir? Blimey, do you suppose it's started? I knew that we couldn't trust those Russkis!"

"Just a routine exercise, I should think," Elton soothed, edging off into the surrounding undergrowth. "Now if you're ready—"

"Here," the constable said loudly, addressing his remarks to the capsule. "Constable Boyle here. What's this about a battle?"

"Battle report follows," the voice answered. "First Grand Fleet, annihilated, casualties total; Second Grand Fleet annihilated, casualties total; Third Grand Fleet . . ."

The voice went on, reeling off statistics.

"This is It, right enough!" Constable Boyle smacked a fist into his palm. "A hell of a fight going on somewhere . . ."

". . . Grand Fleet annihilated, casualties total," the voice droned on. "Sixth Grand Fleet, casualties ninety-eight percent; surviving units retired to defensive dome at station 92, under Yukk siege—"

"Ever heard of these Grand Fleets?" Boyle called to Elton. "That would be your lot, I reckon?"

"Certainly not," Elton said quickly. "Just code

names; you know; the Blue Army versus the Red Army—"

"Never had any use for bloody Reds meself," Boyle stated flatly. "Well, if it's not you Yanks, it must be British units involved. Always knew we were keeping a secret weapon tucked away someplace. Who'd have thought it'd be here in Honduras? But our chaps are in trouble, from the sound of it."

". . . Tenth Grand Fleet; Mobile Command Center Ten ninety-four standing by."

"Ten ninety-four? That's this apparatus here!" Boyle said excitedly. "And its ruddy crew's stepped out for tea!"

"If we hurry," Elton called cheerily.

"I don't like the sound of this," Boyle said. "Looks like the bloody Reds have had all the best of it, so far." He raised his voice to shout into the interior of the capsule.

"What kind of shape are the other blighters in?"

"Yukk Primary Echelon, annihilated, casualties total; Yukk Secondary Echelon, heavy casualties. Yukk Dreadnought *Abominable* operational, standing by off station 90—"

"Yukks, eh? Code name for the Russkis, shouldn't wonder," Boyle said. "And their dreadnought's got a group of our lads hemmed in at someplace called station 92. They'll be wanting a spot of help, sir!"

"Elements of Sixth Grand Fleet under siege at station 92. Besieging Yukk Dreadnought heavily outweighs units in ton/seconds firepower."

"We've got to get cracking, sir!" Boyle yelled. "We can't let the Bolsheviks wipe our chaps out!"

"Awaiting instructions," the voice said. "Three minute alert."

"Here, where's your station complement?" Boyle demanded.

"Station personnel departed to conduct local reconnaissance," the voice stated.

The constable whirled on Elton. "It's clear enough, sir; these chaps have buggered off and left their mates in the lurch. Lucky we happened along. It's awaiting our instructions!"

"Now, constable," Elton said reasonably. "Surely it's not talking to us—"

"Who bloody else? It popped open when we came along, didn't it?"

"I suppose my U-V triggered something," Elton muttered.

Boyle looked suddenly knowing. "Ah-hah, I think I see, sir. Security. You can't take action while I'm hanging about."

"Well, constable," Elton grabbed at the straw, "you don't expect me to violate NATO cosmic security?"

"I'll never breathe a word, sir, cross my heart!" Boyle was standing at attention, chin in, toes out. "We've got to give them a leg up, sir!"

"Out of the question, constable," Elton said, looking around for the first signs of flashing red lights, whooping sirens and pounding military police.

"You're a cool one, sir," Boyle said stiffly. "Have to be, I suppose, in the counterespionage game. But it's not the British way to desert one's mates in time of need."

"One's mates? What in the world are you talking about? We've stumbled into some sort of war games, constable; if we're here when the authorities arrive, we'll end up in a maximum-security prison!"

"I'm saying it's the real thing, sir. Our boys are under fire. They're counting on us, sir!"

"What the devil do you expect me to do?" A strident note had entered Elton's voice, reminding him of his last interview with Dean Longspoon, in which the irascible department head had suggested that Elton spend more time in the classroom and less in what he termed exotic peregrinations. How right, Elton thought, the dean had been.

"We'll fill in for these blinking tea-drinkers!" Boyle proposed. "And I'll have a word for their superiors when this is over!"

"But—but—"

"Two-minute alert," the voice stated.

"I always thought when the chips were down you Yanks would stand with us," Boyle said. "I'm going in—alone, if I have to."

"But—it might be dangerous."

"Chance we have to take," Boyle said curtly. "Coming?"

Elton came slowly across to Boyle's side, looked into the dim blue interior of the capsule, at a maze of pinpoint indicator lights, conduits, push-buttons, fittings.

"Hmmm. Interesting layout. New type oscilloscope, subminiature fluorescents—"

"Awaiting instructions; one-minute alert before reverting to inactive status," the voice said.

"Go ahead, sir!" Boyle urged. "I'm right behind you!"

Elton looked around; there were still no signs of aroused security forces bearing down. He put the suitcase on the ground, sighed and stepped hesitantly through the open entry.

At once, a folding seat deployed from the floor, nudged the back of Elton's knees, and he sat abruptly. Boyle crowded in behind him. Elton stared at the array of tiny dial faces and toggles, packed together like a display in a bargain jeweler's window.

"Say, you've got to hand it to those Air Ministry bods," Boyle said. "Not half crafty, that lot. Not a word in the papers about all this." He was looking around admiringly at the wilderness of quivering needles.

"Thirty-second alert," the voice stated.

"Wonder what that means?" Elton frowned.

"In twenty-five seconds, Mobile Center will revert to permanent inactive status if not activated," the voice said.

"You mean—we'll be out of the fight?" Boyle expostulated.

"Affirmative. Action must be taken within prescribed time limit, in accordance with standard anti-Yukk operational procedures."

"Suppose we don't?"

"Mobile Center will detonate. Fifteen-second warning."

Elton started out of his seat. "Fifteen seconds—let's get out of here!"

"We can't, sir!" Boyle caught his arm. "It's too late now to run! If it blows, it'll take us to kingdom come!"

"What'll I do?"

"Anything, sir! Just jab a button at random!"

Elton dithered, then lunged for the panel, depressed a fat red button directly before him.

Instantly, metal bands snapped around his mid-section, clamping him to the seat. Behind him, Boyle grunted, similarly restrained.

"Prepare for immediate jump to Battle Sector," the voice said emotionlessly. The curved door slid shut with a smooth sigh. The blue glow died, leaving only the jewel sparkle of the instruments.

"Hold on here," Elton yelled, tugging at the seat belt. There was an abrupt jar, an instant's pause —then a silent concussion that seemed to burst painlessly inside his skull. Boyle gave a choked shout—then all was silent and still again.

"S-sir?" Boyle got out.

"What . . . happened?" Elton managed.

"Sir, I've got a feeling . . . we're floating, sort of."

"Nonsense; the thing malfunctioned, obviously. Whatever was supposed to happen didn't. Perhaps it was never intended to. I'm beginning to suspect that we're the victims of the most idiotic practical joke of the decade!" Elton tugged at the seat clasp. "Now I suppose we're trapped here until they decide to come along and—"

"On station, Battle Sector Nine," the voice announced. "Request permission to deploy view screens."

"By all means, deploy the view screens," Elton said wearily. "And, by the way, just who the devil are you? Where are you speaking from? What's this farce all about, anyway? My name is Elton, and I demand—"

"This is the Lunar Battle Computer," the voice said. "I am positioned nine point three four two miles under the Lunar surface feature known as

Mount Tycho. At your instruction, I have placed Mobile Command Center Ten ninety-four on station in Battle Sector Nine, four thousand miles off Callisto, on an intercept course with the Yukk Dreadnought *Abominable*. Request permission to deploy forward batteries."

"You mean—you really—I mean—" Elton tried twice to swallow, make it on the third attempt. "This *is* all some ghastly joke?" he croaked.

"Negative," the voice said flatly. It seemed to issue from a small slot set among the flashing lights—which were now blinking with renewed enthusiasm. A large amber X in midpanel winked on and off frantically.

"Callisto," Boyle said. "I've heard of it. Somewhere near Jamaica, I believe."

"Someone's idea of humor," Elton croaked. He managed a stifled laugh. "Why, if we were really four thousand miles off Callisto, we'd be hundreds of millions of miles away deep in space."

"Space, sir?"

"Callisto is—" he swallowed—"one of the moons of Saturn—or is it Jupiter?"

"Jupiter," the voice said tonelessly.

"Jupiter? Well, now, I knew our lads were holding something back," Boyle said complacently. "You Yanks and your moon shots are all very well, but here we British are, all the way out on Jupiter. Goes to show . . ."

"Goes to show what?" Elton yelped. "Suppose this thing knows what it's talking about? Do you know anything about piloting a satellite . . ." his voice trailed off in a squeak. Two translucent panels which had slid down from slots above, opened out, glowed briefly, then snapped into the crystal clarity of the finest photograph. Against a background of utter black, blazing points of light flared and sparkled. To the left, a brilliant curve of light like an enormous full moon edged into the picture. The screen above showed a similar scene, with the familiar tiny ringed disc of Saturn glowing, bright-edged, off to one side. In the center of the screen a moving blip glowed.

"There you are," Boyle said proudly, indicating Jupiter. "British soil, the whole lot."

There was a loud *ping!*

"What was that?"

"Yukk suppressor rays have locked on Command Center," the voice said in the same emotionless tone. "Likelihood of immediate salvo fire."

"Fire? You mean they're shooting at us? Goodness. Who would want to do that—?"

"Yukk dreadnought on closing course," the Lunar Computer announced. "Request instructions."

"Take evasive action!" Elton yelled. "Get us out of here!"

"Drive mechanism nonfunctional in field of Yukk suppressor rays," the voice said.

"Uh—fire the forward batteries!" Elton yelled.

"Guns nonoperative in field of Yukk suppressor rays."

On the screen the blip grew; it swelled visibly, bearing down at a headlong clip. Elton could make out details of the image now. A clumsy, double-pyramid shape, slabsided, angular, rushing at him from dead ahead.

"Nothing for it but to ram, sir!" Boyle yelled. "God save the Queen!"

Elton lurched forward as the capsule seemed to brake suddenly. The pressure grew. Elton grunted as the seat clamp cut into his stomach.

"Yukk tractor rays now grappling Command Center," the voice said indifferently. "Request permission to self-destruct."

"Not bloody likely!" Boyle bawled. "We're not ruddy Kami Kazis!"

The pressure slacked off. The forward screen went dark, filled by the bulk of the Yukk dreadnought. In the rear screen the stars glittered and winked. A tremor ran through Elton's seat—a sharp jar, a sense of sliding, then silence again.

"We—we've stopped," Elton said uncertainly.

"What do you suppose it means, sir?" Boyle said in a strained voice. "I'd have wagered a fiver we were bound to collide with that monster."

"We're practically bumping into it now."

"We must be hove to alongside," Boyle said.

"I . . . I suppose they'll be along to collect us any minute now," Elton said.

"Captured," Boyle said disgustedly. "Without firing a shot."

"By the Yukks," Elton added. "We'll be brainwashed . . . "

"There'll be help on the way, sir," Boyle said cheerfully. "When the chaps we're filling for get back and find their machine missing, they'll be through to Air Ministry like a shot."

"I wonder what they're waiting for?"

Elton stared at the dark screen, unable to make out details of their captor. "I'd like to get on to the name-rank-and-serial-number part, and possibly get in touch with the Red Cross."

"Pity we're not armed," Boyle said. "We could have put up a spirited defense, and maybe taken a couple of the blighters with us."

Elton didn't answer; he was swallowing hard, running over speeches:

I am a civilian, captain; as a noncombatant, I insist—No, that would be hard to put over under the circumstances. How about: *Well, fellows, the fortunes of war, eh? Wonderful job you did at Stalingrad* . . .

"Maybe if you twiddle the knobs a bit, you can see something of what's going on out there," Boyle suggested. Elton tried the controls beside the dark forward screen; suddenly it lightened; a pitted surface of iodine-colored metal curved before them, sliding slowly past.

"That's better," Boyle muttered. "Don't imagine the Reds had anything like that! Bloody vast thing, isn't it?"

"Bigger than anything we've got," Elton said. "Alien-looking, isn't it? I wonder if Washington knows about this?"

"I should think Whitehall has likely let them in on it, sir."

"Listen," Elton said, "do you suppose that we somehow eluded their radar? After all, we're rather small, and they may have been expecting something their own size."

"You may have something there, sir." Boyle smacked his fist into his palm. "Hard lines we can't activate this blasted pogo stick we're sitting in."

"Look here, Lunar Computer," Elton said. "Isn't there a chance you can get us out of this spot we're in? It appears—"

"All systems now functional," the voice said.

"What! Why didn't you say so!"

"Data not requested," the voice snapped.

"Well, what about it. Can we jump away from here—get back where we started from?"

"Yukk suppressors are activated by high-velocity bodies moving within sensitivity range of instruments," the voice said flatly.

"Suppose we sneak away? Just sort of edge off-stage, so to speak?"

"What about the Commies, sir?" Boyle remonstrated. "If you're feeling a bit better now, we can renew the fight."

"Fight? Look here, Boyle, this has gone far enough. I must have been under the influence of alcohol. What kind of fight can this—this wandering phone booth put up against that Leviathan? No, thank you, I'll be happy just to get back, pay my fines, and leave quietly tomorrow aboard the *S.S. Togetherness* as planned—"

"Sir! Look there!" Boyle's fingers dug into Elton's arm; he pointed to the screen. In the section of the Yukk hull passing across the screen, a vast, gaping rent showed. Inside, Elton caught a glimpse of twisted structural members, buckled deck plates.

"No wonder they paid us no heed!" Boyle blurted. "Looks as though they had a spot of bother of their own." A second vast wound in the immense hull drifted into view. Great, blackened tubes that could only have been weapons hung in their carriages, silent.

"Crikey!" Boyle commented happily. "They've jolly well had it!"

"They're still active enough to deactivate our guns, shut down our engines, and take us in tow," Elton said. "The crew are probably all in the un-damaged part, ready to blast us at the first sign of life."

"What about that, Looney Control?" Boyle barked.

"It's Lunar Control," Elton put in.

"Affirmative," the voice said.

"You see?" Elton said.

"Are they on the lookout for us?" Boyle pressed on.

"Negative."

"Why not?" Elton demanded.

"There are no survivors aboard the Yukk ship," the voice said casually.

"No survivors?" Boyle and Elton echoed together.

"Then," Elton said perplexedly, "who's been operating the suppressor, and tractor rays, and—"

"Yukk defensive armaments activated automatically at the approach of possible hostile bodies."

"Now you tell us!" Elton sagged in his seat. "Well, Boyle, I think that lets us off the hook. We can go back now."

"I wouldn't say so, sir," Boyle cut in. "What about those chaps under siege? We can't just go off and forget them."

"What seige? The Yukks have been wiped out. There's no one here to besiege them!"

"Perhaps they're not aware of their victory, sir! We've got to carry the good news to them. It'll be a feather in our cap, sir."

"I don't care for feathery caps," Elton said. "Let Lunar Control tell them, if it wants too—it seems to be damnably cagy when it comes to withholding information."

"All you've got to do is ask the right question, sir." Boyle's voice was smug. "After all, it's only a machine; admitted that itself. We're the only personnel here—and I say we have a duty to perform."

"All right, all right." Elton addressed Lunar Control. "Can you take us there—to wherever this Lost Batallion is supposed to be pinned down?"

"Station 92," the voice said. "Affirmative."

"All right, I guess we'll give it a try. But creep along slowly, so as not to wake any sleeping electronic dogs. Where is this station 92, anyway?"

"On the surface of the moon Callisto."

"Miserable place to be marooned," Elton said, staring at the bleak expanse of wan-lit, cratered rock below. "Callisto is much too small to support an atmosphere, and at this distance from the sun I imagine the rock never warms much above absolute zero."

The ground was moving up swiftly; the screens swept the close ragged horizon, fixed on the black of the sky. There was a lurch, followed by a thump.

"We're down," Boyle announced. "All right, open up," he called. "And—"

"No!" Elton yelled—too late. The seat clamps snapped back, the doors slid open—and a breath of cool, perfumed air wafted in from outside.

"It's—but—how . . . ?"

"Contact at station 92," the voice said. "You are now within the defensive force dome."

"Oh, that explains it," Elton let out the breath he had been holding. "The dome keeps the Yukks out, and holds the air and heat in."

"Now to spread the good word," Boyle said heartily. "Ready, sir?"

"I suppose you were right about coming over to let them know they've won." Elton stepped out, felt grass underfoot, sniffed the air. "My, won't they be delighted." He stared up at the heavens; Jupiter was a vast, pale crescent moon, glowing in banded pastel colors. Other, smaller moons moved visibly nearby. Vast numbers of fat, close stars glittered overhead.

"I wonder where they are?" Elton squinted into the deep gloom of the Callistan night.

"How many men have survived?" Boyle called to the capsule.

"Seven hundred and five individuals now occupy the redoubt," the slightly bored-sounding voice said. "None of them are Men."

"Did you say," Elton got out, "they're not . . . men?"

"Affirmative," the voice was bland.

"Blimey," Boyle said. "A bunch of ruddy Martians?"

"No wonder the Yukk ship looked alien," Elton groaned. "This is some kind of interplanetary war between intelligent oysters, or something. What are *we* doing mixed up in it?"

"Questions relating to organic motivations are not within my scope," the computer said.

"And the Yukks aren't Commies at all?" Boyle sounded disappointed.

"Negative, in the sense in which you employ the term; however, the Yukk practice a form of communal life, based on—"

"There you are, sir! Commies, as I said. These Reds are a crafty lot. As I see it, we British have made contact with the Martians, who've become our allies. It's a group of their lads out here, and it's our plain duty to carry on."

Elton scrambled back inside the capsule. "I don't know about you, constable!" he yelled, "but I'm leaving."

"Warning," the voice said. "Yukk batteries command entire volume of space within ten million miles. Any attempt to jump will result in approach to Yukk vessel and consequent concentrated automatic Yukk fire with high negative probability of survival of Mobile Command Center."

Elton scrambled back out of the capsule. "Dandy," he said. "Marvelous. Rush to the assistance of our Martian allies, eh? *Now* look at the pickle you've gotten us in!"

"Me, sir? Why, I've merely lent a hand—"

"All right! But here we are—wherever we are—sitting ducks for the Yukk—whatever they are."

"Yukks; some kind of Bolsheviks, I don't doubt. But it's all the same to me. What we've got to do now, sir, we've got to make contact with our side and work out a plan of action."

"Never mind that," Elton said. "We've got troubles of our own. There's got to be *some* way to slip out from under the guns of that derelict."

"Not without first contacting these Martian chaps," Boyle protested. "We can take time to propose a toast or two, exchange cigarettes, that sort of thing . . ." Boyle's voice faded.

He stood, head cocked, listening.

"Do you hear anything, sir?" he whispered.

"Only you, making another fatuous suggestion," Elton replied tartly. "Personally, I favor asking questions of this mobile whatever-it-is until we get some useful answer, and then leaving as hastily as possible."

"There it is again, sir!" Boyle said.

"What?"

There was a sudden quick padding of feet, a loud whoosh!, a sharp chemical odor; Elton took a breath to shout, choked, felt the world swim out from underneath and fall on him like a vast feather mattress.

Professor Elton moved to get away from an unpleasant jogging sensation, discovered fight folds of coarse netting binding his arms to his sides and holding his legs in a tight crouched position. His left ear was pressing into the rough strands, and there was a sharp pain in his neck.

"Help!" he croaked. "Boyle, where are you?"

"Here, sir," a weak voice came back.

"What happened? I'm wrapped up like a mummy in some sort of seine."

"Same here, sir. We were took unawares, it appears."

"By your Martian friends, I suppose?"

"Look on the bright side, sir. We haven't been done in yet. That's something."

They were in a dim-lit corridor, Elton saw. By twisting his head, he made out the silhouettes of slender biped figures with immense heads. He was, he saw, trussed in a net slung like a hammock from the shoulders of a pair of the creatures.

There were shrill shouts from ahead, answering cries from his captors. More of the bipeds crowded around; Elton strained to get a clear view through the mesh, but carried as he was in a head-down position, he was unable to make out any more detail.

There was an abrupt lurching as he was carried up a short flight of stairs. He squinted his eyes against the sudden, brilliant light, then he oofed as the support dropped from under him, slamming him against a cool, hard floor. He pushed at the enveloping net, kicking it free of his feet, fighting it over his head.

"Good Heavens!" Boyle's voice burst out.

"Hang on, Boyle! I'm coming!" Elton shouted encouragingly. He flung the net from him, whirled—

"It said they weren't men," Boyle croaked.

Standing in a semi-circle facing the captives were six exceedingly pretty girls.

"Rubavilup mockerump hifswimp," one of the girls said. Elton reached up dazedly to adjust his tie, his gaze glued to the large greenish eyes in the pert face before him. Below the face was a slender neck, adorned with multiple strands of turquoise-like beads. A close-fitting, short-skirted tunic hugged nicely curved hips; a pair of shapely legs led Elton's eyes to the polished floor, where they paused for a moment, blinked and started back up.

"They're not bad-looking, sir," Boyle said approvingly, "considering they're Martians."

The girl in the center of the group frowned. "Asibolimp hubshut ook?" she asked Elton.

"I'm terribly sorry, Miss," he said. "I'm afraid I don't understand."

"Here," Boyle said loudly. "Who's in charge here?"

"Aridomop urramin ralafoo glip?"

"Who's . . . IN . . . CHARGE HERE . . . ?" Boyle repeated, with gestures. The girls spoke briefly among themselves. One pointed to a door across the room, then took Boyle's arm, urged him on. He jerked free.

"Look here, my girl—" he started, shaking a finger under her nose. A sharp slap sent him back a step; his mouth opened and closed; then he reached for her. An instant later, having described a somersault over the girl's shoulder, Boyle gazed up from a supine position on the floor.

"Ralafoo glip," the girl said and jerked her head toward the door.

"I think when she says ralafoo glip she means it; better do as she says," Elton suggested, starting toward the indicated door.

"All very well for you Yanks, you're used to this sort of thing."

In the inner room, Elton followed gestures toward a massive chair placed against the wall, seated himself gingerly. Something cool touched the sides of his face just in front of his ears, pressed firmly. There was a sharp prickling sensation. Abruptly, his head seemed full with a screech like a tape recorder running backward at high speed. Elton flopped in the chair, caught by the head. As suddenly as it had begun, the screech ended; the clamps retracted. Elton stumbled to his feet.

"What in the name of the Fallen Towers of Hubilik was that?" he demanded, rubbing his ears.

"The language indoctrinator," the nearest girl said.

"I don't understand," Elton stated, staring from the girl to the chair. "How in the name of the Five Sacred Snakes of Bomakook did my sitting in that thing teach you to speak Grimblkpsk?"

"Umma oobabba ungha," Boyle yelled incomprehensibly, pointing at Elton. Two girls seized his arms, thrust him toward the chair. He braced his feet, still shouting nonsense. Elton saw the bright metal clamps swing down and grip the constable's head. They held him as he kicked out wildly, mouth open; then the chair released him. The girls stepped back.

"Now, if you'll behave yourself," the leading girl said to Boyle.

"Calm yourself, Boyle," Elton snapped. "I'm sure your behavior isn't helping us." He faced the auburn-haired girl who had first spoken.

"Now, young lady, if you'll just let me explain: My name is Rflxk ... " he paused, frowning. "Rlfxk? Is that my name?"

"If you're honest, you have nothing to worry about, dearies," the auburn-haired girl said, taking his arm in a firm grip and steering him back out into the hall. "Our detectors showed us something has passed through the screen. Naturally, we couldn't afford to take any chances. After all, you could have been Yukks—just like we learned in Training."

"Us Yukks," Elton managed a chuckle. "Why, my dear, we came here to assist you."

"Fat lot of good it did us," Boyle muttered

behind him. "These bloody Amazons don't want helping."

"Assist us how?" Elton's auburn-haired captor inquired.

"Why, in the fight with the Yukks; but of course—"

"Ixnay, ir-say," Boyle said quickly. "One-day ell-tay em-they ut-way ee-way ound-fay."

"Well, back to the language indoctrinator," a red-head said.

"That won't be necessary," Elton said hastily. "My friend was just ah . . . reciting an old poem. By the way, where are we going?"

"A good luck spell? I hope it's a good one—not that they work."

"You're on your way to see the Mother."

"This is out of our jurisdiction," another added.

The girl holding Elton's arm looked up at him with a reassuring smile; her delicately curved lips were parted, showing even white teeth; her hair looked as soft as angora; her lashes were long and dark. With an effort he kept his eyes from the warm, rounded shape poking against his arm.

"We don't often get visitors from the other domes," she said. "It's kind of exciting, having you here."

"Why did you come?" another asked. "Is it about the fungus competition?"

"Now Nid, the Mother, will handle the interrogation."

The two men followed their escort along the high-vaulted corridor, up more steps and under a filigreed arch into a wide room, where dim light from lamps placed at random among deep chairs glowed on small tables with bowls of exotic fruits, cushioned chaise lounges, and, at the center of the room, a fountain that leaped up to fall back into a shallow pool in which a vast, pale-white figure reclined.

Two of the girls went forward, spoke briefly to the fat woman in the water. Elton could hear an answer in a hearty, policematron voice; the girls twittered again, pointing toward the two strangers.

"Let's have a look at 'em," the fat woman said.

Elton and Boyle moved up to the pool edge, averted their eyes in embarrassment as the matronly figure, totally nude, reached out for a fruit bowl at the poolside, selected a mango-like ovoid, took a large bite, chewed noisily.

"All right," the Mother said. "You did right, girls; they're an odd-looking pair; look a little weather-beaten; not what you'd call beauties; but they're not Yukks, that's easy to see. You there—" Elton knew she was talking to him. He faced her, arranging a faculty-type smile.

"We haven't seen strangers here in a long time," the woman said. "Especially the kind that barge in without warning. Why didn't your Mother call me? Never mind; good experience for the girls. Hearing about something in Training is one thing, actually seeing it's another. Now—" She took another bite of fruit—"you two girls just tell me in your own words what you're doing here."

"What do you mean, you two oof!" Boyle subsided as Elton's elbow caught him in the side.

"Well, ah . . . " Elton started.

"I don't believe I've seen your type before," the Mother said. "Flat-chested, aren't you? And narrow through the hips. You must have a hard time with your babies." She shot Elton a sharp look.

"Oh, ah, terrible," Elton nodded. "Actually, I've never—"

"What dome is it you're from?"

"As a matter of fact, we came here from Shrulp," Elton said. He blinked, trying the name again. "Shrulp?"

"Here, sir, " Boyle put in. "Why not just tell them we're from . . . Shrulp." He looked puzzled.

"I've heard of Mumbulip Dome," the Mother was saying. "And we had a delegation from Rilifub Dome in my Mother's time, after a rock tremor knocked out one of their air plants. They had a terrible time of it, crossing Outside in one of those old Travelers, afraid it would break down any minute; but Shrulp—that's a new one on me. Must be away over on Far Side." The Mother frowned. "You're not here to stir up trouble, I hope?"

"Goodness, no," Elton felt the smile slipping, twisted it back into position. "We understood that you needed help in the fight against the Yukks."

"Praise Mother," the woman made a cryptic sign with her hands, which the girls standing in her line of vision copied. She frowned at Elton. "Where did you get the idea we don't know how to deal with a Yukk?"

"Frankly—" Elton ignored Boyle's look, took the plunge—"the Lunar Battle Computer told us—" he broke off, seeing the expression on the Mother's face.

"Look here, young lady," the Mother snapped. "I'm as devout as the next person, but I won't stand for any superstitious nonsense. Now, I think you'd better explain your invasion of my Dome—and don't take me for a gullible old fool. I showed Mother Rilifub just how far she'd get trying to take the fungus arrangement championship away from us with her slick tricks."

"But it's nothing like that."

"Not that I don't respect the old ways, mind you. If it weren't for you troublemakers, the World would be a peaceful place—and Girl has her place in it. But I'm not standing by to see charlatans get my girls all aroused. First thing you know, they'll be openly advocating Strange Ways—"

A gasp ran through the assembled girls. The old woman ignored the reaction, signaled to a pair of handmaidens standing by. They stepped forward, gripped the fat arms of the Mother and heaved her to her feet. She puffed, wading to shore.

"Tikki, Nid," she said to the attendant girls, "I'm tired. I'll talk to these girls later; they've put me all on edge, and I want to be calm if it comes to a Judgment. Take them along and mind you keep them under close surveillance." She accepted a vast huck towel, draped it across her shoulders, waddled to a chair.

"You'd better give them a blanket apiece and lock them in a storeroom," she added. "You know how crowded we are for space . . ." She shot a hard look past Elton at the girl Tikki. "Yes, I hardly know how we're going to find room for them, with crowding the way it is. But we'll manage somehow. Meanwhile, I intend to check with this Shrulp Dome wherever it is. If they're here to spread Strange propaganda . . ." She gave Elton a look which reminded him of a portly Dean of Women he had once known, who had suspected him of intent to impregnate her charges.

"But we haven't told you—" Elton started.

"Silence!" the fat woman snapped. "I'll talk to you later. Maybe tomorrow."

"See here, we came here to do you a good turn, and without even listening, you're talking about locking us in storerooms."

"If they haven't taught you proper respect for Mother at Shrulp Dome, you'll learn it here!" The Mother said sharply. "Take them away, girls!"

Back out in the corridor, Elton cleared his throat and tried again.

"Pardon me, but aren't you girls concerned about the Yukk dreadnought out there, aiming its guns at you right now?"

"You girls must be overly preoccupied with theology over at Shrulp Dome," the girl the Mother had called Tikki said. "Sure, we know all about the Yukks, but after all . . ." she winked at Elton. "Nobody's ever really seen one. So why should we worry?"

"I don't understand," Elton said. "Here you are, right in the midst of a terrible battle with some sort of ghastly monsters with huge ships the size of mountains—and you don't seem to care."

"If we're good girls, they can't hurt us," the girl dismissed the subject. "Listen, you seem like nice enough girls. The Mother said to lock you in a storeroom, but . . . maybe we could work something out." She turned to speak in a low tone to the girl beside her. They turned into a side corridor lined on both sides with identical doors; it had a deserted air. Through a half-open door, Elton caught a glimpse of an empty room, daintily furnished in bright, flashing colors.

"Look," Tikki said, "I'll tuck you in my room. Even though we're awfully crowded, as the Mother said," she added. "It won't hurt if we double up, if you don't mind sharing the bed. You must be simply worn out from the trip. I'll bet it's just awful outside the Dome," she shuddered.

"Sharing . . . your bed?" Elton asked.

"It will just be for tonight. Your friend will go with Nid. Tomorrow one of the other girls will have you, and the night after that another."

Elton took a deep breath. "Well, if you're sure it won't put you out?"

"It'll be fun," the girl said. "We can just cuddle up and have a nice long talk. I want to hear all about Shrulp."

It was a small, neat room, with fluffy curtains at the window, a shaggy rug on the floor, a flounced spread on the bed, and a rack in one corner on which hung a dozen bright-colored short tunics. Elton's hostess took off her turquoise beads and hung them on the rack, eyeing Elton's battered bush jacket.

"My, those are certainly strange-looking clothes you have on. I suppose you needed them for the trip, but you can get out of them now. I'll draw us a tub. Would you like a little ginger in it or maybe a touch of mint? I always like mint, myself."

"Tub?" Through an open door Elton saw a pink-tiled room, and tropical-looking flowers in planters lining a ten-foot square sunken pool with bright chrome fittings.

"We can just relax and scrub each other's backs," Tikki said. She finished undoing the snaps down the back of her tunic, shucked it off, dropped it in a wall slot, faced Elton wearing a diaphanous one-piece undergarment.

Elton's collar suddenly felt tight. He felt his face break into a silly smile. "Well, whatever you say . . ."

Tikki plucked a small box from a table, offered Elton what looked like a plastic cigarette. He groped, took one, jabbed it at his mouth. Tikki took one, drew on it, blew out perfumed smoke. "I'm afraid you bugged the Mother, with all that talk about the Yukks. She's a dear, really, but very hard-headed when it comes to religion. She says it's time we did away with outmoded concepts and recognized that the Yukks are merely an external-ized personification of an inner yearning for defilement, or something."

"Look," Elton said sharply. "Let's play a little game. We'll pretend I just arrived from . . . from someplace so far away that I never even heard of the Yukks, or the Mother, or the domes—and you tell me all about it," Elton said.

"That sounds like a very strange game," Tikki said doubtfully. She opened the door to an adjoin-ing room, stepped inside; a moment later a sound of rushing water started up. Steam wafted into the room, carrying a scent of Life-savers. Tikki came back, holding a large cake of violet soap.

"Is that what you play back at Shrulp?"

"Yes, we spent a lot of time telling each other things we already know. The trick is to catch the other . . . ah . . . girl in a mistake."

"Well, it doesn't really sound like much fun. If you feel like playing, wouldn't you rather just wrestle? I'll bet you know some interesting holds."

"Maybe later," Elton gulped. "Now, you were

going to tell me all about the Yukks, remember?"

Tikki put a finger to her cheek, nibbled at her lower lip, looking thoughtfully at the ceiling. Elton found the expression perfectly delightful.

So was the slim, tanned body below it.

"Well, nine hundred and sixty-four—or is it sixty-five . . . ? Let me see." Tikki nibbled a fingertip. "It must be sixty-five because I finished Baby Training when I was ten, and Girl Training when I was eighteen, and it was sixty-one then, and that was four—"

"Sixty-five it is," Elton put in. "You're doing fine."

"Anyway, nine hundred and sixty-five cycles ago, when the war with the Yukks was in its nineteenth cycle, there was a great battle fought between two fleets. Now, in those days there were many among the girls who were badly tainted with Strange Ways."

Her voice, Elton noticed, had taken on the tone of a pupil reciting lessons. "Because of this, the girls weren't able to destroy the wicked Yukks, as they deserved. Instead, the Great Mother sent a terrible thing called a Disruptor that caused the machines of the girls to malfunction, and all of the girls were killed or captured—except one ship-load. The captain was a righteous Mother, and so she and her girls were spared. They landed here on the World, and set up the Force Domes, and the defensive screens, to keep the Yukks at bay. That's why it's our duty to tend the Field Generators, and defend girlhood, and weed out any traces of . . ." she blushed, " . . . Strange Ways. Not that anybody has any," she added.

"Any what?" Elton asked.

"Strange Ways," Tikki said primly. "You know."

"But we're playing that I don't know, remember?"

"Here," Tikki said reaching for Elton's top jacket button. "I'll help you get these things off. The tub's ready by now." The steam had formed a pinkish haze at eye level. "Is this what holds it?" She undid the button clumsily. "I'm not very good at this . . ." She undid another button.

"What about the Yukks?" Elton's voice sounded strained. Tikki undid the last coat button and pulled the garment off him.

"Well, the Yukks are evil beings who tried to enslave all Girlhood, once, long ago, before we were driven out of the Heavenly Garden. They were great big ugly creatures, with hair growing all over their faces, and huge, bony hands—six of them, I think—and whenever they could catch a poor, defenseless girl, they'd . . ." Tikki swallowed, her face pink. "They'd do Strange Things to her."

"Strange Things?" Elton's voice was a squeak. Tikki was just finishing the last shirt button. She peeled it back over his shoulders.

"And the terrible power they had was, that they made perfectly nice girls *want* them to do the Strange Things. Even now, there's always the danger that a girl will fall into Strange Ways—like dreaming about a Yukk chasing her, with all six hands reaching for her—and even catching her . . ." Tikki took a deep breath. "That's what makes the Yukks so terrible, and that's why if there really ARE any Yukks, and one of them ever managed to get into the Dome—" Her eyes were flashing with anger; her nostrils flared—"everyone would tear the horrible hairy thing into tiny little pieces before he could spread any Strange Ways!"

"Tiny little pieces?" Elton stammered. He grabbed for his shirt, pulled it back on. Tikki's eyes strayed to his chest. "My you *are* flat-chested," she said, in an envious tone. She put a hand under each of her magnificently formed mammaries, looked sadly down at them. "These DO get in the way . . ."

Elton was backing toward the door. "Ah . . . I've just remembered something," he blurted, fumbling the door open. "Where did they take my friend? I have to find hi—her—right away!"

"Oh, she's just next door," Tikki said. "But—"

Elton whirled to the adjoining door, banged on it, twisted the knob. It flew open. Boyle, shirtless, was just reaching for the tanned curve of his hostess's hip.

"No!" Elton shouted.

Boyle yipped and jumped a foot into the air.

"I've got to talk to you!" Elton hissed, "privately."

"Look here, can't it wait?" Boyle's face had assumed a beefy color. "Bloody cheek, I call it, bursting in here just when I was about to . . . to . . . make friends."

"That's what I have to talk to you about." Elton glanced at Boyle's roommate, then at Tikki, standing in the doorway, looking puzzled. "Do you mind, girls? Just for a moment?" He ushered the girls out, closed the door. "I've made a discovery," he started.

"Me too," Boyle said, smirking. "I think we're on to a good thing. A different one every night, at that. Now if you'd just toddle off, there's a good lad—"

"Do you know what they do to Yukks if they catch one?" Elton cut in.

"Tear 'em to bits, Nid said—that's my young lady. They've no more use for bloody Reds than—"

"Correct," Elton said. "They tear them to pieces. Small, hairy pieces."

"So what's that to do with us?"

"Plenty," Elton said. "We're Yukks."

Boyle was sitting on the bed, mopping at his face with a tiny lacy hanky he had found under the pillow.

"That was a near thing," he said. "Another five minutes—"

"And you'd have stood revealed as the ancient archenemy of girlhood," Elton said decisively.

"But look here, from what Nid said, they've been living here on this Tup'ny world for nine-hundred cycles, whatever those are."

"Nine hundred and sixty-five," Elton corrected him. "I think the term probably refers to Jupiter's revolutions around the sun. That would be about . . . hmm . . . eight thousand two hundred years, Shrulp time."

"Eight blinking thousand years? But that Looney Control affair said the crew had just stepped out."

"They did, too—about the time the ice was melting off Wisconsin. Probably ran into a party of early headhunters or a wandering hyaenodon. I'm afraid Lunar Control has little or no awareness of the meaning of time."

Boyle shook his head. "Eight thousand years with no Yukks? Then how in the Six Rivers of Blue

Mud do they have blinking babies?"

"I'd imagine they have a supply of frozen sperm —or possibly they've developed a method of parthenogenesis."

"How do you suppose this bloody system ever got started?" Boyle looked bewildered. "What this lot needs is a firm masculine hand to put things in order. I've a mind to—"

"To be torn to bits? Please, Boyle, this situation requires careful handling. We've got to get away from here—that much is clear. And there's no time to lose. Sooner or later someone is going to put two and two together."

"And it may as well be me," Boyle said with sudden decision. "Leave that Nid to me for a night or two and I fancy—"

"Strange Ways," Elton said. "That's what they call that sort of thing. I suppose it all started with some sort of idiotic feminist movement, somewhere. The women developed a method of reproducing without men, and declared their independence. Naturally, war followed; a war fought in space."

"Why space? And how? There weren't any bleeding space vessels eight thousand years ago."

"Apparently there were. As a matter of fact, I did a paper once—but never mind that. Being women, the girls wouldn't want to do anything as untidy as fighting a war right there on Earth— and then too, I suppose the important logistical targets were off-planet; control of the spaceways was the key to success. And so a great battle was fought, and both sides virtually wiped each other out. The surviving girls reached Callisto here, and set up these force domes and a defensive screen to keep off what was left of the Yukks; and the Yukks, with only one damaged ship left mounted a siege; then they died off—but the girls never knew."

"I see . . . and back home, everybody made up and forgot the whole thing."

"Not quite; there's still a certain residual hostility. But the economic drain of the war and the loss of personnel plunged society back to a minimal cultural level—and we're only now re-attaining their level of technology."

"All right, granted you're on the right track; what do we do now? Slip out of here and leg it back to the Mobile Whatsit?"

"We don't even know where it is—and anyway, the Yukks have us pinned down, remember? The minute we come out from under the defensive screen, blooie!"

Boyle chewed the inside of his cheek; a shrewd expression settled over his features. "They won't shoot—not if we let them know we're Yukks ourselves."

"Maybe," Elton said, looking thoughtful. "We *could* give it a try, I suppose."

"No time like the present." Boyle went to the door, opened it. Nid and Tikki came in, two slim creatures as unself-conscious as a pair of young antelope.

"What are you two girls talking about in here?" Tikki asked.

"I'll bet you have some important message from your Mother?" Nid hazarded.

"As a matter of fact, we do," Elton said. "Of course, this is a very confidential matter. You mustn't tell anybody."

"Not even Mother?"

"We tell Mother everything," Nid said.

"Even about your—Strange Thoughts?" Elton hazarded.

Nid and Tikki blushed a delicate shade of purple.

"We'll have to confide in you ladies," Boyle said solemnly. "We've got wind of a big push the Reds are planning. High Command is counting on us. We have to go back to our traveler."

"You mean—there really *are* Yukks?" Nid's eyes were large with wonder.

"Absolutely," Elton nodded.

"I . . . I feel all sort of wiggly inside." Tikki put her hands to her stomach.

"Can't you wait till in the morning?" Nid asked anxiously. "It's only a month away."

"No, we have to go right now."

"Even before our bath?"

"Definitely."

"You're such brave girls," Nid said admiringly.

"I . . . I can't go," Tikki said. "I'm afraid I might—" Her lip quivered. "I might turn out to be —unreliable." She burst into tears.

"There, there." Elton patted her shoulder, dismayed. "What's there to be afraid of? You'll be with us."

"You don't know what an awful girl I am," Tikki sniffled. "I have Strange Thoughts all the time . . . and I'm afraid . . . might . . . I might . . . disgrace Mother." Her sobs took over. Nid took her hand. "Now, Tikki, you're not the only one. I don't know a girl who doesn't have a Strange Thought now and then."

"B-but I have them all the time . . ."

"I'll tell you a secret: So do I; but—"

"But I *like* them!"

"Look, we'll keep an eye on you," Boyle said. "You'll have to shut down that salt-water factory now, we've got to get cracking."

Tikki dabbed at her eyes and looked at Boyle resentfully.

"Why, you're the meanest girl I ever met," she said.

Elton stepped up and put a protective arm around her.

"Just leave Tikki alone, Boyle. Can't you see she's upset?"

"Too right," Boyle muttered. "Let's be off, Nid, me lass. No time to waste, you know. Mother's orders and all that."

Nid opened the door and peeked out. "Coast is clear," she said. "What about you, Tikki? Coming?"

Tikki looked up at Elton. "I'll go," she said, still sniffling. "If you'll promise to . . . to watch me."

"I won't take my eyes off you."

"Good. I'll feel safe then." She squeezed Elton's hand. They stepped out and started off along the hall.

Twenty minutes later, the foursome rounded a fountain tinkling in the dark, stumbled past a six-foot hedge, saw the blue glow of the Mobile Command Center ahead.

Elton halted. "There aren't any guards on it, I hope?" he whispered.

"Of course not! Why should there be?" Tikki said aloud.

"Shhh!" Elton cautioned. "This is a top secret mission, remember."

They came up to the capsule sitting quietly, doors open, waiting.

"Looks like everything's shipshape," Boyle said. "Just like we left her."

Elton leaned close to him. "Stand by with the girls a few yards back. I'll try to arrange a truce."

"Right," Boyle moved to comply. Elton stepped into the cramped chamber, settled into the seat.

"Ah . . . look here, Lunar Computer. I'd like to contact the Yukk ship, get a message to their computer; whatever it is that controls the vessel. Is that possible?"

"Messages can be transmitted on the Yukk wavelength."

"All right; I want to tell them I'm taking off, and not to shoot. I want them to know we're on their side. Tell them we're Yukks, just like they are, and—"

"MADAY, MADAY," the metallic voice screeched. "Yukks occupying Mobile Combat Command Center Ten Ninety-four! Executing emergency procedure forty-one!" Elton's seat lifted, dumping him out onto the grass. With a hiss and a sharp *smack!* the doors closed, snipping off the blue glow. There was an abrupt *zing!* followed by a small thundercap. A gust of wind ruffled Elton's hair. The capsule was gone.

"Here!" Boyle yelled. "What do you think you're doing?"

Nid and Tikki stood staring.

"It . . . it went off and left us," Elton said weakly.

"Did I hear it say . . . Yukks?" Nid demanded.

"W-where are they?" Tikki asked, looking around.

"Not we've had it," Boyle groaned. "Stranded, among these Yukk-eating females!"

"What did you say?" Nid demanded.

"Never mind, my dear. You've been as nice a little friend as a girl could have. Now just run along and let me think."

"Hold on, Boyle," Elton said, getting to his feet. "Don't panic." He turned to Tikki. "You girls don't happen to have another Traveler like ours—do you?" he asked hopefully.

The girl shook her head. "I never saw one like that before."

"Do you have any kind of . . . of space vessel?" Elton said desperately. "Anything you can use to travel up there?" He jabbed a finger at the night sky.

"We have one . . ." Nid said doubtfully. "But—"

"That's all we need," Boyle said promptly. "Just lead the way, there's a good girl."

"Well . . . it's a funny time to be going to church."

Distantly, Elton heard the shrill of a siren. Far away, someone shouted.

"Oh, dear," Tikki said. "Someone's discovered you girls have gone out without permission, I'll bet. Mother's going to be upset."

"Let's just hurry along to the ship—quietly," Elton urged. "After all, we can't let anything interfere with the mission, can we?"

"I think we'd better tell Mother," Nid said doubtfully.

"No time," Boyle said. "Every minute counts. Mother will understand, won't she, professor?"

"That's what I'm afraid of. Let's get going!"

"This way," Nid said, and slipped away into the shadows, the others at her heels.

A vast, clumsy pyramidal shape loomed up, the base stretching away into darkness. Elton came up to it breathing hard, listening to the clang of bells, the shouts of *Yukks* and the shrill ululation of the siren.

"They're pretty well stirred up," Boyle said. "How do you reckon we get inside this beast?"

"Where's the door, girls?" Elton inquired, peering through the gloom.

"Over here," Nid called. At Elton's side, Tikki shivered. "It's scary," she said. "I have the feeling the Yukks are right here beside us."

Ahead, Boyle muttered a curse. "Watch that bottom step, professor; rotted through." Elton gave Tikki a hand up, followed her up a short flight of crumbling wooden steps; as he stepped through the wide entry, his shoes clanged on metal.

"Where's the bridge, or the cockpit, or whatever you call it?" Boyle asked in a hoarse whisper.

"You mean the Mother's seat?" Nid asked. "This way . . ."

Elton and Boyle grunted and puffed, clambering up narrow campanionways in the dark, banging their heads on low passages, snorting dust from their nostrils.

"Bit of rum odor about the place," Boyle commented.

"It reminds me of the smell of the Royal Chamber in Cheops' pyramid," Elton said.

"Here we are," Tikki said. "What are you going to do now?"

There was a shout from below, an answering call, then a mutter of conversation.

"How do we close the entry port—the doorway?" Elton hissed.

"That's this big handle over here," Nid said. "Are you going to hold a Service now?"

Elton grabbed the dimly seen lever, hauled it down. There was a growl of metal. Below, a heavy *clang*! cut off the voices.

"Wish there was a bit of light here," Boyle said.

A wavering, yellowish illumination sprang up. Tikki smiled from the panel, where scattered indicator lights glowed wanly. Elton went over, stared at the layout.

"Tikki, do you understand all this?"

"Oh, certainly; we had all this in Training."

"How do you start the engines?"

"Oh, goody, we're going to have a Service." Tikki turned to the panel, reeling off details of the countdown checklist. Boyle came over, holding a thick book in his hand.

"Have a look at this, sir; the log, I imagine."

"Later," Elton said. "You'd better give me a hand here, Boyle. This is pretty complicated."

Boyle listened in silence for a moment.

"Hold up there, Tikki," he said. "Look here, professor, this is hopeless. It would take a ruddy genius to gen up on this drill in the time we've got. You see what we have to do, don't you?"

Elton looked at him. Tikki had stopped her recital and was listening, eyes wide.

"You mean?" Elton said.

"Right! They've got to go along. Couldn't let them back outside anyway, without letting that lot down below in."

"But—that would be kidnapping."

"Tikki!" Nid's voice came suddenly, a shrill yelp. "Look!"

Tikki jumped up. Nid rushed to her, thrust a faded and curled sheet of flexible plastic into her hand. Elton craned to see it.

KNOW YOUR ENEMY! the heading read. Under the legend was a clear, glossy full-length photograph of a nude Yukk.

Tikki looked from Elton to Boyle, back to the picture. "It . . . it looks . . . like the new girls," she said in a quavering voice.

"Just look at that flat chest," Nid gasped. "And those skinny hips; and—and . . ."

There was a heavy thumping from below. Boyle whirled to Nid. "Look here, love, there's no time to give you the full story now; just get this machine going, there's a good girl!"

"We . . . we really ought to go for help," Nid quavered.

"Start the ship up, Tikki," Elton pleaded. "Even if we are Yukks, we're not such monsters, are we now?"

"But I don't . . . I mean, why—?"

"With that crew snapping at our heels, I should think it would be bloody obvious!" Boyle snapped. "You said you know how to operate this thing! Hop to it, or we've bought the ruddy farm!"

"I'm a wicked, wicked girl," Tikki said weakly. "I'll do it . . ."

She went to the control panel, seated herself in the padded chair, punched buttons, closed switches; lights winked and glowed sluggishly; instrument needles stirred from pegs; there was a dry *click* somewhere. Tikki got to her feet.

"There," she said. "But I just don't see how you can think of ritual at a time like this—"

"What ritual? We just want to depart as quickly as possible," Elton reached for Tikki's hand. "I hate to kidnap you like this, my dear, but—"

Tikki shivered and leaned against Elton. "I keep having the Strangest Thoughts . . ."

There was a final thump from below, a screech of reluctant hinges, then a babble of voices. Feet thumped on stair rungs.

"They're inside!" Elton urged Tikki toward the panel. "Quick!"

A girl appeared at the control room door; Boyle jumped at her, came staggering back as she stiff-armed him. More girls crowded into the room; a heavy-set fortyish woman pushed through, stood with hands on hips eyeing Elton and Boyle.

"So, you're Yukks," she said in a loud, deep voice. "You don't look so tough to me!"

Elton lunged for the panel, punched buttons at random. Two of the girls pulled him away.

"A religous nut," the deep-voiced woman barked. "Well, it's too late for that, you! And anyway, you Yukks have no business desecrating the Church!"

"Church? She said it was a ship," Elton stammered. "The only one there was . . ."

Boyle groaned. "It just came to me," he said. "No wonder nothing happened when Tikki twoddled the controls. This must be the ruddy vessel this lot came here in, eight thousand years ago."

"So the story goes," the captain said. "Now let's get moving, you two." She shot Tikki and Nid a hard look. "And there'll be an investigation into the role you girls played in this escapade, too."

"We . . . we kidnaped them," Elton said.

"A likely story." The woman jerked a thumb toward the frightened girls. "Put all four of them under guard and march 'em back to the dorm. It looks like the Mother's going to be sitting in Judgment tonight."

The Mother was reclining in a heavily padded chaise lounge, with a box of pink and yellow candies at one elbow and a plate of cookies at the other. Heavy robes with elaborate flounces obscured her ample contours. She looked at Elton severely.

"Lying to the Mother," she said. "You ought to be ashamed, even if you are Yukks—and I never thought the Enemy would turn out to be so insignificant-looking."

"They're worse than they look," the captain of the guard said. "You see the state they've got this pair of ninnies in," she indicated Tikki and Nid, standing by with drooping expressions.

The Mother's face tightened. "I thought from the first there was something Strange about them." The assembled girls—several hundred of them, Elton estimated, all ages, crowded into the wide Mother's Room—sighed in unison.

"Silence in the courtroom!" the Mother snapped. "This is an open-and-shut case. These two are Yukks—that's plain enough. They led a pair of formerly decent girls astray," she eyed Tikki and Nid. "I'm going to let you two off lightly; cold baths every three hours for the next two days; that ought to cool those Strange Ideas off." She turned back to Elton and Boyle.

"As for you, there's only one way to deal with a Yukk: it's out in the Cold for you—"

The crowd of Girls gasped; a murmur ran through them. Tikki sprang forward.

"That's perfectly horrid!" she cried. "If they're going out in the Cold, I'm going too!" Strong-arm girls jumped for her, dragged her back in line. Nid was sobbing quietly. Boyle shot her a sickly smile. "There, there, lass, don't fret."

Elton cleared his throat. "Just a minute, Mother," he said loudly. "Before you take this drastic step, I think there are a few things you should know."

"What's that? What could a Yukk have to say that would interest a Mother?"

Elton folded his arms, a calm, self-confident expression on his face.

"If you'll clear these others from the room," he said easily, "I'd like to tell you the Facts of Life."

Elton was lounging at ease in a deep-cushioned chair that was a twin to the one the Mother had occupied at the Judgment, eating large hot-house grapes that were being popped into his mouth one at a time by Tikki, while other girls crowded close. Wide double doors opened across the room.

Boyle appeared, shaved, his hair curled, a neat short tunic flapping at his thighs. A bevy of shapely girls surged around him, all clattering at once. Two ran forward, scattered varicolored cushions in a heap by the side of the wide pool set in the floor.

"I've got to give you credit, professor," he said. "You look like a blooming oriental potentate. How in the name of the Nine Gates of Ishalik did you do it?"

Elton wrinkled his nose. "I think they overdid it a bit with the perfume, Boyle," he said easily. "Otherwise you look well."

"The old bitch was ready to shove us outside the dome without even a set of earmuffs," Boyle stated. "We'd have frozen solid before we had a chance to asphyxiate. What did you say to her to rate us all this?"

"Girls, leave us!" Elton said, waving a hand. "You can come back in a few minutes, dears."

They fled, casting longing glances back.

"Well?" Boyle demanded.

"Elementary, my dear Boyle. Surely you noticed the large number of rooms in the dormitory wings? Several hundred in our wing alone, and I saw at least a dozen wings—"

"Don't talk ruddy architecture. Get to the point!"

"This *is* the point. There are only seven hundred and four girls here—and yet the building was obviously designed for many more. And then there was the business of the Mother chattering about the crowded conditions; consigning us to a broom closet."

"That was just a bit of bloody cheek," Boyle said.

"No, it was important to her to give us the impression that the dome was overflowing with girls; these domes don't get along too well with each other, remember. She didn't want strangers to find out her fighting strength had fallen so low."

"Well, if it's low, it's her own ruddy fault. I reckon she's the one that controls the birthrate."

"Hmmm, yes—as far as she can. But did you notice Boyle, that there are no children around? Tikki and Nid are about twenty-one; there's quite a number about the same age. The next grouping is at about the forty-five age level; the older generation, I suppose. Then there are a few old ladies who—"

"But there's no new generation, Boyle, and none of the girls are pregnant."

"So?"

"They've been using an artificial insemination method—using frozen sperm cells, all of the x-x variety—thus only girls were born. But unfortunately, the supplies ran out twenty-odd years ago."

"Blimey! Then—"

"Exactly. After eight thousand years, it was all over—until we came along."

"So now it's up to us?"

"Correct, Mr. Boyle. I suggest we work out some sort of equitable division. It should take us a year or so to work our way through, and then start over."

"Of course," Boyle said doubtfully, "it means we're stranded."

"Not forever. I learned from the Mother that there are very extensive libraries here, well-equipped laboratories—"

"Hold it!" Boyle leaned on one elbow, looking worried. "These little ones we'll be fathering: half of them will be little Yukks!"

"Of course. Things will come back to normal in about twenty years—and by that time I think we'll be ready to retire. We'll set up schools, start training a new generation of technicians. They'll be able to get the old ship going again—or build a new one. We can neutralize the Yukk ship, return to Earth in style with enough technology to make us too rich to talk to." Elton picked up a dusty book from the floor.

"But, this is my greatest prize," he said. "The log book from the ship. It gives an excellent picture of the pre-history of human affairs on Earth from about 15,000 B.C. up until the war seven thousand years later."

"Twenty years, eh?" Boyle mused. "But look here, professor, I just happened to think! All the old bag had to do was take a specimen from one of us—there's millions of germ cells."

"But she didn't know that, Boyle—so we'll just let it be our little secret."

"I think you've hit on it, professor," Boyle called. "Never tell 'em all you know."

"Correct," Elton said. "And in the meantime, we'll deal with our problems . . . one at a time."

Worldmaster

In the boat bay four Deck Police held guns on me while two more shook me down. When they finished, they formed up a box around me.

"All right, this way, sir," the Warrant said. He was a dandified, overweight lad with pale, hard little eyes like unripe olives. Four power guns snapped around to hold on me, rib-high. I stumbled a little and the nearest gun jumped. The boys were a hair more nervous than they looked. As for myself, I was long past the nervous stage; it took all I had left just to stay on my feet with nothing left over to wonder about the curious reception given to a surviving captain paying his courtesy call on his admiral after a twenty-eight-hour action in which two fleets had been wiped out.

Here aboard the flagship everything was as smooth and silent as a hotel for dying millionaires. We went along a wide corridor lit like the big window at Cartier's and carpeted in a pale blue as soft as a summer breeze, took the high-speed lift up to the command deck. There were more DP's here, spit-and-polished in blue-black class A's with white gloves, mirror-bright boots, and chromalloy dress armor. The guns they aimed at me were fancy Honor Guard models with ebony stocks and bright-plated barrels; but they would fire real slugs if occasion demanded. The Warrant came up beside me, smelling a little sweeter than ordinary after-shave. "Perhaps you'd like to step along to the head and tidy up a bit before going in," he told me. "I have a clean uniform ready for you and—"

"This one's OK," I said. "Oh, it's got a few cuts and tears and a couple of scorched spots no bigger than the doily under a demi-tasse, but it came by them honorably, as the saying goes. Maybe I need a shave, but no worse than I did yesterday. I've been a little busy, mister—" I cut it off before it got entirely out of hand. "Let's take a chance and go in. The admiral may be curious about what happened to his fleet."

The Warrant's mouth tightened up as though he had a string threaded through his lip.

"I'm afraid I'll have to insist—" he started. I brushed past him. One of the ratings beside the door leading into the admiral's quarters jabbed his gun at me as I came toward him.

"Go ahead, son, fire it," I said. "You've got it set on full automatic; in this confined space you'll fry all of us blacker than a newlywed's toast."

The annunciator above the door crackled, "Purdy, take those weapons away from those men before there's an accident!" a voice barked. "I'll see Captain Maclamore immediately. Mac, stop scaring my men to death."

The door slid back. I went through into a wide room flooded with artificial sunlight as cheerful as paper flowers and smelling of expensive cigar smoke. From a big easy chair under the windo-rama with a view of a field of ripe wheat nodding under a light breeze, Admiral Banastre Tarleton gave me the old Academy smile, looking hard and efficient and younger than four stars had any right to. Behind him, Commodore Sean Braze glowered, his hands behind his back, big shoulders bulging under his tailor-made tunic, a pistol strapped to his hip as inconspicuously as a rattlesnake at a picnic. A captain with a small crinkled face and quick eyes looked at me from a chair off to the right. I threw a sloppy salute and the braid dangling from my torn cuff flopped against my sleeve. "Sit down, Mac." Tarleton nodded toward a chair placed to half face him. I didn't move. He frowned a little but let it pass.

"I'm glad to see you here," he said. "How are you feeling?"

"I don't know how I'm feeling, Admiral," I said. "I don't think I want to know."

"You fought your command like half the devils in hell, Mac. I'm writing you up for the Cross."

I didn't say anything. I felt dizzy. I was wondering if it was too late to take the offer of a chair.

"Sit down before you fall down, Captain," the man on the right said. Little bright lights were sleeting down all around me. They faded and I was still standing. I didn't know what I was proving.

"Anybody get out with you?" Braze was asking

me. He was a man who wouldn't ask to have the
salt passed without making it sound like a sneer.

"Sure," I said. "My gunnery officer, Max Arena
—the upper half of him, anyway. Why?"

"I saw it on the big Command Screen," Tarleton
said. "A lucky break, Mac. A salvage crew couldn't
have sliced that nav dome away cleaner with cutting torches."

"Yeah," I said.

"Here—" the monkey-faced captain started.
Tarleton flicked a hand at him and he faded off.

"Something bothering you, Mac?" Tarleton was
giving me the wise, patient look he'd learned from
watching old Bing Crosby films.

"Why should anything be bothering me?" I
heard myself asking. "I've just had my ship shot
out from under me, and my crew wiped out, and
seen what was formerly the UN Battle Fleet
blasted into radioactive vapor while the flagship
that mounted sixteen per cent of our total fire-
power pulled back half a million miles and
watched without firing a shot. You've probably
got all kinds of reasons for that, Admiral. Reasons
that would be way over my head. Some of them
might even be good. I wouldn't know."

"Watch your tongue, Maclamore!" Braze said.
"You're talking to a superior officer!"

"That's enough, Sean," Tarleton said sharply.
He was giving me a harder, less contrived look
now. "Sure, you've had a rough time, Mac. I'm
sorry about that; if there'd been any other
way . . ." He made a short, choppy gesture with his
hand. Then he lifted his chin, got the firm-lipped
look back in place. "But the Bloc didn't fare any
better. They're blasted out of space—perma-
nently. It was an even trade."

Maybe my eyelids flickered; maybe I gave him a

look that nailed his heart to his backbone; and maybe I was just a little man with a big headache, trying not to show it.

"An even trade," he repeated. He seemed to like the sound of it. "I watched the action very closely, Mac," he went on. "If the tide had started to turn to favor the Bloc, I'd have hit them with everything I had." He worked his mouth as though he were trying a new set of teeth for size; but it was an idea he was testing the fit of.

"And if the tide had started running our way, I'd have come in, helped finish them off. As it was . . . an even match. The board's clean." He looked at me with something dangerous sparkling back behind his eyes. "Except for my flagship," he added softly.

The wrinkle-faced captain was leaning forward; his hands were opening and closing. Braze took his hands out from behind himself and fingered the pistol bolt. I just waited.

"You see what that means, don't you, Mac?" Tarleton ran his fingers through his still blond, still curly hair, wiped his hand down the back of his neck the way he used to do in the locker room at the half, when he was cooking up the strategy that was going to flatten the opposition. "For the past ten years, both sides have poured ninety-five per cent of their military budgets into their Space Arms, while planet-based forces fought themselves into an undeclared truce. Both sides together couldn't put a hundred thousand armed and equipped men in the field today—and if they did—"

He leaned back, took a deep breath; I couldn't blame him for that; he was breathing the heady air of power.

"I have the only effective fighting apparatus on

or off the planet, Mac." He held out his hand, palm up, like a kid showing me his shiny new quarter. "I hold the balance of power, right here."

"Why tell *him* this, Banny?" the brown-faced captain said quickly.

"Button your lip, Captain," Tarleton snapped. "Keep it buttoned." He heaved himself out of his chair, shot a hard look at me, took a turn up and down the room, stopped in front of me.

"I need good men, Mac," he said. He was staring at me; his jaw muscles knotted and relaxed. I looked past him at Braze, over at the other man. "Uh, huh," I said. "That you do."

Braze took a step in my direction. His carefully lamp-tanned face was as dark as an Indian's. Tarleton's face twitched in a humorless smile.

"How long has it been?" he asked. "Sixty years? Sixty-five? Two giant powers, sitting across the world from each other, snarling and trading slaps. Sixty years of petty wars, petty truces—of people dying—for nothing—of wasted time, wasted talent, wasted resources—while the whole damned Universe is waiting to be taken!"

He turned on his heel, stamped another couple of laps, pulled up in front of me again.

"I decided to put an end to it. I made up my mind—hell, over a year ago. My strategy since that time has been directed toward this moment. I planned it. I maneuvered it." He closed his hand as though he was crushing a bug. "And I brought it off!"

He looked at me, happy, wanting to hear me say something; I didn't say it. He went back to his chair, sat down, picked up the long, blackish cigar from the ashtray at his elbow, drew on it, put it down again, blew the smoke out suddenly.

"There comes a time," he said flatly, "when a

man has to act on what he knows to be right. When he can no longer afford the luxury of a set of mottos as a substitute for intelligence. Sure, I swore to uphold the Constitution; it's easy to die for a flag, a principle, an oath—but that won't save humankind from its own stupidity. Maybe someday the descendants of the people whose necks I'm saving in spite of themselves will thank me. Or maybe they won't. Maybe I'll go down in the book as the villain—a new and better Benedict Arnold. I still say to hell with it. If all it takes to break the cycle is the sacrifice of one man's personal—shall I say honor?—then that's a small price. I'm prepared to pay it."

I heard him talking but it all seemed to be coming from a long way off, remote, unreal. It didn't reach me. I nodded toward the one he'd told to shut up.

"As the man said, why tell me?" I asked him, just to be saying something.

"I want you with me, Mac," he said.

I looked at him.

"I wanted you in it from the beginning, but . . ." He frowned again. I was making him do a lot of frowning tonight. "Maybe you can guess why I didn't speak to you earlier. It wasn't easy sending you out with the others. I'm glad you came through. Damned glad. Maybe it's . . . some kind of sign." His lips twitched in what I guess he thought was a smile.

"It wasn't easy—but you managed it." I wasn't sure whether I said it or just thought it. The roaring in my head was loud now; a hot black was closing in from the sides. I pushed it back. For some reason I didn't want to fall down right now; not here, not in front of Braze and the little man with the darting eyes.

"We used to be friends, Mac," Tarleton was saying. "There was a time . . ." He got up again. It seemed he couldn't stay in one place. "Hell, it's simple enough; I'm asking for your help," he finished.

"Yeah, we were friends, Banny," I said. For an instant there was that strange, hollow feeling, the heart-stopping glimpse back down the yellowed and forgotten years to the old Academy walls and the leaves that were on the cinder track as you walked across, heavy-shouldered in the practice gear, the cleats making you feel tall and tough, and the faces of girls, and the smell of night air, and the fast car bucking under you and Banny, passing a flask back, and then again, across the field while the crowd roared, his arm back, the ball tumbling down the blue sky and the solid smack and then away and running—

"But you found other friends," I was saying, with no more than an instant's pause. "They took you down another path, I guess. Somewhere along there we lost it. I guess today we buried it."

"That's right, we've taken our separate ways," he said. "But we can still find common ground. I didn't make the Navy, Mac—but after I picked it as a way of life, I learned to live with it—to beat it at its game. You didn't. You bucked it. Sure, you made your points—but they don't pay off for those. What do you expect, a medal for stubbornness? Hell, if it hadn't been for me keeping an eye on you, you'd have been—" He stopped. "Suffice it to say I got you your command," he ground out.

I nodded. "I didn't know," I said. "It was a wonderful thing while I had it. I'm grateful to you. And then you took it away. It was a tough way to lose my ship, Banny. In a way I'd almost rather have not had it—but not quite."

He planted himself again, tried to catch my eye. Somehow I seemed to be looking past him.

"I make no apologies," he snapped. "I did what I had to do. Now there's more to be done. I'm going down tonight to make my report to Congress. There are cabinet members to see, the President to be dealt with. It won't be easy. It's not won yet. A wrong word in the wrong place and I could still fumble this. I'm being frank with you, Mac. I need a good man I can trust." He reached out and clapped me on my upper arm—a caricature of the old gesture, as self-consciously counterfeit as a whore's passion. I shook the hand off.

"Don't be a fool," he said in a low voice, close to me. "What do you think your alternative is?"

"I don't know, Admiral," I said, "but you'll think of something."

Braze came over. "I don't like this, Banny," he said. "You've said too damned much to him." He gave me a look like a hired gun marking down a target for later on. The other fellow was up now, not wanting to be left out. He flicked his eyes at me, then at the gun at Braze's belt.

"This fellow's no good for us," he said in a rapid, breathless voice, like a girl about to make a daring suggestion. "You'll have to . . . dispose of him."

Tarleton swung around and looked at him.

"Have you ever killed a man, Walters?" he asked in a tight voice. Walters' tongue popped out, touched his lips. His eyes went to the gun again, darted away.

"No, but—"

"I have," Tarleton said. He walked across to the windorama, punched the control; the scene shifted to heavy seas breaking across a reef under a rock-gray sky.

"Last chance, Mac," he said in a mock-hearty

voice. "The thing happens; it's far too late to stop
it now. Will you be in it—or out?" He turned to
face me, his clean-cut American boy features set in
a recruiting poster smile.

"Count me out," I said. "I wouldn't be good at
running the world." I looked at the other two. "Be-
sides which, I wouldn't like the company."

Braze lifted a lip to show me a square-looking
canine. Walters half-closed his eyes and snorted
softly through his nose.

"What about it, Banny?" Braze said. "Walters is
right. You can't dump Maclamore back with the
other internees."

Tarleton turned on him. "You're telling me what
I can and can't do, Braze?"

"I'm making a recommendation," the commodore came back. "My neck is in this with yours,
now—"

"Another word of mutiny out of you, mister, and
I'll give orders that will have your precious neck
stretched before the big hand gets to the twelve.
Want to try me?" His voice was like something cut
into a plate glass window. He went to his chair and
pushed a button set in the arm.

"Purdy, send those four morons of yours in here
—and try not to shoot yourself through the foot in
the process." He went over and watched the waves
some more. The door opened with a sigh and the
goon squad appeared with the Warrant out front,
fussing over them like a headwaiter figuring the
tip on ten pounds of room-service caviar.

"Find quarters for Captain Maclamore on deck
A," Tarleton said in a flat voice.

The Warrant bustled forward, all business now.
"All right, move along there—" he started.
Tarleton whirled on him.

"And keep a civil tongue in your head, damn you! You're talking to a naval officer!"

Purdy swallowed hard. I turned and walked out past the ready gun muzzles. I didn't bother with the salute this time. The time for saluting was all over.

The medic finished with me and left and I lay back, listening to the small ship noises that murmured through the walls. It had been about an hour now since the last faint shocks that meant contact with one of the chunks of debris that were all that was left of forty-two fighting ships—twenty-two UN, the rest Bloc. At least Tarleton had gone through the motions of picking up what few survivors there might have been from the slaughter—perhaps a few hundred dazed and bloody men, the accidental leftovers of the power plays of Grand Strategy.

I had come through in better shape than most of them, I guessed. With the exception of a few minor cuts and bruises and a mild concussion, aggravated by twenty-eight hours without food or sleep, I was in as good shape as I had been before the fight. My arms and legs still worked; my heart was pumping away as usual; my lungs were doing their job. The brain was still numb, true, but it was working—working for its life.

Tarleton may or may not have meant it when he turned down Braze's suggestion—but he had told me far too much for any man to hear who was arrayed on the opposite side of the fence from the commodore. I didn't need to break out of my cell to look for trouble; it would come to me. Braze was a man who always took the simple, direct course. It had won him a commodore's star; he'd stay with the technique. He'd make his move at the last minute before the ground party boarded the boats for the trip down, to minimize the chance of word getting to Tarleton; he'd have an account of an attempted escape ready for later, if Tarleton got curious—an unlikely eventuality. The admiral would have his hands full digesting his conquests, with no time left over for pondering the fates of obscure former acquaintances.

They'd be going down tonight, Tarleton had said. He'd have a good-sized shore party with him; all of his top advisers—or whatever rat-faced little men like Walters called themselves—and a nice showing of armed sailors, tricked out in dress blues and side arms, as a gentle reminder of the planet-wrecking power orbiting ten thousand miles out.

The flagship carried a complement of two thousand and eleven men—all long-since screened for reliability, no doubt. If I knew Banny Tarleton, he'd have half of them along on his triumphal march. That would call for twenty heavy scout boats. He'd use bays one through ten on the upper boat deck for reasons of ease of loading and orbital dynamics . . . .

I was building an elaborate structure of fancy on a feeble foundation of guesses, but I had to carry the extrapolation as far as I could. I wouldn't get a second chance to make my try; maybe not even the first one—and my quota of mistakes was already used up.

I got up and took a couple of turns up and down the room. I still felt lightheaded, but the meal and the bath and the dressings and the shots and the pills had helped a lot. The plain set of ducks Purdy had provided were comfortable enough, but I missed the contents of a couple of small special pockets that had been built into my own clothes—the ones that had been taken away and burned. The hardware was gone—but with a little luck I might be able to improvise suitable substitutes.

A quick inspection of the room turned up an empty closet, a chest of four empty drawers, a wall mirror, a molded polyfoam chair that weighed two pounds soaking wet, a framed trido-graph of the Kennedy Monument complete with shrapnel scars, and the built-in bunk to which the medics had lowered me, groaning, ten minutes earlier. Not much there to assemble a blaster out of—

I felt the tremor then; the teacup-rattling nudge of a scout boat kicking free. Quite suddenly my mouth had that dry feeling. Boat number two pushed off; then a third. Tarleton wasn't wasting any time. At least there wouldn't be any long, tedious wait to see whether my guesses had been right. The time for action was here. I set my heart rate up two notches and metered a trickle of adrenalin into my system, then went over to the door, flattened myself against the wall to the left of it, and waited.

Seven boats were away now. A couple of minutes ticked past like ice ages. Then there was a soft, stealthy noise outside the door. With my ear against the wall, I could imagine I heard voices. I set myself—

The door slid smoothly back and a man came through it fast—a big, thick-shouldered DP with pinkish hair on an acne'd neck—a use-worn Mark

XX gripped in a freckled fist the size of a catcher's mitt. I half turned to the left, drove my right into his side just behind the holster hard enough to jar the monogram off the hanky in my hip pocket—not fancy, but effective. He made an ugly noise and went down clawing at himself like a cat, and I was over him, diving for the gun that skidded to the wall, bounced back into my hand, and I was rolling, bringing it up, seeing the lightning flicker and feeling the hard tight snarl of the weapon in my hand as I slashed it across the open doorway. The man there fell into the room, hit like a horse falling in harness, and the air was full of the nauseous stench of burned flesh and abdominal wounds.

I got up, stepped to the redhead, kicked him hard above the cheekbone; he gave up the attempt to loop the loop on the rug. At the door, I gave a quick glance both ways; nobody in sight. There was another gentle shock. Number eight? Or had I missed one . . . ?

It was a hot two minutes' work to get the un-bloodied uniform off its owner. It wasn't a good fit, but I buckled everything up tight, strapped on the gun in a way that I hoped would conceal the fold I'd taken in the waistband, tried the boots: too big. I didn't like touching the other fellow, but I did. My feet complained a little, but they went in, shrinking from the warmth of the dead man's shoes. The redhead was still breathing; I thought seriously about putting a burst into his head, then settled for strapping his ankles and wrists and wadding a shirt sleeve in his mouth. It cost me an extra minute and a half. So much for the price of a human life.

Out in the corridor things were still quiet; Braze's work again. He wouldn't have wanted witnesses. I locked the door and headed for the boat.

Four more boats were away by the time I reached the steel double doors that sealed U deck off from the main transverse. I pushed against them, swore, kicked the panel. It gave off a dull clang. I kicked it again, then yanked out the power gun, set it for a needle beam, heard sounds on the other side, slammed the weapon back in its holster in time to see the door jump back and a square-jawed DP plant himself flat-footed in the opening, gun out and aimed.

"Thanks, brother—" I started past him. He backed, but kept me covered. A confused scowl was getting ready to settle onto his face. "Hold your water, paisan—"

"Knock it off," I rapped. "Jeezus—can't you see I'm missing formation? My boat—"

"What you doing on U deck—"

"Look—I had a side-kick, see? I wanted to see the guy. OK, satisfied? You want me shot for desertion?"

"Go on," he waved the gun at me, looking disgusted. "But you'll never make it."

"Thanks, buddy—" I struck off at a dead run . . . .

I had lost count, not sure whether it was eighteen or nineteen—or maybe twenty, too late . . . .

I rounded the last corner, came into the low-ceilinged boat deck, felt a throb of some kind of emotion—fear or relief or a mixture—at the sight of thirty or forty blue-uniformed men formed up in a ragged column, filing toward the black rectangle of Number Two loading port. I dropped

back to a walk, came up to the column, moved
along with them. One man looked over his shoulder at me with a blank expression; the rest ignored
me. A middle-aged Warrant with a long leathery
face saw me, snarled silently, came back.

"You're Gronski, huh? Nice to see you in formation, Gronski. You see me after breakaway; you
and me got to have a little talk about things; OK,
Gronski?"

I looked sullen; it wasn't hard. It's a lot like
looking scared. "OK, Chief," I muttered.

"By God, that's Aye, aye, Mr. Funderburk to
you, swabbie!"

"Aye, aye, Mr. Funderburk," I growled out. He
spun with a squeak of shoe leather and walked
away. The man in front of me turned and looked
me up and down.

"You ain't Gronski," he said.

"What else is new," I snarled. "So I'm helping
out a pal; OK?"

"You and Funnybutt are gonna get along," he
predicted and showed me his back again. I kept
my eyes on it until it was safely tucked away in the
gloom of the troop hold. Wedged in between two
silent men on the narrow shock seat, I held my
breath, waiting for the yell that would mean somebody hadn't been fooled. I wondered what lucky
accident had made Gronski late, what other lucky
accident had assigned him to a detail with a
Warrant who didn't know his face . . . .

But calculating the odds on what was already
accomplished was just sorting over dry bones. The
odds ahead were what counted. They didn't look
good, but they were all I had. I'd taken them—
and play the angles as they fell like Rubinstein
cutting the original sound track of the *Flight of the
Bumblebee*.

We berthed at Arlington Memorial just after midnight, and as soon as he had the platoon formed up
on the ramp, Funderburk called me over. I
answered the summons with a certain reluctance;
I had closed and locked the door to the room
where Braze's gun-boys were awaiting discovery,
but there was no way of knowing how long it
would be before someone went around to check.
The trip down had taken about two hours and a
half. Of course, even if the room had been opened,
that didn't necessarily mean that anyone would
have found it necessary to advise the admiral—
    Or did it?
    "Gronski, I got a little job for you," Funderburk
barked. "A couple of the brass up front had a little
trouble with the turbulence on the way in; looks
like they kind of come unfed. It don't look good all
over the officers head. Maybe you could kind of
see about it."
    "Sure; I mean, aye, aye, Mr. Funderburk. Do I
get a mop or just wipe it up with my sleeve?"
    "Oh, a wise one, huh? Swell, Gronski. You and
me are gonna see a lot of each other. You want a
mop, you scout around and find one; take all the
time you want. But I kind of advise you to be all
finished in twenty minutes because that's how
long I'm giving the detail for chow. I don't guess
you'll miss the flapjacks, unless you got a tougher
appetite than most."
    "I'll finish in ten; save me a stool at the bar."
    Funderburk nodded. "Yeah, I can see you and
me are gonna click good, Gronski. See you on the
gig list." He turned and walked away—just like

that. I didn't wait around to see if he'd change his mind. I walked, resisting the impulse to run, to the utility shack behind the flight kitchen, went through it and out the side door and around to the front, crossed a patch of grass and pushed into a steamy odor of GI coffee and floor wax. A door across the room was lettered MEN. Inside, I forced the door to a broom closet, took out a pair of coveralls and a push broom.

Back out in the pre-dawn gloom ten minutes later with my hair carefully rumpled and a layer of mud disguising the shine on my boots that showed under the too-short cuffs, I moved off briskly; in half a block I found a blue-painted custodial cart lettered UNSA. It started up with a ragged hum; I wheeled it away from the curb and headed for the lights of the main gate.

The boy on the guard post was no more than eighteen, a snub-nosed farm lad, still getting a kick out of the side arm and the badge and the white-painted helmet liner. I pulled up to him, gave him a sheepish grin, waved toward a cluster of glare signs half a block away, wan in the misty night. I picked a name from a bilious pink announcement looming above the others. "Just slipping down to Maggie's for a pack of bolts, Lootenant," I told him. "Boy, a man really gets to hankering for a smoke—"

"You guys give me a swiftie," the kid said. "Where do you get them big ideas? You think the government buys them scooters for you birds to joy ride on? Climb down offa there and try stretching your legs one time."

"You're too sharp for me, Lootenant," I admitted. He watched, arms folded, while I wheeled the cart over to the side, parked it beside the guard shack. I gave him a wave that expressed the emotions of a game loser bowing to superior guile, and ankled off toward the bright lights. At the corner, I looked back; he was still looking military, savoring the satisfaction of rules enforced. I hoped he wouldn't remember the base pass he hadn't asked to see until I was hull down over the horizon.

By the light of a polyarc over a narrow alley behind a row of vice parlors, I sorted through my worldly goods; the odds and ends that a trusted killer named Gronski had had in his pockets when he set out on his final assignment. It wasn't much: a key ring, a white plastic comb clogged with grime, a wallet with a curled UNSA ID bearing an unflattering view of what had never been a pretty face, some outdated credit cards from the less expensive bean and sex joints around Charleston, South Carolina, six cees in cash, and a pair of halfhearted pornographic snaps of a tired-looking girl with ribs. I pocketed the money, went along the alley to a public disposal chute, and put the loot down into the odor of hot iron and fruit rinds.

Clothes were my first problem. When Tarleton got the word that I was gone a cordon would move out through the town as fast as a late-model Turbocad riot car could roll. It would be nice if I could be over the bridge and into D.C. proper before then. Nobody got into the megalopolis nowadays without a full scope and NAC. A set of baggy overalls might be good enough to get me past a recruit pulling the graveyard shift on a Class Two passenger depot; I'd have to do a lot better to satisfy the gray-suit boys on the front door to the Capitol.

Tarleton would figure me to make a run for the
hills; for the West Coast, maybe, or the anonymity
of the Paved State that had once been called the
Land of Flowers. He'd assume that for the
moment my objective would be limited to
survival; he wouldn't expect me to walk deeper
into his net; not now; not until I had lain up for a
while to lick my wounds and lay my plans . . . .

Or so my second-guessing bump told me. Maybe
it was as transparent as a bride's nightie that I'd
head for important ears to pour my story into.
Maybe the gunnies were just around the next
corner, waiting to cut me down. Maybe I was
already a dead man, just looking for a place to
stretch out.

And maybe I'd better stop being so Goddamned
smart and get on with the job at hand, before I got
myself picked up for loitering and did ninety
standing on my ear in the vag tank.

Halfway down the wrong side of a street that
had been classy about the time the sailmakers in
Boston began to decry the collapse of civilization,
a dim-lit window hung with two-tone burlap
sports jackets and cardboard shoes caught my
eye. There was a dust-dimmed glare strip along
the top, lending the display all the gaiety of a
funeral in the rain. It wasn't the smartest haber-
dashery in town, but it wouldn't be the best wired,
either. I went to the end of the street, took a left,
found an alley mouth, came back up behind my
target. Aside from kicking a couple of rusted cans
and clipping a shin on a post and swearing loud
enough to wake up the old maid at the end of the

block, I came in as slick as a travelling salesman making a late house call. The lock wasn't much: a mail-order electro job set in perished plastic. I put a hip against it and pushed; the door frame damned near fell in with me.

It took five minutes to look over the stock and select a plain black suit suitable for the county to bury a pauper in. I added a gray shirt that looked as though it would hold its shape as long as nobody washed it, a tie with a picture of a Balinese maiden, a pair of ventilated shoes with steel taps on the heels that would be all that was left after the first rain. The cash register yielded three cees and some change. I wrote out an IOU, signed it, and tucked it in under the wire spring. That meant that half an hour after the store opened, Tarleton would have a description of my new elegance—but by then it wouldn't matter. I'd either be across the bridge or dead.

Three streets farther up the gentle slope above the river, I found what I needed: it was a blackened brick front holding up two squares of age-tarnished plastex and a door that had once been painted red. The left window bore the legend IRV'S HOUSE OF TATTOO ARTISTRY and the right balanced the composition with a picture of a mermaid seated on an anchor holding a drowned sailor. I walked past once, saw the glimmer of a light in a side window visible along a two-foot airspace that ran back on the right. There seemed to be no activity in the drinking establishment next door; I slid into the alley; walked over bottles, cans, things that squashed, other things that crunched. If there were any dead bodies I didn't notice them.

At the rear, there was a small court walled by taller buildings on either side, a high fence with a gate letting onto a wider alley. The light from the side window showed up a few blades of green spring grass poking up among cinders. Two concrete steps led up to a back door. I stood on the bottom one and knocked, two short, one long, two short. Nothing happened.

A bird let off a string of notes somewhere, stopped suddenly as though he had just discovered he was in the wrong place. It's an uncomfortable feeling; I know it well.

I rapped again, same code, only louder. Still nothing. I stepped back down, found a pebble, threw it at a closed shutter up above, then went back and put an ear against the door. Sounds came, faint and ill-tempered. I heard the bolt rattle; door opened half an inch. There was heavy breathing.

"It's a hot rasper," I said quickly. "Marple up on the avtake before the fuzz gondle."

"Ha? Wha—?" A clogged voice started, broke off to cough. I leaned on the door. "I got to see Irv," I snapped. "Transik apple ready, tonight for sure." The door yielded. I stepped into an odor of last month's broccoli, last week's booze, and a lifetime of rancid bacon fat and overdue laundry. A fat citizen in a gray bathrobe with a torn sleeve thumbed uncombed gray hair back from a red eye set in gray fat. The fingernail was gray, too. So was his neck. Maybe he liked gray.

"You run the skin gallery?" I asked him.

"What's the grift, Jack?" He pulled the knot tight on the robe, shot a look out the door, pushed it shut. I watched his right hand.

"I need a job done," I told him. "They sent me to you."

He grunted, looking me over. The hand lingered on the belt.

"You mentioned a name," he said.

"Maybe you'll do," I said. The hand moved then, slipped inside the robe, was halfway out again with a Browning before I clamped down on his wrist. He shifted, slammed his left at my stomach; I half turned, took it on the hip, jerked the hand out, bent it back, and caught the gun as he dropped it. He didn't make a sound.

"No need for the iron," I told him. "I want papers—fast. Let's step along to your workshop. Time is of the essence."

"What kinda gag—"

I hit him on the side of the head with the gun hard enough to stagger him. "No time for talking it up. Action. Now." I motioned toward the curtain that hung in the kitchen entry.

"You got me wrong, mister!" He was rubbing his face; his hard palm made a scratchy sound going over the stubble. "I run a legitimate little art tattoo parlor here—"

I took a step toward him, rammed the gun at his belly. "Ever heard of a desperate man, Irv? That's me. Maybe every tattoo joint on the planet isn't in the hot paper line, but I'm guessing this one is— and I get what I want or you die trying. Better hope you can do it."

He worked his mouth, then turned and pushed through the curtains. I followed.

It took Irv an hour to produce a new ID, a set of travel orders, a Geneva card, and a special pass to the Visitors' Gallery at the House. Once he got into the swing of it, he was the true artist, as intent on perfection as Cellini buffing a pinhead blemish off a twenty-foot bronze.

"The orders are OK," he told me as he handed them over. "The G-card, too. Hell, it's pra'tically genuine. The pass—maybe. But don't try to fool nobody but maybe some broad in a bar with that ID. Them Security boys will have that number checked out—"

"That's OK. The stuff looks good. How much do I owe you?"

He lifted his shoulders. "Hundred cees," he said.

"Add fifty for getting you up," I said. "And another fifty for the crack on the head. I'll mail it to you as soon as I hear from home."

"The crack on the head's for free," he said. "How's about leaving the Browning. You don't get them with Cracker Jacks any more."

I nodded. "Let's go down." He went ahead of me down the stairs, back through the kitchen, opened the door. I took the magazine out of the gun, tossed it out into the yard, handed him the Browning. He took it and thrust it away out of sight.

"The guy worked on your hands was good," he said softly. "Navy?"

I nodded. He ran a hand through the gray hair.

"I worked with a lot of Navy guys in my time," he said. The red eyes were as sharp as scalpels. "You done time on a lot of quarterdecks, would be my guess. You don't need to sweat me. I don't know no cops."

"Give me three hours," I said. "Then yell your head off. Maybe you could use the Brownie points at headquarters."

"Yeah," he said. I went out and the door closed on his still-gray face.

It was a brisk ten-minute walk to Monticello Boulevard. I made it without attracting any attention other than a close look by a pair of prowl car cops who would never know how close they came to a bonus and promotion, and a business offer from a moonlighting Washington secretary holding a lonely vigil at the Tube entry. A wheel-cab cruising the outer lane answered my wave, pulled off on the loading strip.

"You licensed for D.C.?" I asked him.

"Whattaya, blind?" He pointed to a three-inch gold sticker on his canopy. I got in and he gunned off toward the lights of the bridge.

"You know Eisenhower Drive?" I asked.

"Does a mouse know cheese?" he came back, fast and snappy.

"Number nine eighty-five," I said.

"Senator I. Albert Pulster," he said. I saw his eyes in the mirror, watching me. "You know Pulster?"

"My brother-in-law," I said.

"Yeah?" He sounded impressed—like a car salesman getting the low-down on a ten-year-old trade-in. "Pulster's a big noise in this town these days," he said. "Three years to election and you can't open a pictonews without you get a mug shot of the guy. He's parlayed that committee into a clear shot at the White House."

The control booth was a blaze of garish light across the wet pavement ahead. The white-uniformed CIA man was leaning out, letting me catch the dazzle of the brass on his collar. The cab pulled up and the panel slid down, letting in the cool river air. I handed over the ID and the orders directing me to report to Ft. McNair a day earlier. He looked them over, turned, shoved the card into the scope that transmitted the fingerprint image to the CBI master file, read off the name that popped onto the four-inch screen. It would be mine; the only risk at this point was that Tarleton had already put a flag out on it . . . .

He hadn't. The guard held out a plain plastic rectangle.

"Right thumb, please," he said in a bored voice. I gave it to him; he pressed it on the sensitive plate, shoved it into the same slot, got the same result. All right so far. If he stopped now, I was in; if he went one step farther and checked out the crystal pattern of the card itself . . . .

"Hey," the driver shot a look at me. "He says he's Pulster's brother-in-law."

"So?"

"I never heard of Pulster having no brother-in-law."

The CIA man gave him a heavy-lidded look. "Let's you leave us do our job, fella; you stick to watching those traffic signs." He handed me my phony papers, pushed the button to raise the barrier, waved us on across. My driver drove fast, shoulders hunched. He didn't talk any more all the way out to Eisenhower.

Number nine eighty-five was a big iron gate with twin baby spots mounted up high on an eight-foot

fieldstone wall that looked solid enough to with-
stand a two-day mortar bombardment. A graveled
drive led back between hundred-year oaks to a
lofty three-story facade, gleaming a well-tended
oyster-white in the faint starlight. There was a
porte-cochère high enough to clear the footman on
a four-horse carriage, wide enough for three
Caddies abreast. There were more windows than I
remembered on the west front at Versailles, a
door reminiscent of the main entrance to Saint
Peter's Basilica, wide steps that were probably
scrubbed five times a day by English butlers using
toothbrushes. Or maybe not; maybe the servant
problem had even penetrated as far as the Pulster
residence.

I thumbed a button set in the black iron plate,
jumped when a feminine voice immediately said,
"Yes, sir?"

"How do you know I'm not a madam," I snapped
back.

"You don't have the build for it, sweetheart,"
the voice said, sharp now. "You want to tell me
what it's all about, or do I just call a couple sets of
law to help get you straightened out?"

I squinted, spotted the eye up in the angle of the
iron curlicue at the top of the gate.

"I want to see the senator," I said. "Wake him
up if you have to. It's important."

"Would there be a name?"

"Maclamore."

"Uh-huh. Army?"

"Navy. Captain Maclamore. Six-one, one ninety
stripped, brown hair, brown eyes, and a nasty dis-
position. Hop to it."

"Not even one little old star? Captains we
usually take in batches of nine on alternate Wed-

nesdays, and this being Thursday . . . well, you see how it is."

"You're cute," I told the eye. "With a couple more like you I could start a finishing school for snake charmers. Now run along and tell Albert you're keeping his favorite relative waiting out in the hot sun."

"Like that, huh," the voice said coolly. "You could have said so. What are you trying to do, lose me my job?"

"It's a thought," I admitted. There was no answer. I took a couple of steps, turned, took two back. The tension was building up again now. My small cuts and burns were hurting like big ones; it was time for another load of those nice drugs Purdy's medic had fed me. Instead all I had was the withdrawal symptoms, a let-down of the past few hours' fever-bright energy into a high singing sensation back of the eyes and a tendency to start arguments with disembodied voices . . . .

There was a buzz and a click and the gate rolled back. I went through it, saw a small white-painted wagon rolling along the drive toward me on fat rubber wheels. It stopped and the voice was back.

"If you'll step aboard, sir . . . ?"

I did and the robocart whisked me up to the steps, past them, along to a ramp that slanted up behind shrubbery to an open entry. I got off and went through it into a wide, airy hall full of a melancholy yellow light from wide stained-glass panels above a gallery trimmed in white-painted wrought-iron. A waxed and polished girl with a pert brown face, pouty purple lips, and a cast plastic hairdo came out of a carved door, waved toward a chair that looked like a Scottish king might have been crowned in it once.

"If you'll just be seated, Captain—"

"Still mad, huh? Where's his bedroom? I'll overlook it if his hair's not combed—"

"Please, Captain Maclamore!" She did a bump and grind, showed me a fine set of big white teeth, came up close and let me get a load of the hundred cee an ounce stuff she wore behind the ear. "The senator will be with you in just a moment . . ." Her voice changed tone on the last words; she'd noticed the bruise on my jaw, the patch of singed hair, the small cuts beside my eye where an instrument face had blown out. I worked up a quick smile that probably looked like the preliminary to a death rattle.

"A little accident on the way over," I said. "But it's all right. I got the other fellow's number."

A bell jangled then—or maybe it purred; it just seemed to me like a jangle. The light was too bright, too sour; the tick of an antique spring-driven clock pickled at me like a knife point. My cheap, stiff clothes rasped on my skin—

Feet rattled on the stairway behind me. I turned, and Senator I. Albert Pulster, short, dapper, red-faced, hair neatly combed, came across the floor, held out a hand worn smooth by shaking.

"Well, Mac; a long time. Not since Edna's funeral, I think . . . ."

I shook the hand. It felt hard and dry, but no harder or dryer than my own.

"I've got to talk to you, Albert," I said. "Fast and private."

He nodded as though he'd been expecting it. "Ah . . . a personal matter . . . ?"

"As personal as dying."

He indicated the door the girl had come out of. I followed him in.

Pulster's face looked hollow, as though all the juice had been sucked out of it by a big spider, leaving only a shell like crumpled tissue paper. All that in three minutes.

"Where is he now?" he asked in a voice as thin as his face.

"My guess would be that he's in a closed-door conference with some of his friends from the Hill. Naturally, he'll try to do it the easy way first. Why walk over Congress if he can bring them in with him?"

A little life was showing in Albert's eyes now; a little color was coming back into his cheeks. He leaned forward, clasped his hands together as though he was afraid they'd get away.

"And he doesn't know you're here?" His voice was quick now, emotionless, stripped for action.

"I'd guess he knows by now that I got off the ship. Beyond that—it depends on how good his intelligence apparatus is. He may have three squads with Mark X's trampling across the lawn right now."

Albert's mouth twitched. "No he doesn't," he said flatly. He fingered the edge of his desk, pulled out a big drawer, swung it up on spring-balanced slides, pivoted it to face me. It was a regulation battle display console, the kind usually installed in a two-man interceptor; it showed four stretches of unoccupied lawn with fountains and flowers. Below it was a fire-control panel that would have done credit to a five-thousand tonner.

"A man needs certain resources in these troubled times," Albert said. "I've never proposed to furnish a sitting target for the first Oswald who might rap at the gate."

I nodded. "That's why I joined the Navy; too dangerous down here." I pushed his toy back to him. "He's counting on putting this over fast and smooth: The public will wake up and it will be all over. The right publicity in the right places—now —will kill him."

Albert was shaking his head, looking shocked. "Publicity—no! Not a word, Mac. Good lord, man—" He clamped his teeth and breathed through his nose, looking at me, through me; then he focused in, blinked a couple of times.

"Mac, there's no time to waste. What kind of force would it take to neutralize the flagship?" he snapped out. "Assuming the worst: That Tarleton heard of the move, was able to communicate with the vessel, that she was fully alerted."

"A couple of hundred megaton seconds," I said. "With luck."

"I have no capital ships at my disposal," Albert thought aloud. "I do have over one hundred battle-ready medium recon units attached to National Guard organizations in the Seventeenth District." He looked at me hard. "What do you mean, Mac— 'with luck'?"

"Tarleton stripped the ship to make his Roman Holiday. There'll be skeleton crews on all sections. I don't know who he left on the bridge; he brought all his top boys down with him—he'd have to, otherwise he might find himself looking down his own Hellbores. Assuming a fairly competent man, he'll be able to lay down about fifty per cent fire-power—and as for maneuverability . . ."

"We can saturate her," Albert said. "Run her gauntlet, grapple to her, force an entry, and sweep her clean. And then—" Albert stopped, let his expression slide back to the casual. "But we'll worry about that later. Our immediate need—"

But he'd already done the damage. "You said 'after,'" I told him. "Go on."

"Why, then, of course, I'd restore matters to normalcy as soon as possible." He gave me a sharp look, like a pawnbroker wondering if the customer knows the pearls are real. "I think you could anticipate an appointment to star rank—perhaps even—"

"Forget it, Albert," I said softly. "With fast action and the kind of luck that makes sweepstakes winners we might be able to get together enough firepower to hit her once—now—while he's off-balance, before he expects anything—and knock her out. You've got your hundred boats; if you can swing the North American Defense Complex into it, we just might blanket her defenses with one strike—"

"Mac, you're raving," Albert said flatly. "You don't seem to understand—"

"That ship's a juggernaut hanging over all of us. I think a call to Kajevnikoff might bring their South American Net into it, too—"

"You're talking like a traitor!" Pulster got to his feet, his face back to its normal shade now.

"I'm taking that ship intact!" He tried to get his voice under control. "Be sensible, man! I'm offering you command of the strike force! You needn't expose yourself unnecessarily, of course; in fact, I'd expect you to command from a safe distance, then move in after boarding by my troops—"

"You're wasting time, Pulster," I told him. "Start the ball rolling—now. One word—one hint to Tarleton, and he'll neutralize every resource on the planet before you can say 'dictator.'"

"What do you mean—dictator!"

"One's like another as far as I'm concerned. In fact, between you and Banny, I might even pick him. I came here to stop something, not barter it."

Albert's hand went to his console, stopped self-consciously. He was thinking so hard I could almost smell the wiring burning. I took a step toward him, slid a hand inside my coat as though I had something hidden there.

"Get away from the desk, Senator," I said. He backed slowly—toward the window.

"Uh-uh. Over there." I indicated the discreet door to the senatorial john.

"Look here, Mac. This is too big to toss away like an old coat. The man that controls that vessel—controls the planet. It's almost in our hands! You did the right thing, coming here—and I'll never forget it was you who—"

I stepped in, hit him hard under the ribs to double him over, brought a right up under his jaw hard enough to lift his toes off the floor. He went back and down like a shroud full of baseballs, lay on his back with one eye half open. I didn't check to see whether he was breathing; I hooked a finger in his collar, dragged him to the toilet door, half threw him inside, set the latch, closed it. I looked around the room. There was a mirror on one wall with a table with flowers under it. I went over to it and a hollow-eyed bum in a sleazy greenish-black suit and a wilted collar looked out at me as though I'd caught him in the act of murder.

"It's OK, pal," I said aloud, feeling my tongue thick in my mouth. "That was just a warm-up; almost an accident, you might say. The rough part's just beginning."

Back out in the big, sad, empty hall, I told the
girl that the senator had suffered a sudden pain in
the stomach. "He's in the john," I said bluntly.
"Hiding, if you ask me. Pain in the stomach, ha! A
great thing when a fellow can't come to his own relations when he's had a little run of bad luck."

The look that she'd varnished up for VIP use
melted away like witnesses at a traffic smash. I
made it to the door without a guide; no little cart
appeared to ride me out to the gate. I walked,
wondering how long it would be before she went
in—and whether she would know which button to
push on the console to sweep the drive with fire.

But nothing happened; nobody yelled, no bells
rang, no guns fired. I reached the gate and the big
electrolock gave a buzz like a Bronx cheer as I
went through. I looked back at the eye; if it had
been a mouth, it would have yawned. There's
nothing like a little poverty to make a man in-
visible.

My last two cees bought me a cab ride as far as
Potomac Quay. I made the three blocks to the
Wellington Arms on foot, trying not to hurry even
when sirens came screaming across from Pennsyl-
vania Avenue and three monojag cop cars raced
overhead, heading the way I'd come. It was a fair
guess Miss Linoleum had overcome her maidenly
modesty sufficiently to force the door not many
minutes after I made it off the grounds.

I went up the broad pseudo-marble steps past a
Swiss admiral with enough Austrian knots to
equip a troop of Dragoons, in through a twelve-

foot-high glass door, crossed a stretch of polished black floor big enough for the New Year's Yacht Show. Under the muted glare strip that read INQUIRIES I found a small, neat man with big dark eyes that flicked over me once and caught everything except the hole in my left sock.

"I have some information that has to be placed in the Vice-President's hands at once," I told him. "What can you do for me?"

He reached without looking and slid a gold-mounted pad and stylus across to me, spun it around so that *Wellington Arms* was at the top, the pen poised ready to be written with.

"If you'd care to leave a message—"

I put my face closer to him. "I'm a little marked up; you noticed that. I got that way getting here. It's that kind of information. Take a chance and let me talk to his secretary."

He hesitated; then he reached for a small voice-only communicator, gold to match the pad. I waited while he played with buttons out of sight over the counter, murmured into the phone. Time passed. More discreet conversation; then he nodded.

"Mr. Lastwell will be down in a moment," he said. "Or so he says," he added in a lower tone. "You've got time for a smoke. You may even have time for a chow mein dinner."

"It's a corny line," I said, "but minutes could make a difference. Maybe seconds."

The clerk gave me another X-ray look; this time I figured he caught the hole in the sock. He leaned a little across the counter, squared up the pad.

"Political?" he murmured.

"It's not show biz," I said mysteriously. "Or is it?"

That satisfied him. He went off to the other end of the counter and began making entries in a card file. Probably the names of people to be shot after the next election. I looked at the clock; slim gold hands pointed at gold dots representing half-past one. There was a lot of gold around the Wellington Arms.

He came through the bleached teak doors from the bar, a thin, tired-looking man, walking fast, frowning, shoulders a little rounded, eyes whisking over the room like mice. He saw me, checked his stride, looked me over as he came up.

"I'm Marvin Lastwell. You're the person . . . ?"

"Maclamore. Is the Vice-President here?"

"Eh? Yes, of course he's here. If he were elsewhere, I'd be with him, hmm? What was it you had, Mr.—er—Maclamore?"

"Do we talk here?"

He looked around as though he were surprised to find himself in the lobby. "Hmm. There's a lounge just along—"

"This is private," I cut him off. "Let's go where it will stay that way."

He sucked his cheeks in. "Now, look here, Mr.—er—Maclamore—"

"On the off chance this could be important, play along this once, Mr. Lastwell. I can't spill this in front of every pickup the local gossip ghouls have planted in this mausoleum."

"Hmm. Very well, Mr.—er—Maclamore." He led the way off along a corridor carpeted in dove gray pile deep enough to lose a golfball in. I followed, wondering why a mild-looking fellow like Marvin Lastwell thought it necessary to carry a Browning 2mm under his arm.

The penthouse at the Wellington was no more ornate than Buckingham Palace, and smaller, though not much. Lastwell showed me into a spacious, dim-lit library lined with the kind of leather-bound books lawyers keep around the office to impress the customers and maybe open once in a while on a rainy afternoon when trade is slow, just to see what they're missing. Lastwell went behind a big dark mahogany desk, sat down fussily, pushed a big silver ashtray with a cigar butt off to one side, flicked on a lamp that threw an eerie green reflection back up on his face, giving his worried features a look of Satanic ferocity. I wondered if he'd practiced it in front of a mirror.

"Now, Mr.—er—Maclamore," he said. "What is it you wanted to tell me?"

I was still standing, looking at the cigar butt, probably left there by the last ward-heeler who'd dropped in to mend a fence. It looked as out of place on Lastwell's desk as a roulette wheel at a Methodist Retreat. He saw me looking at it and started to reach for it, then changed his mind, scratched his nose instead. I could feel a sudden tension in him.

"Maybe I didn't make myself clear," I said. "It was the Vice-President I wanted to see."

Lastwell curved the corners of his mouth up in a smile like a meat-eating bird—or maybe it was just the light.

"Now, Captain, you can hardly—" He caught himself, clamped his jaw shut. The abrupt silence hung between us like a shout.

"Like that, huh?" I said softly.

He sighed; his hand hardly seemed to move, but now the Browning was in it. He held the gun with that graceful negligence they only get when they know how to use them. He motioned with his head toward a chair.

"Just sit down," he said in an entirely new voice. "You'll have a few minutes' wait."

I moved toward the chair he'd indicated; the gun muzzle followed. It was too late at night to start thinking, but I made the attempt. The cigar was the skinny, black brand that Tarleton smoked. I'd probably missed him by minutes. He hadn't been close behind me—he'd been a good jump ahead. He's had time to give his pitch—whatever proposition he'd worked out—to the Veep. It had been a risky move, but it seemed the Veep had listened. He'd mentioned me; as for how much he'd said, the next few seconds would tell me that.

I reached the chair, but instead of sitting in it, I turned to face Lastwell. The gun twitched alertly, holding low on my chest. That could be design—or accident.

"Maybe your boss would like to hear my side," I said, just to keep him talking. "Maybe my angle's better."

"Shut up and sit in the chair," Lastwell said, in the tone of a tired teacher talking to the oldest pupil in the eighth grade.

"Sit in it yourself," I came back. "The graveyard's full of wise guys that didn't stick around to get the whole story. Did Tarleton tell you I was Weapons Officer aboard *Rapacious*? Hell, the whole tub's wired to blow at a signal from—"

"You were captain of *Sagacious*," Lastwell cut in. "Save your lies, Maclamore—"

"Not two years ago, I wasn't, when she was fitted out—"

"Save it, I said." Lastwell let his voice rise a decibel and a half; the gun jerked up as he spoke, centered on my chest now. I gave him a discouraged look, leaned forward as though about to sit, and dived across the desk. The Browning bucked and shrieked and a cannon ball hit me in the chest and then my hands were on his neck, sinking into doughy flesh and we were going down together, slamming the floor, and the gun bouncing clear, and then I was on my knees, with Lastwell bent back under me, his mouth open, tongue out, eyes bulging like lanced boils.

"Talk it up," I ground out past my teeth. I gave him a quarter of a second to think it over, then gave him a thumb under the Adam's apple. A sound like a rivet scoring a brake drum came from him.

"He . . . here . . . half hour . . ."

I gave him enough air to work with but not enough to encourage enterprise.

"Who's here now?"

"No—nobody. Sent . . . them away."

"How many are in this?"

"Just . . . the two of them . . ."

"Plus you. Where are they?"

"They're . . . gone to see . . . others. Back soon . . ."

"Tarleton coming back here?"

"No . . . to his place." Lastwell gulped air, flopped his arms. "Please . . . my back . . ."

I smiled at him. "Get ready to die," I said.

"No! Please!" What color was left went out of his face like dirty water down a drain.

"Tell the rest," I snapped.

"He's . . . expecting you . . . there . . . if don't get you . . . here. State Police . . ."

"Say your prayers," I ordered. "When you wake up in the next world, remember how it felt to die a dirty death." I rammed my fingers in hard to the carotid arteries, watched his eyes turn up; he slumped and I let his head bump the carpet. He'd come around in half an hour with a sore throat and a set of memories that he could mull over at bedtime for a lot of sleepless nights.

I left him where he was, picked up the gun, tucked it away. There was a chewed place across my coat front where the needles had hit, a corresponding rip in the shirt. The chromalloy plate underneath that covered the artificial heart and lungs showed hardly a scratch to commemorate the event. Six inches higher or to the left, and he'd have found unshielded hide. It wasn't like Banny Tarleton to forget to mention a detail like that. Maybe he was slipping; maybe that was the break that had let me get this far. Maybe I could ride it a little farther; and maybe I was already out on the skim ice, too far from shore to walk back.

I'd tried to stop Tarleton with indirect methods; they hadn't worked. Now there was only one direction left: Straight ahead, into the trap he had laid.

Now I'd have to kill him with my own hands.

I rummaged in Lastwell's closet, found a shapeless tan waterproof and a narrow-brimmed hat. The private elevator rode me down to the second floor. The silence in the corridor was all

that you'd expect for a hundred cees a day. I
walked along to the rear of the building, found a
locked door to a service stair. There was a nice
manual knob on it; I gripped it hard, gave it a
sharp twist. Metal broke and tinkled and the door
swung in. The luxury ended sharply at the
threshold; there was a scarred chair, a dirty coffee
cup, a magazine, cigarette butts, on a concrete
landing above a flight of narrow concrete steps. I
went down, passed another landing, kept going.
The stairs ended at a wooden door. I tried it,
stepped through into the shadows and the hum of
heavy equipment. A shoe scraped and a big-bellied
man in a monogrammed coverall separated
himself from the gray bulk of a compressor unit.
He frowned, wiped a hand over a bald head,
opened his mouth—

"Fire inspector," I told him briskly. "Goddam
place is a deathtrap. That your chair on the
landing?"

He gobbled, almost swallowed his toothpick,
spat it on the floor. "Yah, it's my chair—"

"Get it out of there. And police those butts while
you're at it." I jerked my head toward the back of
the big room. "Where's your fire exit?"

"Hah?"

"Don't stall," I barked. "Got it blocked, I'll bet.
You birds are all alike: Think fire regulations are
something to wrap your lunch in."

He gave me a red-eyed look, hitched at his shoulder strap. "Back here." His Potsdam accent was
thick enough to spread on pretzels like cream
cheese. I followed him along to a red-painted
metal-clad door set a foot above floor level.

"Red light's out," I noted, sharp as a mousetrap.
There was a big barrel bolt on the door at chest

height. I slid it back, jerked the door open. Dust
and night air whirled in.

"OK, get that landing clear, like I said." I
hooked a thumb over my shoulder and stepped out
into dead leaves. He grunted and went away. I
eased my head above the ragged grass growing
along the edge of the stair well; a security light on
the side of the building showed me a garbage disposal unit, a white-painted curb, the squat shape
of a late-model Turbocad parked under a row of
dark windows. I slid the Browning into my hand,
went up, across to the car. It was a four-seater,
dull black with a gold eagle on the door. I thumbed
the latch; no surprise there: It was locked. I went
down on my left side, eased under the curve of the
hood. There were a lot of wires; I traced one,
jerked it loose, tapped the frame; sparks jumped
and a solid snick! sounded above. I crawled back
out, pulled open the door, slid in behind the wheel.
The switch resisted for a moment; then something
snapped and it turned. The turbos started up with
a whine like a waitress looking at a half-cee tip.
The Cad slid out along the drive, smooth as a
porpoise in deep water. I nosed out into the bleak
light of the polyarcs along the Quay, took the inner
lane, and headed at a meticulously legal speed for
Georgetown.

The fire of '87 had cleared away ten blocks of
high-class slums and given the culture-minded ad-
ministration of that day the perfect excuse to
erect a village of colonial-style official mansions
that were as authentic as the medals on a
vermouth bottle. Admiral Banastre Tarleton had

the one at the end of the line, a solid-looking red-brick finish that disguised half an inch of flint steel, with lots of pretty white woodwork, a copper-sheathed roof made of bomb-proof polyon, and two neat little cupolas that housed some of the most sensitive detection gear ever sidetracked from a naval yard. I picked it out from two blocks away by the glare of lights from windows on all three floors.

There was an intersection nostalgically lit by gas flares on tall poles; I crossed it, slowed, moving along in the shadow of a row of seventy-foot elms with concrete cores and permanentized leaves. The moon was up now, shedding its fairy glow on the bricked street, the wide inorganic lawns, the stately fronts, creating a fragile illusion of the simple elegance of a past age—if you could ignore the lighted spires of the city looming up behind.

The last house on the right before Tarleton's place was a boxy planter's mansion with a row of stately columns and a balcony from which a queen could wave to the passing crowds. It was boarded up tight; not everybody was willing to give up the comfort of a modern apartment a mile up in the Washington sky for the dubious distinction of a Georgetown address. Half the houses here were empty, shuttered, awaiting a bid from a social-climbing freshman congressman or a South American diplomat eager to get a lease signed before the government that sent him collapsed in a hail of gunfire.

There was a sudden movement among moon shadows on the drive opposite the Tarleton house; a heavy car appeared—armored, by the ponderous sway of its suspension as it trundled out to block

the street. It was too late for me to think up any
stunning moves that would leave the opposition
breathless; I cut the wheel hard, swung into the
artificial cinder drive that led up to the bright-lit
front of the Tarleton mansion. Behind me, the
interceptor gunned its turbos, closed in on my
rear bumper. Men appeared in the wide doorway
ahead; I caught glimpses of others spotted across
the lawn that was pool-table green in the splash of
light from the house. They ringed me in as I
braked to a stop. I set the brake hard, flung the
door open, stepped out, gave my coat belt a tug,
picked out a middle-sized fellow with a face as
sensitive as a zinc bar-top.

"Those clowns in the armor better get on the
ball," I told him. "I could have waltzed right past
'em. And those boys you've got out trampling the
flower beds: Tell 'em to hit the dirt and stay put;
they're not in a tango contest—"

"Where do you fit the picture, mister?" His
voice was a whisper; I saw the scar across his
throat ear to ear. He was a man who'd looked
death in the eye from razor range. He was looking at the car now, not liking it much but pushed
a little off-balance by the eagle and the words
OFFICE OF THE CENTRAL BUREAU OF INTELLIGENCE.

I started around the front of the car, headed for
the stairs. "Hot stuff for the admiral," I said.
"He's inside, right?"

He didn't move. I stopped before I rammed him.

"Maybe I better see some paper, mister," he
whispered. "Turn around and put the mitts on
top of the car."

"Pull up your socks, rookie," I advised loudly.
"You think I carry a card when I'm working?" I
crowded him a little. "Come on, come on, what I

got won't wait." He gave—about a quarter of an inch. "Any you boys know this mug?" he called in his faint croak. His face was close enough to mine to give me a good whiff of burned licorice; he was on the pink stuff. That wouldn't make him any easier to take.

I saw heads shake; two or three voices denied the pleasure of my acquaintance.

I hunched my shoulders. "I'm going in," I announced. "I got my orders from topside—"

Someone came out through the open door, saw me and stopped dead. For an instant I had trouble placing the horsy, weather-beaten face under the brimless cap. He opened his mouth, showing uneven brown teeth, said, "Hey!" It was Funderburk, the Warrant from the flagship. I took the first half of a deep breath, nodded toward him as casually as a pickpocket saying good morning to a plain-clothes cop.

"Ask him," I said. "He knows me."

Funderburk came down the steps, three or four expressions chasing each other over his face.

"Yeah," he said. He nodded, as if vastly satisfied. "Yeah."

"You make this bird?" the scarred man whispered.

I tried to coax a little moisture into my dry mouth. My minor wounds throbbed, but no worse than an equal number of nerve cancers. I was hungry and tired, but Scott probably felt at least as bad, writing the last page of his journal on the ice cap; my head throbbed a little, but one of those ancient Egyptians whose family doc had sawed his skull open with a stone knife would have laughed it off.

"Sure," Funderburk said from under a curled

lip. "Gronski. Anchor man of the section. Two months ago they plant the slob in my outfit, and I guess I ain't hardly seen the guy three times since." He spat, off side, but just barely. "The commodore's number-one boy; better play it closer than a skin-diver's tights, Ajax. He's a privileged character, he is."

There was a mutter in which I caught the word "Braze." I poked Ajax with a finger.

"I'll mention you were doing a job," I said. "But don't work it to death." I brushed past him and past Funderburk, went up the steps and through the door. No power guns roared. No large dogs came bounding out to sample my leg. Nobody even hit me over the head with a blackjack. So far so good.

One man was walking behind me, one on my right. I went across the wide, Wedgwood blue reception hall, past a gilt-framed mirror that showed me a glimpse of a pale, unshaven face with eyes like char-wounds. I looked like Mussolini, just before the crowd got him. The stairs were carpeted in wine red which somehow didn't clash with the walls; maybe it was the soft yellow light from a tinkly glass chandelier that hung on a long gold chain from somewhere high above. The banister was wide and cool and white under my hand. The footsteps of the two goons thumped on the treads behind me.

I passed a landing with a tall double-hung window with lacy curtains and dark drapes, a painting of a small boy in red velvet pants, a weathered-oak clock that didn't tick. Then I was

coming up into a wide hall done in dusty green
with big white-painted wood panel doors with
bright brass knobs. A man sat in a chair at the end
beside a curved-leg Sheraton table with a brass
ashtray from which a curl of smoke went up under
a green-shaded lamp. There was a power gun in
his lap. He watched me come, his hands on the
gun.

One of the doors was open; voices came from inside. I felt like a man striding briskly toward the
gallows, but the thin bluff I was riding couldn't
survive any doubts or hesitations at this point. I
went on, turned in at the lighted door and was in a
big, high-ceilinged room with a desk, heavy
leather-covered chairs, bookcases, a bar in one
corner. Three men standing there looked around
at me. Two of them I'd never seen before; the third
was a captain whose name I couldn't remember.
He frowned at me, looked at the others.

"Where's the admiral?" the man behind me
said.

Nobody answered. The captain was still
frowning at me. "I've seen you before," he said.
"Who are you—?"

"Guy named Gronski," my escort said. "The
commodore's dog-robber."

"You have a message from Commodore Braze?"
one of the other men asked sharply.

"I want to see the admiral," I said, looking stub-
born. "I've already told Ajax this is a red-hot
item—"

"You can tell it again!" the third man snapped.
"I'm Admiral Tarleton's aide—"

"And I'm bad news from back home," I snarled.
"I'm not up here to jackass around with a front
man!" I whirled on the captain. "Can't you people

get the message? This is *hot!*"

The captain's eyes went to the door in the wall behind me. "He's just stepped down the hall," he said uneasily. "He's—"

"Never mind that, Johnson," the aide snapped out. "I'll inform him—"

"We'll both inform him," the captain said. "I'm assigned here as exec—"

"Save the jurisdictional wrangles until later," the other man cut in. "If this is as important as this fellow seems to think—"

"It's worse," I barked. "I'm warning you bastards somebody's gonna suffer . . ."

The aide and the captain slammed down their glasses and stamped out of the room neck and neck. I poked a finger at the two who had escorted me. "All right, get back on post," I rapped out. "Believe me, when I tell the admiral . . ." They faded away like shadows at sunset. The man at the bar had his mouth open. I walked across to him, looking confidential.

"There's one other little thing," I started as I came up to him—and chopped out with the side of my hand, caught him across the cheekbone. He almost leaped the bar. Glasses went flying, but thudded almost silently to the rug. I dragged him behind the bar, went across to the connecting door, gave the knob a hard twist. I almost broke my wrist.

Out in the hall, the two who had gone out were nowhere in sight; the gun-handler still sat in his chair beside the lamp. I gave him a hard look as though wondering whether he'd shaved that morning, strode along to the next door, reached for it—

"Hey!" He came out of his chair, gun forward. "Get away from that door!"

I turned toward him as he came up, jumped sideways and kicked out. The burst caught me across the shin, slammed me back against the wall. My head hit hard and brilliant constellations shimmered all around. I clawed, swam up from abysmal deeps where light never penetrated, saw him stepping back, the gun still aimed. Someone yelled; a high, tight string of words. Feet pounded. There was a harsh reek of burned synthetics. I rolled over on my face, got my hands under me. I was staring at the big white door when it opened inward. Admiral Banastre Tarleton stood there, a Norge stunner in his hand. Without pausing to calculate the odds, I planted both feet against the wall behind me, launched myself at his knees. I heard the soft whisper of the Norge as I hit, and the crisper sound of something tearing in his leg, and then we were down together and the stunner hissed again and my left side was dead, but I rolled clear, scrabbled with one arm, saw a man in the doorway just as I caught the edge of the thick metal panel, hurled it shut with what was left of my strength. The dull boom shut off the outside world as completely as the lid of a coffin.

I looked around. Tarleton was on his back, his head propped up at an awkward angle against the leg of a canopied four-poster bed. His face was as white as bleached bone, and the Norge was in his fist, aimed square at my face.

"I don't know how you got here, Mac," he said in a voice forced high by the agony of a broken knee. "I must have more traitors in my organization than I thought."

"Glad to see you still have your sense of humor, Banny," I said. I thought about trying for the Browning, but it was just a thought. The stunner held on me as steady as a deck gun. There was a little sensation in the shoulder where it had caught me; a feeling as though a quarter of beef had been stitched on with a dull needle to replace the arm. My legs were all right, with the exception of the burned plastic and scorched metal below my knee where the power gun had seared it.

"A traitor is a revolutionist who fails," Tarleton stated. "We won't fail."

"Now it's 'we,'" I noted. "A few hours ago it was all 'I.'"

"I'm not alone now, Mac. I've talked to people. Not a shot will be fired."

I nodded. "How does it feel, Banny? In a few hours you'll own the world. You and Napoleon. Take it apart and put it back together to suit yourself. More fun than jigsaw puzzles any day. And you'll have CBI men walking ten deep around you. No more broken legs from wild-eyed reformers who walk into your bedroom past what you call an organization." I was talking to hear myself, to keep my mind off what was coming, to defer for another few seconds the only end the scene could have.

"You moved fast, Mac. I thought"—the gun wavered, then steadied—"thought I had a few secrets."

"Tough, not being able to tip your hand. All that power—if you just don't give it away before the hook's set."

There was a muffled pounding, faint and far away. Tarleton jerked his head up. I could almost make out voices, shouting.

"Get over there," Tarleton ordered. "Open that door."

I shook my head. "Open it yourself, Banny. They're your friends."

He moved, and his cheekbones went almost green. The gun sagged and my hand was halfway to the needler before he caught it. There was greasy-looking sweat on his face. His voice was a croak.

"Better do it, Mac. If I feel myself blacking out, I'll have to shoot you."

I didn't say anything. I was wondering why he hadn't shot already. He stared at me for five seconds, while I waited . . . .

Then he twisted, reached up and back, fumbled over the bedside table, and suddenly sound was blasting into the room:

"—open! The fire's into the stairwell! Can you hear me, Admiral? We can't get the door open—"

"Benny!" Tarleton snapped as the shout cut off. "Blast the door down; I'm hurt. I can't get to it!" He flipped keys.

"I got him," the voice snapped. "Admiral, listen to me: You have to get it open from your side! There's nothing out here bigger than a Mark X; it'll never cut that chromalloy!"

"Get in here, Benny!" Tarleton's voice was a hoarse roar. "I don't give a damn how you do it, but get in here!"

There were many voices yelling together now.

"—out of here!"

"—too late; let it go, Rudy!"

"—all roast together!"

"—son of a bitch is out of his mind!"

There was a loud crash, as though a heavy table had gone over, scuffling noises, a crackling roar. Banny flicked it off. His eyes were on mine. "Jacobs was always a little careless with a weapon," he said in a voice like dry leaves.

"A good man," I said. "Reflexes like a cat. Damn near got my knee cap."

"And morals to match. It was my fault; I should have warned him about the house. Genuine antiques; wood, varnish, cloth. With the right draft there'll be nothing left but a red-hot shell in half an hour."

"You've been forgetting a lot of things, Banny. Like telling your boys where to aim to stop me. You wouldn't have liked the look on Lastwell's face when he put a burst into my chest."

"You must have wanted to get me pretty badly, Mac." He tossed the stunner aside. "It looks like you get your wish. Save yourself—if it's not too late."

He watched me get to my feet; my paralyzed shoulder felt as though my Siamese twin had just been sawed off, and I missed him. The dead hand bumped my side.

"Just the one way down?"

"Service stairs at the back."

There was a tiled bathroom visible through a half-open door; I flipped on the water in the big old-style bathtub, came back out and hauled a wool blanket off the bed.

"Get going, damn you," Tarleton said in a blurred voice. "No . . . time . . ." His head went sideways and he hit the floor with a thud like a split log. That was good; it would be easier for him that way. He'd been keeping himself conscious on pure will power; he wouldn't be needing that now.

The blanket wanted to float. I shoved it under, remembering the sound of the fire bellowing in the hall. I could almost hear it through the sound-proofing now. Precious seconds were passing . . . .

Back in the bedroom, Banny Tarleton lay on his side, his mouth open, eyes shut. He didn't look like a world-beater now; he looked like a fellow who had had a bad dream and fallen out of bed.

He was heavy. I pulled him onto the blanket, rolled him in it with a double fold over his head, hoisted him onto my shoulder—a neat trick with one good arm, when I couldn't tell the shoulder was there, except for the feeling of needles prickling along the edge of the paralyzed area. The door seemed a long way off. I reached it, put my working hand against it; it hissed. That didn't change anything: I thumbed the electro-lock, heard the grumble inside the armored panel. The knob turned, and the door bucked back against me, driven by a solid wall of black-and-orange flame. I shielded my face as well as I could with one hand and a flap of blanket and walked out into it.

The sound was all around me like the thunder of a scarlet Niagara. Under my feet the floor boards were warped and buckled. Pain slashed at me like gale-driven sleet, like frozen knives raking at my face, my back, my thighs. . . .

A section of plaster fell in front of me with a dull boom, drove back the flames for an instant and through the smoke I saw the once-white balustrade beside the stair, a smoking writhe of blackened iron now. Through a dervish-mad whirl of pale fire, I saw the chandelier, a snarl of black metal from which glass dripped like sun-bright water. The clock stood upright on the landing, burning proudly, like a martyred monk. Beside it, the boy in red pants curled, fumed, was gone in a leap of white fire. Charred steps crumbled under my foot and I staggered; the smell of burning wool was rank in my throat. I could see the varnished floor below, with fire running over it like burning brandy on a pudding, a black cresent moving out

behind to consume the bright wood. Somewhere
above there was a thunderous smash, and the air
was filled with whirling fireflies. Something large
and black fell past me, bounced along the floor
ahead. I stepped over it, felt a ghostly touch of
cool air, and suddenly the flames were gone from
around me, and over the surf roar of the fire I
heard thin cries that seemed to cover from a
remote distance.

"Sweet mother of Christ!" a high, womanish
voice wailed. "Look at the poor devil! He's burned
as black as a tar mop!"

There was a smoke-blurred figure before me,
and then others, and then the weight was gone
from my back and I took another step but there
seemed to be something wrong with my feet, and I
was falling, falling, like a star burning its fiery
path across a night sky. . . .

I was afloat in cool waters, listening to the distant
rumble of thunder portending gentle rain. Then
the rumble was a voice, coming from far away on
some frosty white mountain top sparkling in the
blue sky. I was flying, soaring down from the icy
heights—or was it the cool translucent depths
from which I floated up toward light, warmth,
pain. . . .

I opened my eyes, saw a vague, cloudy shape
hovering over me.

"How are you feeling, Mac?" Admiral Banastre
Tarleton's voice asked me.

"Like a barbecued steer," I said—but no sound

came out. Or maybe I grunted.

"Don't try to talk," Tarleton said quickly. "You breathed a lot of smoke; got some fire in your lungs. You're lucky they were made in a factory."

I had the impression someone had come up, muttered to Tarleton. Then he was back.

"You're at Bethesda. They tell me you're out of danger. You were out for eighteen hours. Second degree burns on the face, the left hand, the back of your thighs. The coat you were wearing helped. Some kind of expanded polymer job. Bio-prosthetics are having a swell time clucking over how their work stood up to the fire. Both legs were melted back to bare metal, and the right elbow was fused. They'll have a new set ready for you in about two weeks, when the bandages come off. You won't even have scars."

I tried again, managed a croak. My throat felt like rawhide dried in the desert sun.

"You'll be wondering about how certain things have gone, Mac," Tarleton went on. "Funny thing, after the fire there seemed to be a certain temporary loss of momentum in the movement. I guess my little band of gentleman-adventurers used up all their drive running out on me when things got hot. My own perspective got a little warped: I had to keep reminding myself that in a society of maniacs, the sane man has a duty to rule. And those lads who got the hell out when the flames got knee high; they did the sane thing. You can't fight that. It took a crazy man to walk through the fire for me."

It was a long speech. I had a long one of my own ready: I was going to tell him all about how it had been a mistake to rush me to the hospital, because as soon as I could walk I'd have to come after him to finish what I'd started; that sick or well, sane or crazy, there were things loose in the world that were worse than man's animal ferocity, and one of them was the ferocity of the Righteous Intellect; and that the most benevolent of despotisms rotted in the end into the blind arrogance of tyranny. . . .

But all I managed was a whimper like a sick pup.

The frosty haze was closing in again. Tarleton's voice came from far away, as far as the stars:

"I have an appointment with the Vice-President now, Mac. I'll have to explain some things to him. Maybe he'll understand, maybe not. Maybe things have gone too far. Whichever way it goes, I'd like to leave one thought with you: Theories are beautiful things—simple and precise as cut glass —as long as they're only theories. When you find in your hand the power to make them come true . . . suddenly, it's not so simple. . . ."

Then he was gone, and the snow was drifting over me, silent and deep.

It was hours later, I don't know how many. I was half awake, reasonably clearheaded, wondering if Tarleton had really been there, or if I had dreamed the whole passage. There was a Tri-D screen by the bed, playing the kind of soft music that's guaranteed not to intrude over the bridge-table conversation. It stopped abruptly in mid-moan and a voice harsh with excitement broke in:

"We interrupt this program to bring you the following bulletin: The Vice-President has been assassinated and the Secretaries of Defense and State and the Attorney General as well as a number of lesser officials cut down in a burst of gunfire that shattered a secret meeting of the National Defense Council at 2:19 P.M. Eastern Standard Time today—less than ten minutes ago. An unofficial statement by a newsman who was first on the scene indicates that a heavy caliber machine pistol smuggled into the Capitol by Admiral Banastre Tarleton was the massacre weapon. Tarleton, still heavily bandaged from yesterday's fire and with a cast on his leg, is reported to have died in the answering fire from a Secret Service man who broke down a door to gain entry to the room. A spokesman for the CBI stated that Admiral Tarleton, a national hero since his destruction of Bloc naval forces in a deep space battle two days ago, apparently broke under the double tragedy of the loss of the majority of his forces in the fighting, followed by the disastrous fire which swept his Georgetown home—"

The sound cut off then; I got an eyelid up, made out the hovering figure of a man in pale green hospital togs. He fumbled at my left arm, made soothing noises, and things got vague again. . . .

Voiced picked at me. I came back from soft cool shadowland, saw faces floating like pink moons above me. I recognized one of them: Nulty, Under-Secretary of Defense.

". . . ranking surviving officer," he was saying. "As senior line captain since the terrible loss in Monday's engagement . . . assured you'll be fit for duty in three weeks . . . temporary rank of vice admiral . . . grave crisis . . ." His voice faded in and out. Other voices seemed to come and go. Time passed. Then I was awake, feeling the artificial clearheadedness of drug-induced alertness. Nulty was sitting beside the bed.

" . . . hope you've understood what we've been saying, Maclamore," he said. "It's of vital importance that the flagship be fully operational as soon as possible. I've posted Captain Selkirk to her as acting CO until you could assume command. We don't know what the Bloc may be doing at this moment, but it's vital that our defensive posture not be permitted to deteriorate, in spite of the terrible tragedies that have struck us."

"Why me?" I managed.

"All but a handful of staff officers of flag rank were lost in the fight," he said in a voice that quivered with tension and fatigue. "The President agreed; you're Academy trained, with vast operational experience—"

"What about Braze?"

"He . . . was one of those lost in the assassination."

"So now *Rapacious* is my baby . . .?"

"I'm hoping you'll be able to board her within a day or two. I've ordered special medical facilities installed, and the surgeon general has agreed you can complete your convalescence there. I have reports for you to read, Maclamore. The Bloc is aware of the confusion here. They'll be wasting no time . . ." His face was close to me, worried.

"What will you do, Admiral?" he demanded. "You'll be commanding the entire surviving armed force of the UN. What will you do . . .?"

A man in green came then and whispered, and Nulty went away. The lights went off. It was late; the shadows of evening were long on the walls.

I lay in the darkness and pondered my reply.